Also by Kimberly Belle

The Last Breath

The Ones We Trust

The Marriage Lie

Three Days Missing

Dear Wife

Stranger in the Lake

My Darling Husband

The Personal Assistant

Young Rich Widows (collaborator)

the
PARIS
WIDOW

KIMBERLY BELLE

PARK
ROW
BOOKS

PARK
ROW
BOOKS™

Recycling programs
for this product may
not exist in your area.

ISBN-13: 978-0-7783-0797-6

The Paris Widow

Park Row Books
22 Adelaide St. West, 41st Floor
Toronto, Ontario M5H 4E3, Canada
ParkRowBooks.com

Printed in U.S.A.

To Bella.
This one's all for you.

PROLOGUE

Nice, France

What seems to us as bitter trials are often blessings in disguise.
—*Oscar Wilde*

At Nice's Côte d'Azur Airport, the pretty woman coming down the Jetway looked like every other bleary-eyed traveler. Rumpled T-shirt over jeans with an indeterminate stain on the right thigh, hair shoved into a messy ponytail mussed from the headrest. A backpack was slung over her right shoulder, weighed down with items that weren't technically hers but looked like they could be. She'd sorted through them on the seven-hour flight, just long enough to make the contents feel familiar.

"Don't lose it," the Turkish man said when he hung it on her arm, and she hadn't.

The Jetway dumped her into the terminal, and she trailed behind a family of five, past gates stretched out like spider legs, along the wall of windows offering a blinding view of the sparkling Mediterranean, a turquoise so bright it burned her eyes.

The backpack bounced against her shoulder bone, and her heart gave a quiet little jingle.

She made it through passport control without issue, thanks to her careful selection of the agent behind the glass. A man, first and foremost. Not too old or too young, not too handsome. A five to her solid eight—or so she'd been told by more than one man. This one must have agreed, because he stamped her passport with an appreciative nod. Frenchmen were like that. One smile from a woman out of their league, and they melted like a cream-filled bonbon.

She thanked him and slid her passport into her pocket.

In it were stamps to every country in Europe and the Americas, from her crisscrosses over every continent including Antarctica, from her detours to bask on the famous beaches of Asia, Australia, the South Seas. More than once, she'd had to renew the booklet long before it expired because she'd run out of empty spots for customs agents to stamp. She was particularly proud of that, and of how she could look any way you wanted her to look, be anyone you needed her to be. Today she was playing the role of American Tourist On A Budget.

At baggage claim, she slid the backpack down an aching shoulder and checked the time on her cell. Just under six hours for this little errand, plenty of time, assuming she didn't hit any unexpected roadblocks. If she didn't get held up at customs, if the taxi line wasn't too long, if traffic on the A8 wasn't too awful, which it would be because getting in and out of Monte Carlo was always a nightmare at this time of year. *If if if.* If she missed the flight to London, she was screwed.

A buzzer sounded, and the baggage carousel rumbled to a slow spin.

At least she didn't look any more miserable than the people milling around her, their faces long with jet lag. She caught snippets of conversation in foreign tongues, German, Italian, Arabic, French, and she didn't need a translator to know they were bitching about the wait. The French were never in a hurry, and they were always striking about something. She wondered what it could be this time.

Thirty-eight eternal minutes later, the carousel spit out her suitcase. She hauled it from the band with a grunt, plopped the heavy backpack on top and followed the stream of tourists to the exit.

Walk with purpose. Look the customs agent in the eye. Smile, the fleeting kind with your lips closed, not too big or too cocky. Act breezy like you've got nothing to prove or to hide. By now she knew all the tricks.

The customs agent she was paired with was much too young for her liking, his limbs still lanky with the leftovers of puberty, which meant he had something to prove to the cluster of more senior agents lingering behind him. She ignored their watchful gazes, taking in his shiny forehead, the way it was dotted with pimples, and dammit, he was going to be a problem.

He held up a hand, the universal sign for *halt*. *"Avez-vous quelque chose à déclarer?"*

Her fingers curled around the suitcase handle, clamping down. She gave him an apologetic smile. "Sorry, but I don't speak French."

That part was the truth, at least. She *didn't* speak it—at least, not well and not unless she absolutely had to. And her rudimentary French wasn't necessary just yet.

But she understood him well enough, and she definitely knew that last word. He was asking if she had something to declare.

The agent gestured to her suitcase. "Please, may I take a look in your luggage?" His English was heavy with accent, his lips slick with spit, but at least he was polite about it.

She gave a pointed look at the exit a few feet away. On

the other side of the motion-activated doors, a line of people leaned against a glass-and-steel railing, fists full of balloons and colorful bouquets. With her free hand, she wriggled her fingers in a wave, even though she didn't know a single one of them.

She looked back at the agent with another smile. "Is that really necessary? My flight was delayed, and I'm kind of in a hurry. My friends out there have been waiting for hours."

Calm. Reasonable. Not breaking the slightest sweat.

The skin of his forehead creased in a frown. "This means you have nothing to declare?"

"Only that a saleslady lied to my face about a dress I bought being wrinkle resistant."

She laughed, but the agent's face remained as stony as ever.

He beckoned her toward an area behind him, a short hallway lined with metal tables. "*S'il vous plaît*. The second table."

Still, she didn't move. The doors slid open, and she flung another glance at the people lined up outside. So close, yet so far.

As if he could read her mind, the agent took a calculated step to his left, standing between her and the exit. He swept an insistent arm through the air, giving her little choice. The cluster of agents were paying more attention now.

She huffed a sigh. Straightened her shoulders and gave her bag a hard tug. "Okay, but fair warning. I'm on the tail end of a three-week vacation here, which means everything in my suitcase is basically a giant pile of dirty laundry."

Again, the truth. Miami to Atlanta to LA to Tokyo to Dubai to Nice, a blur of endless hours with crummy movies and soggy airplane food, of loud, smelly men who drank vodka for breakfast, of kids marching up and down the aisles while everybody else was trying to sleep. What she was wearing was the cleanest thing she had left, and she was still thousands of miles from home.

She let go of the handle, and the suitcase spun and wobbled, whacking the metal leg of the table with a hard clang. Let him lug the heavy thing onto the inspection table himself.

She stood with crossed arms and watched him spread her suitcase open on the table. She wasn't lying about the laundry or that stupid dress, which currently looked like a crumpled paper bag. He picked through her dirty jeans and rumpled T-shirts, rifled through blouses and skirts. When he got to the wad of dirty underwear, he clapped the suitcase shut.

"See?" she said. "Just a bunch of dirty clothes."

"And your other bag?"

The backpack dangling from her shoulder, an ugly Tumi knockoff. Her stomach dropped, but she made sure to hold his gaze.

"Nothing in here, either. No meat, no cheese, no forgotten fruit. I promise."

She'd done that once, let an old apple sink to the bottom of her bag for a hyped-up beagle to sniff out, and she'd paid for it with a forty-five-minute wait at a scorching Chilean airport. It was a mistake she wouldn't make again.

"Madame, please. Do not make me ask you again."

The little shit really said it. He really called her *madame*. This kid who was barely out of high school was making her feel old and decrepit, while in the same breath speaking to her like she was a child. His words were as infuriating as they were alarming. She hooked a thumb under the backpack's strap, but she didn't let it go.

And yet what choice did she have? She couldn't run, not with those senior agents watching. Not with this pubescent kid and his long grasshopper limbs. He'd catch her in a hot second.

She told herself there was nothing to find. That's what the Turkish man had promised her with a wink and a smile, that nobody would ever know. He swore she'd cruise right on through customs. And she had, many, many times.

As she slid the backpack from her arm with another dramatic sigh, she hoped like hell he wasn't lying. "Please hurry."

The agent took the bag from her fingers and emptied it out on the table. He took out the paperback and crinkled magazines, the half-eaten bag of nuts with the Japanese label, the wallet and the zippered pouch stuffed with well-used cosmetics that had never once touched her face. He lined the items up, one after the other, until the contents formed a long, neat row on the shiny metal surface. The backpack hung in his hand, deflated and empty.

She lifted a brow: *See?*

But then he did something she wasn't expecting. He turned the backpack upside down, just…upended the thing in the air. Crumbs rained onto the table. A faded receipt fluttered to the ground.

And there it was, a dull but discernible scraping sound, a sudden weight tugging at the muscles in his arm, like something inside the backpack shifted.

But nothing else fell out. There were no internal pockets.

"What was that?"

"What was what?" With a clanging heart, she pointed to the stuff on the table. "Can I put that back now? I really have to go."

The agent stared at her through a long, weighted silence, like a held breath.

Hers.

He slapped the backpack to the table, and she cringed when he shoved a hand in deep, all the way up to his elbow. He felt around the sides and the bottom, sweeping his fingers around the cheap polyester lining. She saw when he made contact with the source of the noise by the way his face changed.

The muscles in her stomach tightened. "Excuse me. This is ridiculous. Give it back."

The agent didn't let go of the backpack. He reached in his

other hand, and now there was another terrifying sound—of fabric, being ripped apart at the seams.

"Hey," she said, lunging for the backpack.

He twisted, blocking her with his body.

A few breathless seconds later he pulled it out, a small, flat object that had been sewn into the backpack lining. Small enough to fit in the palm of his hand. Almost like he'd been looking for it.

"What is this?" he said, holding it in the air between them.

"That's a book." It was the only thing she could think of to say, and it wasn't just any book. It was a gold-illuminated manuscript by a revered fourteenth-century Persian poet, one of the earliest copies from the estate of an Islamic art collector who died in Germany last year. Like most of the items in his collection, this one did not technically belong to him.

"I can see it's a book. Where did you get it?"

Her face went hot, and she had to steady herself on the metal table—the same one he was settling the book gently on top of. He turned the gold-leafed paper with careful fingers, and her mind whirled. Should she plead jet lag? Cry or pretend to faint?

"I've never seen it before in my life."

This, finally, was the truth. Today was the first time she'd seen the book with her own eyes.

The agent looked up from the Arabic symbols on the page, and she didn't miss the gotcha gleam in his eyes. The way his shiny forehead had gone even shinier now, a million new pinpricks of satisfied sweat. His gaze flitted over her shoulder, and she understood the gesture perfectly.

He was summoning backup.

She was wondering about French prison conditions.

His smile was like ice water on her skin. "Madame, I must insist you come with me."

ONE

STELLA

Paris

I grab Adam's hand and tug him hard to the left, dragging my husband into a somewhat sketchy Parisian alleyway. Smooth beige limestone stretches up on either side of us, darker at the bottom with grime from passing bikes and cars—not that many could fit through here at one time. The alley is no wider than a one-way street.

Adam falls into step behind me. There are no sidewalks here, just a narrow street with a bend up ahead and tall buildings rising on both sides, and we stick close to the walls just in case. We've been dodging Parisian traffic long enough to know that cars in this city don't stop.

I pause to point to a pile of brown goo wedged in cobblestones. It's late June, and smells of the city summer roll on a light breeze: baked bread, geraniums bursting into bloom, heated tarmac, dog poop.

"Don't step in that."

Adam's sole misses it by half an inch, but he doesn't complain about the close call or the sketchy alleyway, and he doesn't bother mentioning the many cafés and restaurants we passed along the way. When it comes to food, I like things that are off the beaten path.

"I just hope it's still here," I say, even though I've already prepared him for the possibility it might not be. My husband loves a good plan. He likes beginning every morning with a mental run-through of the day's agenda, one that leaves little room for spontaneity. His calendar is a color-coded work of art. He does best when I give him advance notice of any deviations.

But it's not like I could call ahead for a reservation. The last time I was here was ages ago, and I don't remember the restaurant's name or the exact address, only the general location. There's a very real possibility the restaurant no longer exists.

"It better be, because I was promised food so good that it'll make me fall to the ground."

A painfully chic Parisian I once knew told me that about this place, and I didn't understand her zeal until she made me try the *galette trois fromages* and I almost died. *Falling to the ground* is a Frenchism for *faint*, and my friend was right. That first bite was practically orgasmic.

Up ahead, a motorcycle comes squealing around the corner, a dark figure in head-to-toe black gunning the engine in our direction. We press ourselves to the wall and wait for him to whiz by, close enough to stir my clothes and hair. Adam's fingers wrap around mine tight like a glove.

"How much farther?" he says once the growling engine has faded. His dark shades, the ones he bought at a junky tourist shop in Portofino, have slid down his nose. He looks at me over the brim. "I'm starving."

I grin and tug him onward. "Almost there. And you're always starving."

My husband's endless appetite is one of the quirks I love about him, along with his knobby fingers and wonky pinkie toes, his habit of talking to himself in the car and in the shower, and that look he gets on his face when he's haggling for a precious antique: victory mixed with boyish wonder. These past few days in Paris, we've bounced from café to *brocante* to *boulangerie* to *marché aux puces* to *crêperie* all day long, with an occasional peek at the Seine or the Eiffel Tower in between—all of which was fine by me. I've seen all the sights anyway, multiple times.

"I'm not meeting you in Europe to play tourist," I told him when we began planning this adventure, a tagalong vacation tacked onto Adam's work trip. "I'm coming so we can experience life like the Europeans do. Eat where they eat. Shop where they shop. Learn a couple of key phrases so we can speak to them in their own language. Believe me, when it comes to getting a reservation or having a shopkeeper help you out, a few phrases go a long way. I want people to see us and think we're locals."

Not that Adam is one of *those* Americans—the ones who don white running shoes under baggy jeans and a polo, or bitch in shouty voices about how nobody here speaks any English. Adam lives in slim-cut pants and battered brogues, and there's not a shirt in his wardrobe that isn't collared. He prefers restrained over flashy, dark tones over bright patterns or colors. It's another thing I love about him, that he dresses like he stepped out of an Italian movie set in the 1950s. When he walks into an antique store anywhere in the world, the shopkeepers think he's one of them.

And his French is excellent.

The alleyway opens onto a small square, a steady stream of honking cars and growling bikes weaving aggressively around a pretty park the size of a postage stamp. People mill around on the sunken grass, getting dragged by dogs on leashes or chatting by a bubbling fountain. Well-dressed people, women with blowouts and high heels, men in linen jackets complete with elbow patches. This is the 6th arrondissement, a district filled with palaces and ancient churches and million-dollar apartments, like the ones that line this square. You can tell by the windows hung with overflowing flower boxes, by the ornate Art Nouveau railings on the shallow balconies, their double doors flung wide to let in the breeze.

Adam's gaze is focused lower to the ground, scanning the restaurants on the bottom floor. "Which one?"

I point to a tiny terrace under a yellow-and-white-striped awning, where three rickety café tables are jammed between concrete planters bursting with hot-pink bougainvillea. To the right, a plain wooden door stands open. No sign, no posted menu. And not one single solitary tourist.

In other words: perfection.

"Grab that one," I say, pointing to the table at the end, where an elderly couple just finished their coffee. The woman is already standing, already gathering up her things, while her husband wedges a colorful euro note between the cup and saucer. "I'll go in and tell the chef to get busy."

We have allotted an hour for this meal and not a second more, to comfortably make our 5:00 p.m. flight. If we'd asked the hotel concierge, he would have directed us to Café de Flore or Les Deux Magots, infamous tourist traps that charge twenty euros for a cup of halfway decent coffee. Last meal, best meal, I promised Adam, and the perfect way to cap off what's turned out to be the trip of a lifetime.

Amsterdam. Malta. Bilbao. The Amalfi Coast. Luxembourg. Paris. Six countries, ten stops, twenty-one glorious days zigzagging through my favorite spots in all of Europe, places I've been to dozens of times. Only this time I'm seeing them with Adam.

Another thing I adore about my husband? He loves to travel as much as I do.

I step inside the restaurant to a dizzying scent, coffee and cheese and sizzling meat. It's still on the early side, but the staff is in full swing, bustling preparations for the lunch crowd. My French consists of mostly nouns, and I apologize as best I can for our hurry, stumbling over what I hope conveys the message that I couldn't leave Paris without introducing my husband to the best galettes in all the city. The waiter looks bewildered, his slow head shake indicating he's still trying to puzzle out meaning from my torrent of horrendous grammar, but the chef's wink tells me he got the message.

Adam is settled by the time I return, his back pressed so far into the bougainvillea that it hangs over both shoulders, long braids of fuchsia flowers trailing down his crisp white shirt. He's scrolling through something on his phone, his big body balanced on the flimsy wooden café chair, and I pause for a moment to drink him in. That defiant cowlick in his dark hair, his scruff that's a few days beyond a five-clock shadow, his long legs outstretched in the morning sunshine.

My husband is beautiful, but the most beautiful thing about him is that he doesn't know it. He doesn't notice all the eyes that flit to him whenever he walks into a room, doesn't register all the head tilts. I pointed it out to him once back when we first started dating, and he said it was me, that those people were looking at *me*. I fell a little in love with him that day, because even when he's aware of the attention, he doesn't think it's for him.

"Galettes are on the way," I say, sinking onto the chair across from Adam. Something beige and green flashes on the screen of his phone, a photograph of something ancient. Some kind of architectural antique, I'm guessing, the kind he sells in his shop. "Admiring your new babies, I take it."

Parquet floors and terra-cotta tiles smooth with age. Mantels and columns carved with fleurs-de-lis. Gilded mirrors and stained-glass windows and Louis XIV doors—those are his babies, gorgeous, complicated pieces reclaimed from Parisian apartments and country estates, from castles and châteaus. It's what he was doing here before I arrived, buying centuries-old artifacts for the Francophile architects who frequent his Atlanta shop, enough pieces to fill a whole shipping container.

He tosses his sunglasses on the table, holding his phone so I can see. "Hey, gorgeous. Take a look at this one."

I lean in and look at the screen, the heart pendant Adam gave me in Venice bouncing against my chest. "What am I looking at?" A complicated slab of matte white and shiny gold. "What is that?"

"It's a wall molding. That's twenty-four-karat gold leafing, and it's original, which is a miracle, considering its age. Late nineteenth century, salvaged from a home that once upon a time belonged to a French industrial family. They sold off most of their properties in the Great Depression. Do you know what they call the first upstairs floor in a Parisian apartment building? The 'noble floor.' Antoine told me that."

"Who's Antoine?"

"Antoine Bernard. He owns a shop similar to mine in the 18th. I met him a couple of years ago at the Saint-Ouen market, and he's become my ears on the ground for pieces like these, a dime a dozen here but the kind Americans pay top dollar for." Adam drops his gaze to his cell phone screen, tapping it with a long finger. "Anyway, I bought eight."

"And you got them for a steal, didn't you?"

He gives me a lopsided grin. "How'd you know?"

"Because you have that look on your face."

"What look?"

That look when his eyes go all bright and dancing, when his cheeks turn pink and shiny.

"Satisfied and proud and a little bit stunned, all at once. It's the same look you get after a really hot—" I grin and lift a brow, but I don't say the word out loud.

"Oh, you mean orgasm?" His voice is a whole decibel louder than it needs to be. "A really hot orgasm?"

I shush him, sending a pointed glance to the couple beside us, sharing a slice of tarte tatin.

"This is Paris, Stella. I'm pretty sure you can say the word *orgasm* out loud here." He really leans into the word again, his grin growing wider. This is not a smile fit for lunch terraces or antique shops. "But you're not wrong. Deal hunting does feel a lot like sex. Same buildup of excitement and adrenaline, same release of endorphins when you score."

A pretty blonde with a flock of swirling butterflies tattooed up a bicep brings us our food, more galettes than the two of us could ever eat, wild mushroom and artichoke and sharp chèvre, a Florentine thick with wilted spinach and melted cheese. I sit back and let Adam take the first bites, smiling at his sounds of appreciation, which were much like mine the first time I tried them.

"You did not oversell this place," he says once he's tasted them all. "These galettes are freaking delicious."

I think about the million things we have to do when we get home. The hours Adam will spend catching up at the shop and the fundraiser I'm supposed to help cater tomorrow night, the laundry and the lawn and the mountain of mail we'll have to sort through. I think these things, and I don't want to leave.

"So," he says, dragging his knife through the mushroom galette, cutting off another generous slice, "what was your top best?"

It's something we do often—at the end of a day, an experience, a trip—name the thing that stood out to us the most. That one, singular moment that will become a top cherished memory. I don't have to even think about it.

"That's easy. You almost getting mowed down by that bicycle in Amsterdam. You squealed like a little girl."

Even now, weeks later, the memory makes me giggle. Adam stepping into the bike path that cuts through the middle of the Rijksmuseum, thinking it was a sidewalk. The oncoming cyclist leaning on his bell, the screaming and flailing of arms—mostly Adam's as he leaped out of the way. I've never seen him move so fast.

"That asshole came out of nowhere, and I'm pretty sure that bike was electric, which how is that even allowed? He must have been doing fifty miles an hour."

"Dutch bikes and trams, I told you to watch out for those things." I pause for a bite of artichoke, grinning at him across the table. "What was yours?"

He takes a moment to think, staring out into the square, his gaze climbing the buildings on the opposite side, snagging on the prettiest one. On the second floor, the windows are thrown open, the sheer curtains just inside billowing in the breeze.

"You think they're all going to be so cliché. Everywhere we went, I mean. We've both seen them before, and they're all so recognizable—listed in every guidebook and travel site as Must Sees, pictured on everybody's social medias. Notre Dame, Amsterdam's canals, the pastel buildings on the Italian coastline. You know going in these places are going to be tourist traps, but then you get there and you don't care. They're exactly like you thought they would be and, at the same time, the most beautiful thing you've ever seen."

I fall silent, because how many times have I tried to explain why my blood pumps hotter, why my heart beats more fiercely in a foreign land? A million, at least. For me the allure of a faraway place is a visceral, emotional thing. I've never been able to find words that give it enough weight. And now Adam just did. Without even trying, he found the exact right words.

I stare out into the square, where the sun sneaks through gaps in the cluster of trees and paints the grass and cobblestones with gold, and I sigh. "You want to stay another night?"

"I wish we could."

"I wish we could stay here forever."

Adam reaches across the table and grabs me by the necklace

he gave me in Venice, a bloodred heart of glass set in a diamond cage, and gently tugs my face toward his. "I changed my mind, by the way," he says, not letting me go—my gaze or the heart. Looking at me in that way of his that heats my skin and blood. We've been married three years, together for four, and my husband can still do that to me.

"It's you," he says, and my own heart gives a little lift.

"Me, what?"

"You're my top best. Every moment of these past three weeks with you. *Je t'aime à la folie.*"

Another funny Frenchism: *I love you to madness.*

I smile and we kiss, and it's the kind of kiss you see in the movies, the kind where two lovers sitting in a busy Parisian café kiss like they're the only two people on the terrace. I love my husband to madness, too.

Later, in the weeks and months following this perfect moment, I will change my mind. Adam's top best—every moment of these past three weeks crisscrossing through Europe, just us two—will become mine, too. The whole blissful trip my most cherished memory.

Every single moment until what happened next.

TWO

"Shit." We've almost made it back to the opposite end of the alleyway when Adam lurches to a stop. He pats his chest, his pockets, the top of his head. "I left my sunglasses at the café."

The sunglasses we bought in Italy because he'd left the previous pair on yet another sunny terrace, somewhere in Spain. They're cheap and ugly, and he bought them at the first place he saw, a corner store so jam-packed with wares that they spilled out onto the sidewalk. Piles of buckets and shovels and blow-up toys, hanging net bags filled with balls, turnstiles of flip-flops and plastic sunglasses in every imaginable color. Adam pulled a black pair from the display and paid without trying them on. They are too narrow for his face and sit crooked on his nose.

I snake my arm through his and give him a tug in the direction we were headed. "I'll buy you a new pair at the airport. A *nice* pair."

But Adam's feet stick to the sidewalk. He shakes his head, jutting a thumb over his shoulder. "I'll only lose them. And I want *that* pair."

"Which cost what—six euros? You paid for them with change from the bottom of my purse."

"So? Somewhere in China there is a child who was taught fine motor skills in order to screw those glasses together. They're my favorite souvenir." He smiles. "I have very happy memories of that afternoon on the beach."

Skin warm from the Italian sun, sand and pebbles shifting underneath our shared towel, the taste of coconut oil and lemon gelato as we made out like a couple of teenagers. There were a million people on that beach that day, music and laughter and kids screaming as they kicked up sand, but it was all background noise. *Farei qualsiasi cosa per te*, Adam said to me at one point, his breath tickling my neck, and I teased him about his Duolingo skills. He told me I wouldn't laugh so hard if I knew what those words meant. *Farei qualsiasi cosa per te—I would do anything for you.* And then he took me back to the hotel and showed me.

Now I laugh and slap him on his stomach, flat as a galette despite being filled with four of them. "You big ol' softy. Fine, come on. We'll go back."

We've only made it a couple of steps into the alley before he stops again. He checks the time on his cell, and because I know my husband, I check the time, too.

"It's not quite quarter to one," I say, because I already know what he's thinking, "which means we have more than four hours before takeoff. The hotel is three blocks away. Even if we don't rush, we can make it back by one. We have plenty of time."

He humors me with a thoughtful pause, even though I can tell by his tight lips that it's purely for show. Adam's mind is already whirling, adjusting the times on his mental schedule. "Maybe. But we still need to get all our stuff from upstairs."

"It's all packed. The suitcases are by the door."

"Except for the things in the safe."

Our passports, some jewelry, a few thousand in cash because Adam is as old-fashioned as his beloved antiques. He refuses

to go anywhere without emergency cash, enough to last him
at least a week.

"The safe will take two seconds to empty out, and the airport is only a thirty-minute drive. And that's *with* traffic, which
the concierge said we likely wouldn't have this time of day."

"*Likely.* He said *likely.*"

I swallow down a sigh, the frustration more at myself than
at Adam, because it's not like we haven't had this argument
before. Even though I planned this outing with a generous
buffer. Even though I know that when Adam feels stressed for
time, rationality doesn't prevail. My husband doesn't want to
be on time for things. He wants to be early because being late
for anything, even for a party, gives him hives.

He reaches out a hand, wraps his fingers around mine. "I'm
a freak, okay? I know this. But please, humor me on this one?
I'll feel better if we divide and conquer. I'll run."

I laugh. "How about this? You take a *leisurely stroll* back to
the café and fetch your glasses, and I'll go back to the hotel and
grab our luggage and everything from the safe. By the time
you make it back, the doormen will be loading everything
into the back of a cab."

"Thank you." He picks the necklace off my chest and tugs,
pulling me in for a kiss. "See you in ten, back at the hotel."

"You bet." He sets off in a brisk jog back down the alleyway.
I call out to his retreating back, "You don't really have to run."

He laughs and tosses a wave over his shoulder. "You know
I do."

And then, just like that, he's gone.

Unlike my agenda-obsessed husband, I take my time.

The alleyway spits me out on the Rue Saint-Sulpice, and I
double back half a block to the crosswalk so I can stroll on the
sunny side. I pause at a window to take in a tower of macarons,
tiny cushions in every imaginable color. My mouth waters at

the smell, vanilla and butter and sugar, but I don't go inside. Adam loves macarons as much as anyone, but if he makes it back to the hotel before I do, I'll never hear the end of it.

Up ahead, the Church of Saint-Sulpice towers over an entire city block, and I stop on the sidewalk, shade my eyes with a hand and admire its sculpted dome. It's my favorite church in all of Paris, much more interesting than the more popular Notre Dame or Sacre Coeur, and much less of a tourist trap. A few days ago, Adam explained how the sundial works, when the sun shines through the stained-glass windows exactly at noon, lighting up the brass line embedded in the floor and prompting the church bells to peal out the time. I didn't tell him I knew this already because I'd once been there at noon on the dot.

Or that I could lead him to the best place to see the Eiffel Tower light up at night without once consulting Google Maps, or could walk the route from our hotel to the Place Vendôme without a single wrong turn. Or that once upon a time, I knew the way into every Place To Be in this city—the restaurants with monthslong waiting lists, the nightclubs with lines that wrapped around the block, the designer shops that stocked just enough of the latest it-bag but let me walk out with one dangling from an arm. There wasn't a line or a list I couldn't get past in Paris, but this was years ago, a lifetime before I met Adam.

"Excusez-moi."

It's a woman. Silk dress, sensible leather pumps, a fluffy white poodle on an orange leash. The epitome of Parisian chic, her shoulders drooped slightly with age. I smile and step backward, giving both of them ample room to pass.

Once, on an overnight flight from JFK to Marrakech, a sharp bout of turbulence shook the Airbus so hard it knocked me to the ground. That's the first thing I think when the ground underneath us pitches. The jolt feels the same, a violent wave of pressurized air that sends me flying into the building behind me. One second I'm standing there, watching the woman and her dog pass by on the sidewalk; the next, my shoulder bone slams the bricks with a hard *thwack*, pain radiating down my arm and back. I register a scream before I realize it's mine.

I press myself flat to the building until the ground stops shaking, my fingertips searching for purchase on the flat facade. My brain tries to make sense of what just happened.

An earthquake?

No, that can't be right. My eardrums are ringing, not just from the shock but a thundering clap. A boom that shook the streets and jolted me backward. My chest heaves with realization. *Oh, my God.* This was an explosion.

A few feet away, the poodle is losing its mind, barking and dancing around the elderly woman, sprawled face down on the sidewalk. I hear its incessant yipping just before I notice everything else. Screams. Car alarms. And in the distance, sirens. A swell of sound pushing through the ringing in my ears.

I push myself off the wall and rush over. *"Madame. Ça va?"*

More *how's it going* than *how are you*, but I can't come up with the French word for *hurt*.

Beyond her, the glass walls of a bus stop fall to the ground, shattering into a million beads of glass that scatter across the sidewalk and street. They glitter in the sun like diamonds.

The woman doesn't respond, so I grab the dog's leash and tug it away from its owner, crouching over her, my mind rolling through the first-aid steps, beginning with assess. Did she hit her head? Injure her neck or her spine? I take in her limbs spread every which way, the way her shoulders rise and fall with breath, thank God, but the rest of her is still.

Rolling her over can do more damage than good—I've done enough first-aid trainings to know that. Plus, she's at an age where bones can shatter at the simplest fall, and this one was far from simple. This was a blast that shot her into the concrete.

I look around, scanning the street for help. A bewildered

man climbs out of his car, stopped crosswise in the middle of the road, like he slammed the brakes hard enough to skid sideways. Farther up the sidewalk, three people break into a sprint.

Shit.

I turn back to the woman, conjugating the French word for *break* in my head—*casse, casses, casse, cassons, cassez*—when she moans. She rolls onto her side, and the dog lunges for her face, licking a cheek stained with dirt and smudged lipstick but, thankfully, no blood.

"Oh, thank God," I say, and it's enough for her. She answers in rapid-fire French, something about a sister and a lunch date and one word that tingles every hair on the back of my neck: *terroristes.*

Is that what this was, a terrorist attack? *Jesus.*

She bats a crepey hand in my direction, gesturing for me to help her to her feet. I'm careful to support her in case she did break a bone. Her hands are scraped, there's a thin line of blood snaking down her shin and, judging by the steady stream of French tumbling out of her mouth, she's probably in shock. I don't catch even half of it.

"English?" I say, but she doesn't so much as pause. I let her ramble on, thinking back to that ominous word. *Terroristes.*

It wasn't all that long ago that this city suffered through a string of them, coordinated attacks after some magazine published an offensive cartoon. I remember the signs plastered all over the city and every website—*je suis Charlie.* For Parisians like this lady, people who lived through the horror, the attacks are fresh enough that her mind would automatically go there.

I see it, too, on the faces of the people stepping out into the street, ducking their heads out of shops and upstairs windows. Not *what's wrong?* but *again?* A mixture of resignation and disgust.

I do a slow spin, taking in the street. The stopped cars, the sunny square, the ancient buildings of brick and limestone. If it weren't for the *boom* still echoing in my bones and the disheveled old lady stumbling away with her poodle, I might think I'd imagined it. Across the street, the church bells peal out a solemn song—1:00 p.m. It's the time I was supposed to be ready and waiting for Adam at the hotel.

I pull out my phone and call him, alarm beginning to prickle in my limbs. His phone rings four times, then shoots me to voicemail.

"Babe, call me. There was just a big explosion, and I want to hear your voice. I love you. Call me."

I hit End and follow it up with a text message: CALL ME, in all caps.

I slide the phone back into my bag and turn in the direction I just came from. The way Adam would be coming from once he fetched his sunglasses from the table. I stare up the pretty street, half expecting to see him jogging toward me, his face filled with fear and relief. A breeze kicks up, shaking the leaves in the trees, but otherwise, the street is quiet and empty.

Too empty.

It's then I spot it, the thick column of smoke swirling into a clear blue sky. It rises like a black ghost over the treetops and zinc-tiled roofs, a billowing streak of filth and fire.

I see it, and I start running.

THREE

The alleyway is thick with people—a surge of bodies swarming out of the smoke. I push up on the tips of my toes, but I'm five and a half feet on a good day and all I see are heaving chests and panicked faces. A steady stream of people coming at me, a human stampede jostling me backward. My lungs singe with the charcoal odor of fresh fire.

I catch garbled snippets of French as they pass, a lot of it curse words. *Putain de bordel de merde.* Loosely translated, *holy motherfucking shit.* Their expressions—tense, dazed, relieved to be alive—tell me I'm headed the right way.

It hits me again, all at once, what happened. An explosion. A bomb. I think it and my legs go limp with fear. These people are running from disaster, from danger, and so far none of them are Adam.

My heart seizes with slippery terror, and I tell myself he's back at the hotel by now, probably annoyed because I'm not there. I see him trudging up to our room at the end of the fourth floor, hear him call my name into the room, empty except for the suitcases lined up by the bathroom door. I see him tick in the passcode to the safe, where the cash and our passports are still tucked away securely inside. I see his forehead wrinkle first with irritation, then worry. He must be thinking the same thing I am right now.

Surely not. What are the chances?

A woman rams into me, a head-on collision that pushes me back an entire foot. She's carrying a child on her hip, a little girl of about two or three who's wailing loud enough to pierce an eardrum. Both of them are covered in white dust.

"Pardón," I say automatically, at the same time Adam's laughter rings through my mind. "Such a Southern belle," he's always teasing me. "Why apologize for something that's not your fault?" Adam is from Chicago, where people are nice but not *that* nice. The woman shoves past me and then she's gone.

I lean into the stream of people and push myself through. Forward motion. I search for him in the faces I pass.

Find him.

Then again, maybe he's called me back by now. There's no way I would have heard my phone ring in this overcrowded alleyway, no way I would have felt it buzzing in the messenger bag against my hip, not with all this shoving and jostling. My heart gives a hopeful jingle. Maybe all my worry is for nothing.

I thread a hand in my bag and feel around for my cell. The little side pocket where I keep it for easy reach—empty, which means it's bouncing around at the bottom of my bag. I search for it while I push into a bottleneck of people crowding the bend in the alleyway, praying for it to buzz to life in my fingers, or at the very least, be overflowing with text messages.

Hey, gorgeous.

I'm back at the hotel, where are you?

I'm worried.

I'm fine.

Please, for the love of God, let Adam have called me back.

My fingers make contact with something hard and smooth, and with a throaty sob of relief, I pull it out and swipe up with a thumb. I'm unlocking the screen when the alleyway suddenly darkens, and I look up to find a staggeringly large man looming over me. He barks at me in a Germanic language, pointing over my head, and I understand enough of it to get the gist. I'm going the wrong way.

I gesture past him, deeper into the alleyway and beyond, the square. "My husband," I say in English, because translating those words is too much right now, and so is the gash in his hairline. It oozes a stream of ruby red down the right side of his cheek, dripping off his jawline into what was once a crisp white collar. The blood is still flowing, the fabric heavy and sticking to his skin. Whoever this man is, he needs stitches.

There are more guttural words, more gesturing to the alleyway behind me, but he turns just enough to let me squeeze past.

The man behind him isn't as accommodating, though, and he shoulder-butts me hard enough to knock the air from my lungs. My bag catches on something—a hand, his arm. The strap pulls tight across my chest like a seat belt, tugging me back the way I came, and I jab the pointiest part of my elbow into soft flesh—a stomach, I'm guessing from the grunt that comes as a result. But the tension releases, and the bag slaps against my hip.

I lurch back into the oncoming stream of bodies so dense I can barely breathe.

My cell buzzes in my fingers, and my heart revs at the number sitting atop the text app. Ten new texts.

As I push through the crowd, I hold my breath and tap the icon with a shaky finger, my stomach falling when I see the names that float to the top. A colleague, my few friends, my boss, people who know I'm here and saw the news on CNN.

But there's nothing new from Adam. No *Hey, gorgeous*, his

standard opening line. No missed calls. My CALL ME text is still marked delivered but not read.

Tears burn in my eyes, but I wipe them away and tell myself he's fine. Adam is *fine*, and unlike my news-obsessed friends and colleagues, he's probably oblivious to the afternoon's drama.

Or no—he'd be like me, running into the thick of things. To search for me, to help. He's probably rescuing someone, wiping tears and blood with the tail of his shirt. That's the kind of guy Adam is, the kind who would risk his own life to save others.

I tap his contact card and hit Call, then press it to my ear and pray. The line takes forever to connect, and I think of all the other millions of worried people in this city. The cell towers are probably overloaded with people like me, trying to track down their loved ones.

I'm about to hang up and try again when, by some miracle, the line finally connects. It rings four sluggish times before sending me to voicemail.

His familiar voice squeezes in my chest. "Hi, this is Adam. Please leave me a message."

"Adam, please please *please* call me the second you hear this. There was some kind of explosion, and it was nearby and now I can't find you and…I'm so scared, babe. Please call me. *Please.*"

I hang up and then send another all-caps text. My hands are shaking as I hit Send, a combination of fear and adrenaline that zings through my blood as I stare at the screen. Six seconds pass, then ten, then more. There are no dancing dots, no indication he might have seen the message. Another text marked delivered, but not read.

I feel it in my stomach, the dark spread of dread.

"Hey, Siri, call the Hôtel Luxembourg Parc."

This time, the connection is almost immediate. "*Bonjour,* Hôtel Luxembourg Parc. How may I direct your call?"

"*Bonjour,* this is Stella Knox. My husband and I are staying in room 413. His name is Adam Knox. I'm hoping you can help me look for him."

"Would you like me to connect you to the room?"

"Yes, but can you check to see if he's checked out first?"

"*Mais oui*, of course, madame. One moment, please." A pause filled with the clicking of a keyboard, a soft hum. "I see that Housekeeping reported the room as still occupied at quarter to one. Are you aware of our checkout time?"

I pull the phone away from my ear and check the clock—1:13. That gives Adam a window of some thirty minutes since I saw him last, plenty of time to fetch his glasses from the café and the bags from upstairs, to wonder where I am, to call me the fuck back.

"Can you have Housekeeping check again? Or maybe he's already downstairs. In the lobby somewhere. He's tall, dark hair. He's wearing jeans and a white button-down."

"I see at least ten men here who look like what you describe."

"Just yell out his name. Adam Knox. Yell it really loud."

"Madame. I can't just—"

"Please. Help me find him. *Please.*"

A pause, and then she does it, asks if anyone there is named Adam Knox—first in French, then in English. I hold my breath and wait, terror lingering in my stomach like an ulcer.

"I'm sorry, madame. There is no one here answering to that name."

My lungs deflate and so do my bones, my legs nearly folding underneath me. I slump against the wall of the alley like a rag doll. "Keep trying, please. And please call me back at this number as soon as you find him. Can you do that?"

"I... Yes, madame, of course."

I rattle off my cell phone number and pocket my iPhone, giving myself another pep talk. Adam is probably already on his way upstairs, or probably he's dragging our luggage into the elevator, or maybe he's got his glasses but lost his phone. Wherever he is, he's *fine*. Everything is okay. It's got to be okay.

By now the alleyway is starting to empty out, and it occurs to me this is both good news and bad. Good because fewer people means a clear path, more bodies behind me than blocking my way. But bad because the last stragglers coming down the alleyway are more injured than the ones earlier on. More cradled limbs and contusions, covered in more grime and blood. The walking wounded.

And still, not one of them has been Adam.

Up ahead, the alleyway opens up, and I break into a jog, my necklace bouncing against my chest. I drop it inside my T-shirt without slowing down, zigzagging around the last few stragglers limping by. One of them, a man of about my age, staggers straight at me, looking like he just climbed out of a coal mine. His face is covered with soot, all but two white lines fanning out from the corners of his eyes. Tears, maybe, or sweat. He reaches for me with a moan, and I lurch to the right—horrified, both by his appearance and my response. Any other day I would stop and help this man, but not today. Today all I can think about is finding mine.

At the end of the alley, I stop and stare into the square.

Sunlight tries to pierce through the foggy smoke, which hangs over the square like an angry storm cloud. It's louder, too, filled with the sounds of shouts and swirling sirens. In the middle of the square, the trees rise up like jagged ghosts around a fountain that's still clattering, and it's the strangest sensation. I can almost see myself standing here, stiff with shock, taking it all in. Like I'm floating outside my body.

The square is like a war zone. Like those disaster sites you see on the news. Like the footage from ground zero.

Only this is real. This is really happening, right now.

It takes me a full ten seconds to pick the figures out of the fog, to register that the dark smudges and lumps are bodies.

Stretched out on the sunken grass. Slumped on the hoods of parked cars. Lying on the pavement between trash and debris, next to mounds of rocks and giant chunks of concrete. I scan the shapes for one that looks like Adam, but there are too many, the smoke too thick. It singes my throat and clogs my lungs. I cough into an elbow.

And then my gaze moves to the hole where a café once stood. Where less than an hour ago Adam and I sat at a tiny table pushed up against a planter overflowing with bright pink bougainvillea. Where we scarfed down the most delicious galettes and thumbed through pictures of French antiques on his phone. Where he kissed me like we were the only two people in Paris. Now there's literally nothing left of it except the memories inside my head.

The terrace. The restaurant. The patrons and the winking chef.

All of it is gone.

FOUR

I stand at the edge of the square, my eyes and throat burning as bright as the flames licking out an upstairs window, two stories above where the restaurant once stood. A gaping hole in what was once a block-wide stretch of smooth, four-story limestone, now a black cave of dangling wires and charred concrete. I think of the couple eating salads next to us, the waitress with the butterfly tattoos, the people going about their day in the apartments just above, and my stomach roils with shock, with horror.

"Oh, my God. Oh, my *God*." My voice sounds flat, as if it's coming from a long way off, from someone else. The smoke seems to grow thicker, more suffocating.

Or maybe that's the panic seeping in.

A man with wheat-blond hair races by in a full-on sprint, and I grab him by the sleeve, lurching him to a stop so abrupt, it drags us both into the street.

"Aidez moi s'il vous plaît." *Help me, please*—but in an accent so lousy, it's questionable to even call it French.

The man looks confused, and though he stays put, he clearly doesn't want to. He tosses a glance in the direction of the burned-out restaurant. Except for the light coating of dust on his shoes and hem of his jeans, the bright streak of fresh blood on his T-shirt—not his, I don't think—he's like me. Clean. Uninjured. This man came here after the blast.

He gives a hurried shake of his head. "My French is bollocks. You mind trying that again in English?"

British, I realize with a pang of relief. We speak the same language.

"Help. I need help." I pull out my cell and show him the screen saver, my all-time favorite picture of Adam and me, taken on a sunny terrace in Amsterdam. "I'm looking for this man. Have you seen him?"

He squints at the screen, scrunching a nose that's been broken more than once. "Maybe? Hard to know for sure. So far the bodies I've carried out haven't all been—" he swipes a hand down his face, which contorts in a grimace "—recognizable."

I breathe through another wave of nausea. This man said *bodies*—plural. Unrecognizable ones. This man might have carried my husband out, but he doesn't know for sure because the bodies were *unrecognizable*.

"These…" My voice trails off, and for a long moment I can't finish. Even thinking about it makes me nauseous, but somehow I force the word over my tongue. "These *bodies* you carried out. Where did you put them?"

He gestures to the sunken middle of the square, where the fountain shoots up a steady stream of water, oblivious to the day's drama.

"On the lawn over there, mostly. If you have any medical skills, some of those folks could probably use some help. Or at the very least, some comforting."

I'm off before he's finished the last sentence, my sneakers kicking up dust in the ash-covered street. A mangled chunk of stainless steel lies directly between me and the lawn—an oven? A sink? I skirt around it, almost tripping over a chair, one I recognize from the restaurant, same as the ones Adam and I sat in not long ago. The force of the blast must have blown them here, a good thirty feet away, right before it rained down a thick gray dust. It covers everything, the streets and sidewalks and balconies, the buildings and oblivious fountain. The bodies stretched out on the grass.

"Adam!" I scream his name into the square.

I leap down the steps onto the lawn, scanning the faces. There are at least a dozen of them, and I take in the length of their legs and arms, the color of the hair I can see under the matted ash. Adam is tall, well over six feet, and bulkier than the typical Parisian male, who tends to be lean. There are only a few here with Adam's proportions—one by the bushes on the far end, another cradling his head on a bench, a body lying motionless on the other side of the fountain. But none of them are him.

"Adam."

The man on the bench looks up from his hands, and I flinch, at the same time I'm thanking God it's not Adam. One eye is swollen completely shut, and there's a gash that runs the length of his cheek, dripping blood down his neck and into his collar. So much blood that it's a wonder he's still conscious.

I hand him a scarf I dig out of my bag—an Hermès Adam found at a steal during one of his treks through the market—and he takes it, pressing it to the wound on his face.

I hold my phone in front of his face. *"Cet homme. Le voyez-vous?"* This man. *Do you see him?*

"Oui. Je le vois." I see him.

Shit. And this is the problem with my high-school French; I was always crap at past tense. *Sees.* He *sees* Adam on my phone.

The man really does look awful. He's going to need stitches, and soon. Guilt pings, because I think this, and yet my concern remains with Adam.

"Do you see this man, *there*?" I ask it in French, then in

English, and I look like an idiot, over-gesticulating at the remnants of the restaurant, but it gets the point across.

"Ah," he says as understanding hits, and God bless this man, he takes another look at my phone. He presses my scarf to his face, shaking his head. *"Non."*

There's more, a rush of French I don't understand, but I'm already turning away, pivoting to face the others in the grass. I try not to linger too long on their bloody faces, their shredded clothes, the way too many of them are not moving at all. A teenager wearing a scooter helmet. A young woman curled up on her side. An elderly man staring up at the sky.

I zigzag from body to body, shouting his name. A few of them stir, but none are who I'm looking for, and I don't know whether to be relieved or terrified when I've made it to the last one and Adam is not among them. My chest goes tight, my heart a clenched fist, and I scream his name until my throat is on fire. "ADAM."

A female voice barks at me, a torrent of angry, rapid-fire French that ruffles the hair on the back of my head. I whirl around, and she's young, hair slicked back into a severe bun. Sweat drips from her temples in shiny streams down cheeks free of makeup. I take in her uniform: the dark cargo pants, light blue polo shirt, boxy navy cap with white piping. The patch on her sleeve says *gendarmerie*, but this is not the badass kind guarding the Élysée Palace with bulletproof vests and automatic rifles. This is the kind who helps little old ladies cross the street.

"I'm looking for my husband." I don't bother with attempting it in French, as I'm too flustered, far too horrified by the state of the people I just saw on the grass. "He came to get his sunglasses from the restaurant, and now I can't find him anywhere."

"Go back to your hotel." Her English is impeccable though

heavily accented, her pronunciation all pursed lips and throaty *R*s. "Your husband is probably there."

"I already called the hotel, and he's not. He's not answering his phone, either." I tap my phone screen just in case, flip it around so she can see. No calls or messages.

She doesn't so much as glance at it.

"I am to clear people to make room for emergency services. They will have someone who will maintain a list of missing persons. If you were a witness to the bombing, they will want to talk to you. In the meantime, I need you to wait over there." She points to the far corner of the square, as far away as possible from the blown-out restaurant.

Two little words hit me: *the bombing.* Not an explosion, a *bombing.* It's one thing to hear it from a little old lady who passed me on the street, another thing entirely for it to come from a member of the gendarmerie.

"So that's what this was—a bombing?"

She realizes her mistake with a sharp shake of her head. "Explosion. I wanted to say *explosion.* But again, madame, you must get out of the way."

When still I don't move, she presses a hand to my shoulder and gives me a forceful nudge, moving me back and away, putting even more distance between me and the restaurant. I refuse to leave this place, not before I find Adam.

A siren swoops from the square's northwest corner, the promised emergency services van, and the cop pushes me harder. I think about the British man I flagged down earlier, about the bodies he carted to the grass, the medical help and comforting he told me they needed. I dig in, my soles sliding across the ash-covered bricks.

"*Wait.* I'm trained in CPR. I know how to administer oxygen, stem bleeding, use an AED." She frowns, and I add, "AED stands for *automated external defibrillator.* I also know how to do the Rautek Maneuver."

A tactic to drag an unconscious victim out of the danger zone, even ones that far outweigh me—like the two-hundred-pound man who dropped dead on a flight to Abu Dhabi. I have other skills, too, like how to coach a pregnant woman through labor or what to do when someone goes into cardiac arrest, though that's probably not as useful here.

The cop releases her grip on my shoulder. "Okay. But only helping. No getting in the way."

I nod my agreement, and she pushes past, taking off in a jog toward the northwest corner, where troops are piling out of a van.

I return my attention to the people on the sunken grass, more now thanks to the British man, half walking, half carrying a woman to the opposite side of the fountain. She's covered in dust and now so is he, his hair and clothing turned a light, pallid gray since I saw him last. He settles the woman gently onto the ground, then peels her arm from around his neck, but she doesn't want to let him go. She grabs on to his hand with both of hers, her mouth moving nonstop.

I'm watching them when he spots me and straightens, gesturing me over with his free hand. "I need a translator."

I skirt around the fountain, moving closer. "I think you're overestimating my French, but I'll try."

"It's a hell of a lot better than mine, that's for sure." He gestures to the woman on the grass, still grasping his hand in both of hers. Still talking, her gaze locked on the Brit.

I clock her at about my mother's age, somewhere in her mid-to-late fifties, though much more well-preserved. Botox, lashes, fresh blowout under a thick dusting of ash. She gives his hand a hard shake, staring up at him with wide, panicked eyes, her breakneck French always circling back to the same word: *chat*.

"She's asking you about her cat." I pause to listen, picking a few key words out of the steady stream, trying to piece them together in a way that makes sense. "I think she's saying that he jumped out the open window. Something about *trois*—three. The third floor, maybe? Or no—maybe she means *toit*, which I'm pretty sure is a rooftop."

The Brit gives me an amused look, making a sound deep in his throat. He swipes his face with a sleeve, leaving a dark streak on his cheek. "A cat on a rooftop is the least of my worries. Not until we get all the people out, and even then." He turns to the woman and pries his hand free, giving hers a supportive pat. "Tell her I'll watch out for her pet."

He turns and jogs off before I can agree, and what is it that Mr. Rogers said? To look for the helpers. The Good Samaritans like this man, an innocent Brit who was likely here on holiday when he heard the *boom*. Instead of running away, he's running into the fray, taking the steps by twos and threes on the way back to the café. How many of these people has he carried out? How many lives has he saved? I watch him until he's out of sight, disappearing back into the blown-open building.

And then I squat down to deliver his message in broken French. It comes out in stops and starts, lots of *ummm*s and pauses while I search for words, but eventually the woman gets my gist. She settles back onto the grass with a sigh of relief.

I scan her body for injuries. "*Ça va?* Are you okay?"

She tells me she's fine, and I show her the picture of Adam on my phone. "Have you seen this man? My husband, *mon mari*. I don't know where he is. *Je ne sais pas.*"

She pats my knee with a filthy hand, giving me a slow shake of her head. "I'm sorry," she murmurs—*je suis désolé*—but I hear that word, *désolé*, and suddenly I can't do this anymore. I can't hold back my tears. I fall backward onto the grass and sob.

Me, too, I think. *I am desolate, too.*

By now the square is bustling with people, police in tactical gear, firemen with shiny yellow jackets, more gendarmerie swarming in from every side street. They unroll crime scene tape and haul long metal barriers from the back of a van, arranging both in a generous perimeter around the café. Above their heads, tattered awnings flap in the breeze.

And then I see him, talking to a fireman on the far end of the square. A tall man with dark hair and broad shoulders. I take in his bright white shirt, his slim-cut jeans, and my bones go soft with relief.

I leap to my feet and take off across the square.

FIVE

ADAM

Capri, Italy
Eighteen days earlier

No man is rich enough to buy back his past.

—Oscar Wilde

"It's not all that difficult," I say, cranking the handle of the winch to adjust the sail, white silk billowing against a bright blue sky. A couple of football fields to our right—starboard side, as I keep explaining to Stella—the island of Capri sparkles like a jewel in the distance. "You just have to know how to make the wind hit the sail at the right spot so it lifts the boat and slides us through the water. It's simple physics, really, a combination of aerodynamics and hydrodynamics. A piece of cake once you learn how to feel the vessel."

And not just any vessel, a thirty-eight-foot Dehler some jokester christened *Feelin' Nauti*, a masterpiece of teak and fiberglass. It's a lot of boat to handle on my own, but I grew up on the shores of Lake Michigan. I've been on sailboats all my life.

Stella pushes up from the bench where she's stretched out,

her skin almost as white as the hotel's terry-cloth towel, but her freckles are out in full force. "Red hair and sunshine do not mix," she said with a roll of her eyes when she saw them, slathering on another thick layer of SPF.

"I hate to tell you, but physics isn't simple. I freaking *hated* physics, almost as much as I hated my teacher, Mr. Batista. He was a real pervert, by the way. He said if I showed him a picture of me in a bikini, he'd bump my C up to an A minus."

I look over with a grin. "And did you?"

"Hell, no. I reported him to the principal. Mrs. Strickland was all *I am woman hear me roar* feminist fierceness, and she fired him on the spot. After that I was known as the girl who got Mr. Batista's skeevy ass fired, and I *still* got a C. Like I said, physics is not simple."

I keep a steady hand on the helm, but my gaze skims downward, over the lavender fabric barely covering her oiled-up skin, and my blood sizzles in a way that's not just from the sun. It's from the thrill of slicing through open water. Of bending the wind to your will and the freedom of nature and speed. Of Stella in that lavender bikini.

"Poor Mr. Batista never knew what he was missing."

She laughs. "And he never will."

We come around a cliff to the south side of the island, where dozens of sailboats like ours leave wispy trails in the turquoise water. Just beyond, three craggy rock formations rise up from the Tyrrhenian Sea like soldiers standing guard over the island—the iconic Faraglioni.

I point across the bow. "Marina Piccola, two o'clock."

Stella sits up on the bench, taking in the jumble of colorful parasols, the neat row of changing cabins, and Siren's Rock, where Ulysses was supposedly seduced. Where we spent yesterday afternoon sunning on its rocky beach, watching the boats bob by while she told stories of the celebrities who used to come here. Oscar Wilde. Grace Kelly. Jacqueline Onassis.

Elizabeth Taylor and Sophia Loren. During the La Dolce Vita days of the late 1950s, Marina Piccola was their playground. As a former flight attendant, Stella is the most well-traveled person I've ever met, and that's really saying something, given my line of work. She makes a great tour guide.

"Who knew you were so good at this?" she says now, pushing up from her towel to snap yet another picture. "Or that sailing was so sexy. You're looking mighty fine behind that wheel."

"It's a helm. And just wait until you see my Palomar knot."

She laughs. "Such a nerd. I bet you went to sail camp, too, didn't you?"

Sail camp and tennis camp and swim camp, adventure camps and golf camps and pretty much every other camp you can think of. My parents weren't the Capri kind of wealthy, but despite their spectacular divorce, they had more than enough—of money and of me and my sister, Julia. Every summer they got rid of us by shipping us off to back-to-back camps, followed by endless bickering about whose turn it was to foot the bill. Julia likes to joke that we were expensive pawns, but it's not really a joke. It's also why the two of us are so close, why I will do whatever it takes for her and her daughter, Babs, even if it means crossing a line or two.

"Whoa. Look at that one," Stella says, pointing at a white-and-tan yacht sitting high and huge in the water.

"That's the *Flying Fox*. At 450 feet, it's the world's largest charter superyacht. Most expensive, too, since it cost a million dollars per foot to build. And see that platform at the very top? That's the helipad. There's also an onboard hammam, sauna, pool, gym, movie theater, and an entire wall in the dining room that's a giant aquarium. Oh, and a permanent DJ alcove."

"For when Tiësto comes to visit, I suppose."

"Or for when he charters it, which Jay-Z and Beyoncé did not all that long ago, for the bargain-basement price of four million dollars a week."

"Such peasants. Who's the owner?"

I shrug. "Nobody knows. For a while there, it was rumored Jeff Bezos owned it, but his yacht is a sailing yacht, a brand-new three-master too tall to pass under the bridge between the Rotterdam shipyard and the North Sea. So, he did what any smart billionaire would do when their yacht gets stuck, and offered to pay to have the bridge dismantled and put back together again after his boat passes through. The Rotterdammers are *pissed*. It's a whole big battle."

Normally, this is Stella's department, spouting off facts like a Lonely Planet booklet, impressing me with her knowledge. But this is one subject I happen to know a lot about, and not just because I like boats.

She looks at me with squinty eyes. "How do you know all these things?"

"I read newspapers."

"Which part, the society section?"

"Ha ha." A sudden gust of wind tugs at the sails, pitching us a couple of degrees to the right, and I scramble to make adjustments. I loosen up the rope, point the bow a fraction south, tiny course corrections that smooth out the ride. "I learned all that from the business section, FYI. Owners of boats like the *Flying Fox* tend to hide their identities behind LLCs owned by multiple layers of trusts. It's legal, but just barely."

"I'm sure it makes for some fascinating reading."

I don't answer, because that's when a ship slips by on the other side of the sails. Another mega yacht like the *Flying Fox*, but darker. Sleeker, its massive body towering above the water. I count the half-dozen men patrolling the upper walkways, the shiny brass letters glinting high on the hull, gold against black fiberglass.

Aphrodite IV.

"Adam, did you hear me?"

I force my gaze away from the boat. "I'm sorry—what?"

She steps up behind me, winding an arm around my waist, pointing with the other one to a spot closer to shore. "I said steer us over there. Let's park this thing and go for a swim."

I nod, heart hammering, and it's a good thing Stella is behind me so she can't see my face. I stand here, trying to breathe, trying to gauge what it means. The *Aphrodite IV* is here, on the coast of Capri, in the same bay Stella and I are sailing at the same exact time. Surely the world is not that small. Surely this can't be a coincidence.

Stella's breath is hot on my back. "Is everything okay?"

"Of course." But my voice sounds hoarse, and I have to clear my throat. "Everything is great."

The *Aphrodite IV*. *Fuck fuck fuck.*

"But your heart." She presses her palm to the center of my chest, holding it there. "It feels like it's going a mile a minute."

I peel her hand from my chest and lift it to my lips, dropping a kiss on her knuckles, stretching the moment long enough to get my shit together. I gesture to the ladder leading to below.

"Grab the bottle of rosé from the fridge, will you? The rental agency said there's cheese and crackers down there, too."

"A boozy picnic, my favorite." She slips past me, disappearing down into the cabin.

While Stella bangs around below, I sail us close enough to see the people behind the yacht's windows, close enough to make out their faces. A blonde maid, cleaning the glass. A chef in a starched white hat in a downstairs galley. A man with dark hair and a broad back in an upstairs room. He's facing the other way, but it's him, I know it. He didn't see me, but I saw him, and that's enough.

I give a yank to the helm, loosen the sails, catch a breeze that will carry us to the shoreline. I need to get us away from here, away from the big yachts. Away from one big yacht in particular. By the time Stella emerges from below, the *Aphrodite IV* is in our rearview.

But not out of my mind.

I think about it for the rest of the afternoon, what it means that they're here. I think about it while Stella and I swim laps around the boat. While we sip rosé and feed on cheese and crackers, followed by sweaty, salty sex on the deck. While the boat spins slow circles on the anchor, offering up views of the sparkling Marina Piccola on one side, the *Aphrodite IV* on the other. A dangerous, dark cloud looming in a sea of blue.

A coincidence, or a shiny black promise of what is to come?

SIX

STELLA

Paris

I stare up at the man I spotted across the square, the one with the dark hair and the long limbs and the white shirt stretched over broad shoulders. His nose is too long. His chin is too pointy. His shirt isn't even white but light blue.

"You're not him. *Dammit.*" I shove my hands in my curls and tug, desperation burning my cheeks like a bad rash.

It's ridiculous to blame this man. Logically, I know this. According to the label on his shirt, he's one of the good guys, a member of the gendarmerie. He and a half dozen of his colleagues are busy corralling the crowd, holding them back so the rescue workers can clear the building of more bodies. By now the square is full of people like me, searching for news of their loved ones.

He blinks at me, and his eyes are kind. "Who are you looking for, madame? Perhaps I can help."

"My husband. Adam Knox. I can't find him anywhere."

The officer gestures to a woman a few feet away, clutching a clipboard to her chest. "Have you spoken to my colleague? She is maintaining a list of missing…"

He says more, but I don't hear it. I'm already lurching in the woman's direction, pushing my way through the crowd. "I need to add my husband's name to the list. Adam Knox."

She hands me the clipboard and a pen. "Write down his full name, height and hair color, clothing description, and your cell phone number."

The top page is already three-quarters full, and it's not the only one. Underneath are dozens of pages filled with scribbles from people like me, clinging to hope. *Astrid Dubois, 172 cm, blonde and blue dress, 06 48 62 44 07. Gregory Gilberto, 2 meter, bald with white and blue striped shirt, +39 31 49 70 4.* At the very bottom, two names are crossed out, a heavy line drawn through the middle. Found? Or found dead?

"Have you looked on the grass?" the woman next to me asks, her words heavy with an Eastern European accent. "That's where they're bringing the people."

I press pen to paper and start writing, not bothering to look over. "Yes, I've looked on the grass. I've looked in the square. I've looked *everywhere*. I called the hotel. I called my husband a million times, and his cell keeps going to voicemail. I've been looking for him for more than an hour now and I don't know what else to do. There's no sign of him anywhere. WHERE IS HE?"

My words spiral into a loud and hysterical shriek, and the people around me go quiet, watching me warily.

The woman who handed me the clipboard shakes her head. "*Madame, s'il vous plaît.* We are doing the best we can."

I hand her back the clipboard and then the tears come on hot and fast, spilling down my cheeks in heavy, hiccuping sobs. It's an open-mouthed, full-body sort of cry, the kind that steals my breath and shocks me with its intensity, just like it shocks this woman. She wraps a gentle hand around my elbow and tugs me away from the crowd, finding me an empty bench.

I plop onto it, sending up a mini–mushroom cloud of dust, then drop my face into my hands and bawl.

Now what? What the fuck do I do now?

I give in to the tears, picturing Adam wandering the streets of Paris, those awful sunglasses sitting lopsided on his nose. I see him patting his pockets for his phone, and my mind runs through all sorts of scenarios. Innocuous, reasonable explanations for where Adam could be, why he's not answering his phone. That in all the chaos and confusion he lost his cell, or the battery is dead. He is unconscious in a hospital or in the back of an ambulance somewhere. He's back at the hotel, oblivious to the disaster in the square, wondering where the hell I am. He can't reach me with a dead or lost cell phone.

The last thought stirs a ping of relief, of hope, and I pull out my phone and try the hotel again.

"Yes, hello, this is Stella Knox calling again. I'm looking for my husband, Adam."

"Yes, Madame Knox. The manager alerted the entire staff. We know to watch for him. But I'm very sorry to say he's not here."

"Can you transfer me to our room? Maybe he slipped upstairs without anyone seeing."

There's a long pause, and I know what she's thinking. I can hear the desperation in my own voice. I don't need her to point it out for me.

"Of course, madame. One moment, please."

There's a beat of silence, and then the phone rings. And rings and rings and rings. I count them, twelve long beeps while I tell myself he's fine, that when a fireball turned the building inside out, he and his stupid sunglasses were long gone. I tell myself that there must be an explanation that doesn't include death. There *has* to be.

I hang up as someone taps me on the shoulder. A pretty woman in heels and a suit. She holds out a bottle of icy water and a packet of travel-sized tissues. "No offense, but you look like you could use these more than me."

A fellow American, judging by the accent.

"Thank you." I pluck the items from her hands, wedge the bottle between my thighs and peel open the sticker on the tissues, using the first two to mop up my face. Tears and makeup and dust and grime and more tears, which are nowhere near stopping. I pull two more tissues from the packet and blow my nose, then chug half the bottle. The dust and fear have made me desperately thirsty.

The woman doesn't walk away. She just stands there watching me, waiting for me to get settled. And then she offers up a small smile.

"I couldn't help but overhear. Your conversation with the policeman, I mean." She waves a hand in his direction, but he's already moved on. "You said you're looking for someone?"

I nod. "My husband. He went back to the café for his sunglasses and now..."

Now what? The tears strangle me all over again.

"Perhaps I can help," she says, and it's then I fully take her in.

Her hair, brown curls shiny and styled like she just walked out of a salon. Her makeup, thick but impeccable, with berry lips and the kind of heavy-handed contouring you find on a YouTube tutorial. I take in the cobalt blouse peeking out from a dark tailored suit, the baby-pink polish on her fingernails, the man lingering at the edge of the crowd with a camera balanced on a shoulder, watching us.

I know who this woman is. What she's doing here.

"You're a reporter."

My first instinct is to be angry. Reporters make a living by profiting off another person's tragedy. They shove their mics into panicked faces and step into the paths of victims fleeing the scene. They find sobbing women on park benches and broadcast their despair for clicks and views. It's televised rubbernecking, and I want no part of it.

The woman points at her cameraman. He lifts a hand in a wave, but he doesn't come over. Not yet. "That's Steve, and I'm Stephanie. We work for France 24, an international news channel broadcasting around the clock in French, Arabic and English. Our viewers would be very interested in hearing what happened to your husband."

She's not even halfway through her spiel when I'm already shaking my head no. This woman doesn't care about my husband, and she definitely doesn't care about me. Also, what the hell am I supposed to say? I don't *know* what happened to him. I'm not ready to contemplate the worst, especially not on live television.

"I understand your reluctance, but I promise to be gentle. You can say as much or as little as you'd like. But I meant it before, about being of help. Our broadcasts reach three hundred million homes all over the planet, with a combined weekly viewership of 45.9 million. Perhaps one of those people might have seen your husband."

And just like that, I'm up off the bench, lifted by the hope I hear in her words. Forty-six million people. Not all of them will be in Paris, but still. That's a lot of eyes on a picture of Adam. I'll do whatever it takes to find him, including fall apart on live television.

I scramble to open my phone, bypassing the shot of us on my lock screen and pulling up the photograph I snapped just yesterday, a close-up of Adam beaming at me across the breakfast table. Happy. Friendly. A broad smile and face that's handsome enough to be memorable. I pull up the image on my screen and turn the brightness as high as it will go.

After that, things move fast. She gives a thumbs-up to the cameraman, and he hustles over, fiddling with the camera on his shoulder, flipping switches and positioning us for the best shot. They do a couple of quick sound tests, and then she turns to me.

"I'm standing here with…"

She shoves the microphone under my chin. "Stella Knox."

"Thank you for joining me, Stella. I understand your husband is one of the people missing."

"He's not missing. It's just that I can't find him."

Okay, yes. I do realize how this sounds. It sounds like I'm delusional, like I'm grasping at fictional straws, but I don't care. I white-knuckle my phone, pointing the screen at the camera.

"This is him. Adam Nathaniel Knox. K-N-O-X. He's six foot three, has brown hair with a big cowlick and a scar on the left side of his forehead." With my other hand, I draw a half-inch line up mine with a fingernail, remnants from when a horse tried to kick him when he was twelve.

I think of his face when he first told me the story, of his self-deprecating laugh when I said he was lucky he didn't lose an eyeball, and there they are, my damn tears again, gushing like a broken faucet. The reporter glances at the cameraman, and I imagine him zooming in on one as it rolls down my shiny cheek, over the purple splotches that I know have sprouted on my face and neck. People with red hair and porcelain skin do not make pretty criers, as forty-six million people are currently witnessing. But the last thing I care about right now is what I look like.

"It sounds like you have reason to believe he was near the café when it exploded."

I shake my head, quick and decisive. "No, we were there *before*. We had lunch there, but then after we left, he realized he forgot his sunglasses, so he went back. We were supposed to meet back at the hotel, but he hasn't shown up and he hasn't called me yet, either. Maybe he lost his phone. I don't know."

"Lost it in the explosion."

"Or while running away from it. I don't know. That's just

it—*I don't know.* But I do know a person doesn't just disappear. He has to be *somewhere.*"

The reporter's brow crumples, an overly articulated expression of concern for the camera—or maybe for me. For my vehement denials. I know I sound like a madwoman.

"I see. What else would you like our viewers to know about your husband, Stella? What do they need to know about Adam Nathaniel Knox?"

"That he's kind. And so smart. He owns a shop that sells reclaimed antiques to builders and architects. That's what he was doing in Paris, buying pieces for his store. We're supposed to be on a plane right now, but I can't leave this city without him. I can't... I literally don't know what I would do if..."

A fist tightens around my throat, and my lungs do one of those stuttering sobs that sucks down the rest of my words. I close my eyes and disappear into my head for a bit, breathing hard. *Come on, Stella. You can do this. Forty-six million viewers, and all you need is one. Just one person who's seen Adam alive.* The pep talk works. I open my eyes, and my lungs loosen up.

The reporter gives me an encouraging nod, tilting her head toward the camera.

I turn and stare into it, and everything else fades away. The busy square. The smoke and dust. The smell of charred wood and rubber. I don't even care that I just broke down on live television. I see my picture of Adam lit up in the glass, and I put everything I have into what I say next for the camera.

"Please. If you've seen this man or think you have, *please* call me at the Hôtel Luxembourg Parc here in Paris. If I'm not there, you can leave a message with the reception desk, and I'll call you back as soon as possible. I'm begging you, please. *Please* help me find my husband."

The reporter's eyes gleam at my performance. From triumph. I can practically hear her thoughts as they tick through the incoming bounty. Ratings. Promotions and awards. An

Emmy. I'm like one of those weeping parents you see on TV, begging for the safe return of their kidnapped child. This is broadcast-news gold.

She manages to hold her expression steady as she pivots, aiming her solemn face at the camera. "Reporting live from Place Carlou Aubert in Paris, I'm Stephanie Wilbanks for France 24."

SEVEN

It's dark by the time my phone finally dies, the battery wound down from calling the hotel obsessively. After my interview on France 24, the pile of messages blew quickly out of control, people calling with tips, far too many to relay over the phone, and other reporters asking to feature me.

All afternoon long, I let a long line of reporters point their lenses at my ratty hair and splotchy cheeks while I sobbed for their cameras and the world. All that, and still no sign of Adam. Only a thumping headache and a bone-deep exhaustion, like I ran an ultramarathon on no food and zero sleep. The journalists sucked me dry, and then they sucked down the battery on my phone, leaving me no other choice than to leave the square. Alone.

At the Hôtel Luxembourg Parc, the doorman sees me coming. He takes in my dust-covered hair and skin, my clothes coated with sweat and grime and other people's blood, and he frowns because he knows who I am. I'm *that* woman, the poor American tourist whose husband was blown to bits.

"Madame Knox." He whisks open the door with a polite nod.

I thank him and scramble inside, where people are everywhere. Wheeling their luggage across the marble floors, dodging the crowd sipping cocktails on couches and at little round tables, waiting shoulder to shoulder at the bar. Grinning like a literal bomb didn't just go off four blocks from here.

That's not what the cops are saying, by the way—*bomb*. Other than that first female cop I spoke to, the police have steered far, far away from the menacing word. They are calling it "an explosion," and they're quick to point out that because it happened at a restaurant, it could have been caused by something as innocent as a gas leak—though nobody seems to be buying it. That old woman I helped up off the sidewalk isn't the only one I've heard blaming the blast on *terroristes*.

Is that what this was? Did some lunatic blow himself and my husband up as some kind of perverted political statement? If that's true, I don't know how I'll ever get past it. How do you make sense of something so senseless?

I push my way through the crowd to the reception desk, a long stretch of beige marble and polished wood staffed by three pretty Frenchwomen in matching crisp jackets. I step up in front of the one who checked Adam and me in, a thin brunette named Manon.

"I'm so sorry," she says to me in English. "If there is anything I can do…"

She doesn't finish, which is fine by me because I don't want her to. More tears are gathering in my sinuses, and I'm desperate to get away from her and all these people so I can cry in the privacy of my own room.

Manon slides me a thick stack of papers, dozens and dozens of pages. "Many people saw you on television. They have been calling and calling. I took down as many messages as I could, but I'm not sure they will all be very helpful. There were a lot of…" She turns to her colleagues. *"Comment dit-on les fous?"*

The girl next to her winces. "Crazy people."

I look down at the top page, a typed list of names, phone numbers, short messages, most of them in French.

Manon taps a finger next to one halfway down the page, the line highlighted in yellow. "I marked the ones I thought might be useful. There are not so many, unfortunately."

"Thank you. I really appreciate you doing this."

"Also—" she gives me a gentle smile "—Mr. Laurent thought you might be more comfortable upstairs, on the top floor. It's much quieter there. He put you in one of our penthouse suites. The bellman has already moved your luggage. Mr. Laurent transferred the contents of your safe personally to make sure everything is secure. He emailed you the new code."

I blink at her, and for the first few seconds I'm speechless because a penthouse. A new room with fluffed pillows and a freshly made bed. Where the linens smell of laundry detergent, and not Adam. I think about sliding under them alone, without Adam, and it breaks something in me.

"Room 703. It's very beautiful. Your key card will work to open the door." Manon pats my arm, giving me an encouraging nod. "Mr. Laurent says you may stay as long as you need."

I turn away, clutching the papers to my chest and pushing my way through the crowd before she can see that my tears are not of gratitude, but of grief.

Upstairs in the suite that's far too big for me alone, I dump my stuff by the desk and pick up the hotel phone, starting with the first number Manon highlighted in yellow.

A man with a deep smoker's voice answers, *"Oui allo?"*

I sink onto the chair, digging a pen out of the desk drawer. *"Bonsoir, monsieur.* My name is Stella Knox. I think you saw me on TV?"

My words unleash a torrent of broken English mixed with French, but enough that I get the gist. This man claims to have seen Adam yesterday afternoon, at a *boulangerie* in Poitiers. A city a couple hundred miles from here. I thank him and hang up, drawing a black *X* next to the number.

I move on, slowly making my way down the list, defeat dragging me down with each call. A series of wrong numbers, some more dud sightings, nosy rubberneckers eager for an update. So far, not a single useful tip.

And then, finally, on the other end of a number at the bottom of the twelfth page, a woman. I give her my name, ask if she has any news of Adam. She answers in posh French, each word measured and carefully enunciated so I can understand.

"Il a eu ce qu'il méritait."

He got what he deserved.

I slam the phone on the cradle and scream into the empty room. *Adam, where are you?*

EIGHT

My eyes pop open, and I lurch upright on a sharp gasp. Sunlight streams through the gauzy curtains, painting patterns on the unfamiliar carpet, and it takes me a full ten seconds to remember where I am. The hotel. Paris. The explosion. It returns with a terrifying jolt.

Adam is gone. *Gone.*

Je suis désolé. I am desolate without him.

So now it's morning of day two, and I'm on the penthouse floor. Last night after giving up on the list of tips, I roamed from room to room, pulling open drawers and peering into closets, sniffing the pretty bottles of toiletries lined up like glass soldiers on the bathroom shelf, wrestling the brand-new toothbrush out of the packaging after the police took both of ours, because they needed to identify Adam's DNA, and they didn't know which one belonged to him. I slipped on pajamas I tugged from my suitcase, but I couldn't bear to unpack. This room is a pity gift. Unpacking feels like giving up.

I roll to my side and slide my phone from the nightstand, scrolling through dozens and dozens of messages. Friends and family back home, my boss and colleagues, neighbors and people I haven't heard from in years. It seems France 24 isn't the only one broadcasting my face to the world. People are hearing what happened on CNN, Fox, the BBC, all the major television networks and national newspapers, their socials.

Stella Knox, grief-stricken beauty, begs for information on her husband, lost in Parisian explosion.

They're calling me "The Paris Widow," using the same awful picture—splotchy cheeks, mouth wide in midbawl, clutching the picture of Adam on my phone. Sometime during the night, I became the face of this tragedy, but the only thing that matters is that picture of Adam. Adam's image made it to CNN. Millions of people will see his face. Surely one of them can help me find him.

I'm pushing back the covers when the hotel phone rings, a sharp trill coming from the complicated machine on the nightstand. I pick up the receiver, breathless. "This is Stella."

I recognize the voice that greets me as Manon's. "Good morning, Madame Knox. I am very sorry to disturb, but there is an officer here to see you." She pauses, and I white-knuckle the sheets. "A Lieutenant Colonel Collomb."

My heart stops. I can't breathe, no air going in or out. I'm not familiar with rank, but a lieutenant colonel seems high enough that whatever he's come here to say is important. I open my mouth, but my lungs have locked up.

"Madame Knox, are you there?"

"I'm here," I croak. "Please tell him I'll be right down."

I hang up, then shove off the covers and leap out of bed. I've eaten nothing since the galettes, but I still feel it coming, a surge of something sour. I make it to the toilet just in time.

Seven minutes later, I'm in the elevator, a seizure of terror expanding in my stomach. I've had seven whole minutes to think about the police officer waiting downstairs, seven minutes to contemplate what he could possibly have to tell me, and none of it's good.

The doors slide open with a ping, and I burst into the short hallway, running smack into a cluster of Japanese tourists in the middle of an animated conversation. I bounce off one of them, a teenager with braces and pink hair. She squeals as I step on her toe.

"Sorry. Sorry!" I call over my shoulder as I hurry out into the lobby.

I spot him by a far window, a man in a light blue shirt and dark pants, a uniform that by now is a common sight. I've seen enough of them milling around the square and directing foot traffic, have gleaned enough from my interactions to know that the French system is a complicated web of police forces. Gendarmerie, Police Nationale, and La PP, Paris's Préfecture de Police, all of them pitching in to fashion a chaotic kind of order at the blast site. As far as I can tell, it's been all hands on deck.

His head is down, his thumbs ticking away on his cell phone screen, and I try to match his profile with one of the faces I saw yesterday at the square, but I can't. He's not one of the officers who was barking at me to get out of the way, or telling me to fill in yet another form. I take a step, then another, searching his profile for clues. Is he here with good news? Bad? His expression gives nothing away.

I'm halfway across the marble floor when he senses I'm near and turns to look at me full-on. He's somewhere in his late fifties, with close-trimmed hair and blue eyes, bright against the dark circles underneath. They match the ones I spotted on myself upstairs, twin bruises bleeding into the hollow of my cheeks. I'm barely functioning on zero food and a few hours of fitful sleep, and this man looks like he got about the same.

"Did you find him?" I say when I'm close enough. "Did you find my husband?"

The lieutenant colonel pushes to a stand, brushing a crease out of his pants. "No, and that's not what I came to discuss."

His words are thick with a French accent, refined sounds that can't mask the ugliness of what he says next. "Monsieur Knox is still on our list of missing persons."

"Okay, then why are you here?"

My response is rude, I know, and so is my tone, but my husband has been missing for almost twenty-four hours now. Twenty-four hours of clawing my skin off while waiting for word. I have neither the patience nor the energy for social graces.

And neither does this guy, apparently. "My name is Arnaud Collomb. I am a lieutenant colonel on the Paris Police Force. I have some questions about your husband." He peels a business card from his pocket and holds it out to me. "In particular, about his business."

For a long moment, I'm stunned silent. I was expecting information, not questions—least of all about something as benign as Adam's work. I take the card from this man's fingers, running one of mine over the red-and-blue logo, the tiny words printed underneath. *Liberté. Égalité. Fraternité.*

His gaze flits past me, into the din of the lobby. "Perhaps we could find somewhere a little more private."

And this lobby is anything but private, its corners far from quiet. A constant stream of people flowing in and out, seated on plush chairs arranged around tiny tables in the middle, in line for coffee at the café on the far end.

"Let me see what I can arrange," he says, holding up a bony finger. "Wait here."

After a bit of discussion with the hotel staff, we end up in a small room behind the reception desk. A break room, judging by the sideboard piled high with pastries and supplies for coffee and tea. He closes the door, the noise of the lobby fading away with a whoosh. Suddenly, we are alone.

He gestures to the round table in the center of the room, and I collapse onto one of the chairs.

The lieutenant colonel takes his time. He sinks onto a chair, pulls out a pen and a pad of paper, and flips through it for a blank page. His eyes are on the paper when he asks, "How much do you know about your husband's work?"

I frown, unsure where he's going with this. "Um, I know the basics, I guess. Adam deals in antiques. Construction antiques, specifically. Reclaimed doors, old fire surrounds, ceiling and wall decorations, things like that. He sources them from all over, really, but his clients have a thing for European building styles. They especially love Parisian."

"I see. And you have been to his store in Atlanta? Architectural Antiques, I believe it's called."

"Of course. Many times." It's a thirty-thousand-square-foot showroom on busy Piedmont Avenue, the site of a former dairy farm. A complex of offices and workshops stretch out behind the main building, taking up almost three acres. He's owned the property since long before we met.

"So you've seen these construction antiques with your own eyes? You've met his customers?"

"Not all of them, of course, but yes. I've seen him interact with the people at his store. I've even been to a few homes he's worked on, built with products he sourced." I wipe my damp palms on my jeans, squinting at this man over his notepad. "What are you implying, exactly, about his business? Why do you need confirmation?"

"Because while Architectural Antiques might be a legitimate business, it is only a very small part of how your husband makes his money. Monsieur Knox's real business, the one that brings in a great deal of income, is dealing in looted and stolen artifacts."

The accusation is so out of left field, so absurd, that I laugh. The sound is sharp in the tiny room, and loud in my own ears. But the lieutenant colonel's expression doesn't change. He stares at me across the table.

I sit back abruptly. "No. That's not true. Adam sells decorative wall panels and, and…antique mirrors. Cast-iron balcony railings like the ones here in Paris. He doesn't steal these things. He *buys* them."

"That may be true, but I'm not here to talk about the architectural antiques. Like I said, his shop seems to be a legitimate business, but it's only a front. Monsieur Knox is also a broker of sorts. He smuggles stolen goods across international borders, often using forged documents, then sells them to wealthy clients willing to pay top dollar to own a piece of the world's past. Artwork, statues, figurines, jewelry. We call them 'blood antiquities' because they are looted from historical sites—museums, temples—in war-torn countries."

"No." I shake my head, when what I really want to say is *no fucking way*. I look around and grab on to the table to center myself. "No, that can't be true."

"The trade of blood antiquities is a highly lucrative business, the third-largest international criminal activity, surpassed only by drugs and arms dealing. I imagine I don't have to tell you it is also highly illegal."

A thief. This man is calling Adam a thief.

"You may not know my husband, but I do. The only kind of artifacts he cares about are the kind you plaster onto ceilings or incorporate into a staircase. I've never once heard him talk about paintings or figurines."

"Let me ask. What do you have hanging on the walls in your home? Paintings? Mosaics? Do you have any statues or old books lying around?"

"Yes, of course we have those things. But they're not *real*. They're not valuable."

He looks at me, and his lashes are blond and stubby. He narrows his eyes, and they disappear. "Are you certain?"

I nod, even though now I can't stop thinking about the Chagall print Adam brought home from an overseas trip last year, how his eyes lit up when he unrolled it from the cardboard tube. I think about how heavy the canvas was, about how the paint looked flaky in spots, the edges frayed and yellow. I even commented on it, how it looked so *real*.

"That's because it's a replica," he said at the time, "a damn good one. The original's at the Centre Pompidou, but I just loved it so much. I must have sat on that bench and stared at it for hours."

The Chagall is now framed, hanging over the dresser in our upstairs bedroom.

I'm also thinking about the elaborately carved bronze statue high on a bookshelf, a potbellied boy with one chubby arm held high in the air—according to Adam, a replica of the original Roman statue of the childhood version of Bacchus, the god of wine. I think of the marble bust on the side table in a hall, the carved wood box on the coffee table, the collection of Dutch East India Company coins tossed carelessly in a drawer. All fakes—at least, according to Adam.

Still. I make sure to look the lieutenant colonel dead in the eye, and maybe it's because I don't want to believe these things he's saying about Adam, or maybe it's pure instinct. Something is telling me not to tip my cards.

"Yes. I'm one hundred percent certain. They're not real."

"Then you won't mind the Atlanta police searching your house."

"You're joking, right?"

The look he gives me tells me no. He's not joking.

"But I'm not even home. I don't know when I will be." I don't add the rest, words that have echoed through my head for an entire day now: *I'm not leaving this place until I find Adam.*

"Then I suggest you alert someone who has a key. A neighbor, perhaps? In the meantime, I'd like to hear more about what you and Monsieur Knox were doing here in Paris."

"I already told you why he was here, to purchase antiques.

He bought a whole bunch of stuff he is having shipped back. Enough to fill a whole container."

"Who did he buy it from?"

"I don't know."

"Where are the items now?"

"I don't know."

"Which port is the container shipping from?"

"I have no idea."

"Who are his contacts here in Paris? Which antique stores and markets did he visit?"

"I already told you, *I don't know.* I don't know any of these things. I only joined him for the sightseeing part of this trip."

It's been this way since the very beginning. When it comes to work, Adam doesn't ask too many questions, and neither do I. He knows how much I detest my catering job and its endless onslaught of demanding clients, A-list actors with weird diets. Vegan, gluten-free, raw, paleo, alkaline—those are the easy ones. How about a diet that consists entirely of baby food, or only foods of a certain color? It's one of the things I most appreciated about Adam when we met: his willingness to keep our work lives separate from our private lives.

"The only thing I know is that he showed me some pictures on his phone of some wall moldings he bought. Decorative elements he sourced from the walls of a fancy Parisian apartment."

And not just any apartment, an apartment that was located on the first upstairs floor in a Parisian apartment building, also known as the noble floor. The memory comes to me in a flash, Adam telling me he learned that from a colleague, a shop owner he met at the Saint-Ouen market who is his ears on the ground here in Paris. I don't remember the shop owner's name, and I definitely don't mention this little tidbit to the lieutenant colonel. So far, our conversation has only served to put me on edge.

The cop scribbles my answer onto his paper, along with a

few words I can't read upside down. "What is the passcode to your husband's phone?"

"I have no idea."

"You don't know the code to open your husband's phone." He doesn't phrase it as a question, and the condescension in his tone makes me want to flip the table, Jersey Housewife style. "You've never watched him enter it."

"Adam has the latest iPhone. It works on face recognition."

"And the picture on his home screen, do you at least know what that is?"

I don't miss the *at least*, or the way he loads the words up with snark. Sarcasm and disdain, I wonder if they're part of the Préfecture de Police training, just like they seem to be for the scantily clad hostesses at Hôtel Costes. Adam and I had a good laugh after one of them begrudgingly showed us to our table. But now, coming from this man, the insolence isn't the least bit amusing. Heat blooms in my chest, fury beating in time with my heart.

"Yes, I know the picture on Adam's home screen, and you don't have to be so rude about it. It's a picture of me, standing in front of a waterfall. I'm wearing pink shorts, a white tank and a denim baseball cap."

I was a sweaty mess when he snapped it, after a five-mile hike during a spontaneous weekend away to escape an Atlanta heat wave. We rented a cabin perched on the edge of the Nantahala National Forest. We drank too much wine and stayed in bed till noon. I remember every detail of those three blissful days, because that was the weekend Adam first told me he loved me.

And yet this is not what I'm thinking of, but something else. The realization comes to me in drips. "Why are you asking me about his phone? Did you find it?"

"Yes. I wasn't certain until just now, when you confirmed the photograph. One of my officers found it in the wreckage."

He pauses to let that little bombshell land. They found

Adam's phone in the wreckage. His phone survived the blast, but Adam is still nowhere. Missing, or worse. Instantly, my eyes fill with tears.

He puts down his pen, arranging it diagonally across the notebook. "Madame Knox, this phone is not good news for your husband's welfare, as I can see you've already determined. My advice is that you should prepare yourself for the worst."

"The worst. As in…" I can't make myself say it. I can't say the word.

"As in death, yes. Either way, Monsieur Knox has been a key figure in the illegal artifacts trade in Europe. He's brokered millions of dollars' worth in stolen goods in the last year alone. My colleagues and I have been tracking his business for almost a decade now."

A decade. Millions of dollars. I shake my head again; it's all a misunderstanding.

"This business your husband is involved in is dangerous. A seventy-billion-dollar black market run by criminals. When that kind of money is involved, bad things tend to happen."

A chill slips down my spine, a million icy currents shooting across my back. There's a long stretch of silence while I process his words. "What are you saying, that this wasn't some act of terrorism?"

This—because I'm not ready to define it. The explosion. The disaster that left nothing of my husband but his phone.

"That is exactly what I'm saying, Madame Knox. The blast that took out the restaurant was not random. It was not a gas leak but a bombing, meticulously planned and executed." He pauses, and his expression and tone both soften. "We have strong evidence to suggest that your husband was the target."

NINE

I first met Adam at the Scott Antique Markets in Atlanta, a monthly expo down by the airport. I was there with my best friend, Katie, who'd dragged me along with a box of treasures she'd salvaged from a bad breakup, after she'd found her attorney fiancé in bed with one of his paralegals. She responded by piling most of his favorite things on the front lawn, dousing them with lighter fluid and torching them live in a TikTok video that garnered almost a million views.

But the best things, the most valuable things, she packed in a box and brought to sell to a dealer she met online.

The two of us wandered up and down the booths in the North building, joking about how whoever Scott was, he must be a pretty pretentious guy. As far as we could tell, his market was more junk than antiques, a bunch of dealers who'd emptied out their grandmother's dusty attic. The crowd wasn't much better, a mix of retirees, professional bargain hunters and potbellied men who haggled for sport.

And then there was Adam. Tall. Dark jeans sitting low on his trim hips, thick hair shoved to the left with a determined cowlick, a slow smile that almost made him seem surprised when his eyes landed on mine. So out of place in his pressed button-down and battered brogues. So wildly different from anyone I'd ever dated, so *normal*, that for a minute, I was almost dizzy with it. With him.

I was silent while he and Katie came to a deal for the few items that didn't land in the bonfire. Pete's first-edition *Winnie-the-Pooh* book signed by A. A. Milne, a carved cigar box he'd inherited from a great-grandfather, family trinkets and jewelry he'd given her over the years. Adam didn't try to lowball her on any of it—Katie had done her research and knew what the items were worth—and I liked him better for it. Adam gave her a fair price, then slid her a whopper of a check and both of us his business card.

But all that time, I couldn't stop watching him. His easy banter, the old-man clothes that somehow seemed to suit him, his friendly, unassuming smile. He looked like a guy who worked hard and did his own shopping, who played sports and hung out on the weekend with friends. Normal—or as Katie called him, vanilla, but to me that was his charm. After the relationship I was coming out of at the time, I couldn't think of anything I wanted more than vanilla.

"Wait a minute," Katie said, frowning at the name on the check, comparing it to the one on the business card. "I thought my meeting was with Doug."

"It was, until last night, when he ate some bad sushi at the airport. Which, I mean, come *on*. You almost deserve food poisoning for eating airport sushi, don't you think? Anyway, Doug said he really wanted that Pooh book."

Katie waved the check, then folded it in half. "Don't tell Doug, but I would have given him the book for free. If nothing else than for the look on Pete's face when he hears how much it's worth."

"Pete is her fiancé," I explained.

"*Ex*-fiancé. And good riddance. To him *and* his shit."

I grinned. "She made a pretty spectacular bonfire with most of it. Well, with everything but the stuff she just sold to you."

"I'm sorry I missed that." Adam smiled, his gaze holding mine for a beat too long. He turned his attention to Katie. "So are you going to tell him? That you got a small fortune for stuff that wasn't technically yours to sell, I mean."

"Maybe. Probably." Katie paused, squinting at him over the glass case. "Why? Is that going to be a problem?"

Adam held up both hands. "Hey, I'm in the antiques business. Half the stuff in this place comes from questionable sources at best. In this line of business, asking too many questions leads to answers you don't want to hear."

That day, with Pete's betrayal still so fresh and Katie and I out for revenge, it seemed like a perfectly fine answer. Don't ask too many questions. A philosophy I could certainly stand behind at the time—and had, many, many times before.

When Adam called later that same day, asking me to join him for dinner, I didn't ask where he got my number from. I assumed from Katie, but honestly, I didn't really care. There wasn't an answer on the planet that would have changed mine.

Yes.

Now, though, all alone up here in the suite, the lieutenant colonel's accusations thump through my head on repeat, and I think through what I know. A bomb took out half a Parisian block. Police are saying the explosion was anything but accidental. Adam is one of the dozen or so people missing—not only a victim but the target. A claim so outrageous that I dismissed it almost immediately.

Because how ridiculous it is to think such a thing. That all this time I've known him, my normal, low-key husband has led a secret life as an international criminal. That he's involved in a dangerous business that's made him some very dangerous enemies. Before today, before Lieutenant Colonel Collomb's accusations, I would have said Adam is as straight as they come.

But now...

Uncertainty hovers like a bad summer storm.

Asking too many questions leads to answers you don't want to hear.

I'm stepping out of the shower when my phone chirrups with a stream of incoming messages, and the first thing I think is Adam, because this is what hope does. It conjures up outrageous plotlines you believe down to your bones, even while the more logical part of your brain whispers *impossible*.

It's not his name lighting up the screen, but my best friend's, and as much as I love her, as much as I need to hear her voice right now, it's still a punch to the gut. I swipe a thumb across the glass. "Katie. I'm so glad you called."

Her throaty voice comes through my phone, thick with Carolina twang. "You're not gonna be when you hear why I'm calling. I just came from your house, where I went to drop off your welcome-home flowers, though I guess I just ruined that surprise, didn't I?" She laughs, the sound undercut with road noise—the hiss of wind, a motor gunning. Katie is calling from the car. "Anyway, guess who I found asleep on your front porch swing."

I don't have to guess, because I already know. Emily, my mother. A trained pastry chef who can't hold down a job or a husband. Who tends to go off the rails whenever she's between either. I also don't have to ask what she wanted, because it's always the same. Money. A place to crash, just until she's back on her feet. To guilt me into helping her *just this last time, sugar, I swear* only to disappear days later without so much as a goodbye.

Despite everything, worry still pings me behind the breastbone. "How did she look?"

"Honestly? Kind of strung out. She was twitchy and really skinny."

I make a face, groaning. "You didn't let her in, did you?"

"Hell, no. I gave her the flowers and a twenty and sent her

on her way. I also made sure to tell her y'all have a new alarm, one with cameras and sensors on all the doors and windows."

An alarm Adam upgraded last spring, after Emily had jimmied open a bathroom window and helped herself to all our best wine. We came back from a weekend in Florida to find her passed out, naked and sprawled in our bed.

I sigh. "I'm sorry you had to deal with that. With her."

"No, babe. *I'm* sorry. You deserve so much better."

Katie says this every time we speak of my disaster of a mother, and like every time, I love her a little bit more for it. Now, though, I don't have the energy to give my mother another second.

I sink onto the unmade bed, clutching the damp towel to my chest. "Have you seen the news?"

"I just came off thirty-six hours on call. I haven't had time to shower, much less turn on the TV or radio." This isn't unusual, as Katie is in her last year of an oncology fellowship at Emory University. She often disappears for days at a time, either into a hospital or her bed. I've learned to not take it personally. "Why? What's going on?"

"Adam's gone, Katie. He's just…gone."

"What do you mean, Adam is gone? Gone where?"

I fall back to the pillows and tell her what happened, short and fast. About leaving the terrace on the square full of galettes. About Adam realizing halfway to the hotel he'd forgotten his sunglasses and running back. About the blast a few minutes later that still rings in my ears. About the rescue workers and the hole in a city block and the long stretch of frantic, desperate searching that ended with me here, in the pity suite all alone.

When I'm done, Katie is silent for a long time. She clears her throat. "So, what do they think, that he's…?"

She trails off, not saying the horrible word out loud, but it echoes in my head anyway. Dead. *Dead dead dead.* It's so much easier to think I don't know where Adam is. I don't know what happened to him.

"A lieutenant colonel was here earlier, and he told me to prepare for the worst. Those were his exact words, to prepare myself for the worst, right before he told me that Adam brokered in blood antiquities. Can you believe that asshole?"

Another long stretch of silence, then: "Stella Knox, if this is some kind of joke, then you're the asshole and it's not funny. Stop scaring the shit out of me."

"This is not a joke, Katie. Believe me, I wish it was. This lieutenant colonel says he's been tracking Adam for almost a decade. A decade! He says Adam's sold millions and millions of dollars' worth of stolen treasures on the black market."

"Well, clearly this lieutenant colonel never met your husband, because Adam? The same guy who cried real tears when he found the perfect carved stone gazebo at some French château for that lady up in Alpharetta? Because, and I say this with all the love in my heart for your man, but *Adam*? He's not exactly the mobster type."

"I know! That's what makes all of this so absurd. I feel like I woke up in the Twilight Zone. Like I'm tripping on one of Emily's mushrooms. And I haven't even told you the worst part yet." I pause, leaning into the phone, lowering my voice even though I'm in a hotel room all alone. "The lieutenant colonel says Adam was the target."

"The target of the *bombing*?"

"Of course the bombing. What else? Jesus, pay attention!"

I'm yelling at her because what I really want is to be yelling at Adam. I want him to be standing right here, in front of me in this suite, so I can yell at him instead of her. I want him to tell me what the hell is going on.

I press my free hand to my forehead, my hairline still gritty with dust and grime. "Sorry. Sorry! I don't mean to be such a bitch. I think I'm still in shock."

"For God's sake, Stella, don't apologize. I mean…holy shit, it's a *lot*. I'm in shock, too. Did you call the hospitals?"

"All of them. Every single one. I also spoke to every human being in the square, uniformed and plain-clothed and anywhere in between, multiple times. I showed them Adam's picture and begged them to rack their memories. I spoke to dozens of reporters on live TV and left messages everywhere I could think of—the hotel, the police, the American Embassy, the morgue. I filled in a hundred forms and wrote my name and number on hundreds of lists, and still. Not a single text or call about Adam. Nobody can tell me a thing."

I hear footsteps in the hall, and I lurch off the bed and hang my head around the corner to stare at the door. It's the strangest sensation—the hope that it might be Adam. I picture him pushing through the door, that lazy smile when he spots me sitting here, the hand he'd lift in a wave. The image of him is so real, so brilliant and beautiful and *present*, that it pushes my heart into my mouth, and me to my feet. I hold my breath and wait for the doorknob to turn.

"I can move some things around," Katie is saying into the phone, "see if I can find someone willing to switch shifts. If I hurry, I can make tonight's flight."

Her words are like a stream of ice water, slapping me from my fantasy. Katie works stupid hours even when she's not on call, and with patients who wouldn't survive a delay. Breast cancers, skin cancers, soft tissue sarcomas—Katie sees the worst of the worst. I can't do that to them, or to her.

"No, stay. There's nothing you can do for me other than hold my hand, and your patients need you there. Just…promise me you'll pick up whenever I call, will you?"

"Always, even if I'm in surgery. What else can I do?"

"If I text you a list, can you pick up some stuff from the house?" I'm thinking, of course, of the framed Chagall over the bedroom dresser, the bronze of the potbellied boy, the marble bust and carved wooden box, the coins tossed in a drawer. If the police come like the lieutenant colonel predicted, I don't want them to find those.

"Consider it done, and if you change your mind, I'm on the next plane. All you have to do is say the word."

"Thank you. For everything."

"Of course, but, Stella, if it's true what the lieutenant colonel said and Adam really is this…this criminal on somebody's hit list, who's to say they won't be coming after you, too?"

I hadn't thought of this, but it's not unreasonable for Katie to think I might be in danger. I am Adam's wife, and presumably have access to the money and everything else that was Adam's. What if they think I knew about the blood antiquities? What if they think I was helping him?

"Maybe you should come home," Katie says. "Just until you know what's going on."

I lean against the wall, blinking into the empty hotel room. The messy bed, the throw pillows piled on a chair, the windows with the curtains thrown wide.

"I can't, Katie. I'm not leaving Paris. Not until I know without a doubt what happened to Adam. Not until I know the truth."

Katie breathes a long, weighted sigh, and I know that sigh. It's her Sigh of Frustration, because we've had this argument before, many times. Me, doing stupid and reckless things because of a man. Her, begging me to get on the next plane home. She knows from experience that this is a fight she won't win.

"Just promise me you'll be careful, okay? And that you'll call me the second you know anything. The very second."

"Promise. And thank you for worrying about me."

"I'm so sorry this is happening. I love you. Keep me posted."

"I will. Love you, too."

We hang up, and I check my phone for missed calls. I check

my email, my text messages, my WhatsApp, but there's nothing. No new messages or calls. Not so much as a peep from Adam.

If it's true what the lieutenant colonel said, and this bomb was indeed planted with Adam as its target, then how? How did they know where we were going? Adam didn't know I was taking him to that square; I had only a vague sense of the restaurant's location myself. Whoever planted that bomb must have done it quickly, and they must have been following him. Following *us*.

I move to the window, staring down into the busy street, at the people filing past on their way to who knows where, and a migraine builds behind my temples. Those people in their pretty clothes, with their perfumed hair and easy smiles. What a luxury to spend an entire day without a single care. Without once wondering, *Is it true what Katie said? Am I in danger, too?*

TEN

I exchange the towel for a pair of jeans and a T-shirt, then collapse onto the suite's overstuffed couch, looking at the place through Adam's eyes. The delicate tables on carved wooden legs, the artwork clogging every wall, the plush Persians atop marble floors polished to a mirror gleam, the "more is more" decor. If Adam were here, he'd raise his gaze right over all those pretty things to the smooth ceilings where a molding should be.

"When the architecture is solid," he'd say, "you don't need all this extra stuff."

Architecture. *That* was Adam's passion. Not artifacts.

Adam can talk for days about the shape of a corbel or the carvings in a marble fireplace. He wouldn't hesitate to use his brand-new shirt to brush the soot off an antique fireback's carvings so he could better see the artistry. The Adam I know wants to *preserve* history, not exploit it.

I march to the walk-in closet and roll Adam's suitcase and backpack from a back corner—until I go home to Atlanta, this is all I have of him. If there are any nuggets of truth in the lieutenant colonel's accusations, if Adam was brokering anything illegal during this trip, the proof will be in here, in his things. I drop the backpack onto the floor and heave the suitcase onto the bed, working the zipper around.

The smell hits me first, a familiar mix of sandalwood and leather and soap, and suddenly, I am surrounded by him, by his smell, his presence. His absence. I breathe through a wave of despair, of missing him so badly my stomach aches.

I stare into his suitcase, and I'm not entirely sure what I'm looking for exactly. An ominous letter from a disgruntled client? A pile of offshore bank statements? If Adam was earning millions and millions of dollars in commission like the lieutenant colonel claimed, where the hell is all that money? Not in his savings, not in our shared bank account—that much is certain. Even after getting married, we've kept things separate, but I've seen the statements he lets pile up on his desk. I know how much money is in there, and it's for sure not millions.

And we don't live large. It's one of the things I love most about Adam, that he's happy in our three-thousand-square-foot home with a bedroom half the size of the one I'm currently standing in. We don't take private jets to exotic locations. We don't drive luxury cars or drop fortunes on bags and watches. We have a mortgage and two car loans that eat up a good chunk of our monthly income. We do our shopping at Costco and Target. We saved up for months for this vacation.

None of this makes any sense.

I start on the left side, removing the pieces one by one, folding them into neat squares that I organize into piles. Of all my husband's talents, folding is not one of them. Rumpled T-shirts tossed in willy-nilly with jeans and dress pants and shoes. I pick up a hoodie from the top of the pile and slip it over my head, breathing in his scent. He wore it less than a week ago, on the plane from Malta to Paris.

I pick up a tattered paperback and flip through it for loose papers, dump his toiletry bag on the bed and reorganize the contents. I'm shaking out a pair of jeans when something whacks my big toe. It doesn't hurt so much as startle me. I look for it on the carpet, trying to pick it out of the kaleidoscope of swirling shapes and colors, but I don't know what I'm looking for. Something small enough to have fallen from a jean pocket. A coin? All I see on the carpet is my own bare feet, hot-pink nail polish against pasty skin.

I drop the jeans on the suitcase and fall to my hands and knees, feeling around with an open palm. I sweep it back and forth over the fibers, moving slowly in the space between the bed and the wall. Nothing but carpet, so I lie on my back and reach as far as I can under the bed, a one-armed snow angel. My hand is gliding alongside the headboard when my pinkie makes contact with cool metal.

I know before I pull my hand out that it's a ring. A wide band of tarnished gold shaped like a belt buckle. Pretty, but not anything I'd ever purchase for myself.

I sit up on my knees and flip on the bedside lamp, holding it up to the light. There's an inscription on the back, something in Russian, maybe, or Greek, and what I'm guessing are initials on the inside band: *OFOFWW + RRH to WWW* in swirling cursive.

I sit there, staring at the band, holding it up to the light like it's some kind of archaeological find. I hadn't thought about what I would do if I did find something. The ring looks old, and Adam had clearly hidden it in his things. Is it true, then, what Collomb said?

But no—Collomb was talking about relics looted from historical sites, not jewelry. Not a ring. This ring might be made of gold, but it's just a ring. I slide it up my thumb, where it fits nice and snug, then return to the suitcase with renewed vigor, my thoughts bouncing between panic and rationalization. It's only a piece of metal, it's nothing, it's solid gold, it's something. The initials, the initials, the initials. They're what I keep coming back to. Those initials have to mean something.

I search every piece of clothing in Adam's suitcase, feel around in every pocket, but if there's anything else here, I don't find it. I check again as I repack his stuff, neater this time, arranging the stacks like puzzle pieces. When I'm done, I zipper the suitcase and wheel it back to the corner of the closet. Moving on.

On the way back through the bedroom, I heft his backpack from the floor and carry it into the sitting room. The first pass is fast and furious. A quick thumb through his things, the leather notebook Adam is always scribbling in, his electronics and chargers and the little scraps of papers and business cards he stuffs in the inside pocket. Nothing.

I take another pass, slower this time, removing the items one by one and organizing them into neat piles on the desk. I page through every piece of paper, fan the notebooks and checkbooks and the brand-new paperback Adam had bought for this trip and hadn't so much as cracked. There's absolutely nothing remarkable here.

I sink onto the velvet desk chair and peel open his laptop.

This is another reason I doubt the lieutenant colonel. If Adam really did have all these illicit business dealings earning him a top secret income, would he have given me his laptop password?

No. No, he would not.

I tap the cursor on the password line and type in LaBella-Stella1601<3. *Boom*, I'm in.

Adam is a Mac guy. He has a thirteen-inch MacBook Pro, the latest iPhone and iPad, an Apple Watch he uses for workouts, and an Apple iCloud account. Not because he loves the products so much, but because he loves their convenience. Mac machines work straight out of the box. They communicate with each other and sync up without issue, meaning anything he does on another device—send a text message or an email or make a call on his iPhone—will show up here, on his laptop.

I start by tracking his devices. According to his Find My app, his AirPods are at 88 percent somewhere near his laptop; I find them in the front pocket of his backpack. His iPad and Apple Watch are back home, likely sitting on their chargers in the bedroom. Under the icon for his iPhone, three little words hit me like a punch to the gut: *No Location Found.* I picture it sitting in an evidence locker somewhere and wonder why the Paris police would turn off his location services. Is that normal?

The numbers on his email app in the bottom dock top out at 157. I click the icon and scroll through the unread messages, deleting the ones that are spam, paying extra attention to the senders' names. I'm searching for a ping of familiarity, the shop owner in the 18th whom Adam called his ears and eyes on the ground, but none of them ring a bell. His name was French—that's as much as I can remember. Étienne, maybe?

After a few more minutes of this, of finding nothing and no one out of the ordinary, I move on to the folders on his desktop, a combination of work and personal files. I spot one named *Stella*, but when I click it, it's mostly legal files. His will and the mortgage statements, insurance and utility contracts. I back out and flip to his messaging apps.

Fifty-four new messages, most of them from me. His last sent text was at 11:27 yesterday, right before lunch, to one of the employees at the shop. Got a pile of carved corbels and cornice brackets headed your way. Tell Pete if he wants us to hold on to any for his clients, he better let us know asap. These things are going to fly out the door. He must have sent it while I was ordering the galettes.

I check his call log, his browser history, the pictures on his photo app. I scroll through our vacation shots—the canals of Amsterdam and Venice, the beach on Malta, the superyachts dotting the marina in Capri—and my eyes sting with tears at the parade of memories. No activity at all since yesterday morning there, either.

I'm turning to his calendar app when the desk phone rings, and I scramble to pick up. "Stella Knox speaking."

"Mrs. Knox, this is Lucas Fournier calling from the United States Embassy, Citizens Services department. I've been assigned to your case, which basically means I'm here to assist in any way you need. I hope I'm not disturbing."

My body goes warm, my muscles slushy with something that feels like relief. Finally, someone from the embassy returning my calls, to help me navigate the maze of French agencies. An American with a very French name. He even pronounces it like a Frenchman would, though the rest of his words are delivered in an American accent so generic, he could be from any one of a couple dozen states.

"No, you're not disturbing. In fact, I'm so glad you called. Please tell me you've got news."

"I have news, yes, but not as to the whereabouts of your husband, unfortunately. He's still on the list of missing persons, though in the past few hours that number has decreased somewhat. I just got off the phone with the head of the PP, the Préfecture de Police. That's Paris's main police force. The prefect tells me they pulled three more people from the rubble just this morning, though, sadly, one of them was deceased. Your husband is one of the five still listed as missing."

I do the math, and it fills me with nervous energy. "Okay, but two of the people they pulled out were still alive?"

"I understand they're in critical condition, but yes. As of this moment, they are alive."

"So there's still a chance they could find Adam, too? That he could still be…" I can't finish, and I can't sit still. I pop out of my chair and move to the window, pacing back and forth in front of the sheers. "I mean, it's only been a day and a half. They're still looking, right?"

"Yes, they're still looking. The prefect assured me his people will do everything in their power to find the missing five, including Mr. Knox, but I must warn you. The longer this goes on, the longer your husband is not found, the less positive the outlook."

His words are like that ice bucket challenge that was all the rage a decade or so ago, a shocking, frigid shower. The clock is ticking, like the timer on the bomb that blew up a Parisian square and possibly my husband. I hold out my hand in front of me. It's shaking again.

"I'm very sorry," he says. "I wish I had better news to report. I imagine things must be very confusing right now."

Confusing. Lonely. Infuriating. Desolate. Take your pick.

I shove open the sheers and find myself face-to-face with a woman on the other side of the street, blowing cigarette smoke out over the opened French doors of her top-floor apartment. She sees me watching, and I turn away. "Honestly, I'm losing my mind."

"Is there anything I can do? Other than keep you apprised of the investigation, I mean. We can provide translation services, for example, and we have an emergency financial assistance fund. Do you have the ability to stay at your hotel for the duration?"

"Yes. The manager put me up in a suite. He told me to stay here as long as I need. They've been very kind."

"I'm glad to hear it. I'll make sure our ambassador sends a personal thank-you note to the hotel manager."

A text pings Adam's MacBook, and I hurry across the carpet to find a frantic note from someone named Steve. Please tell me that wasn't your wife I just saw on CNN, and that it's some other Adam Knox who's missing. Text me back, man. News out of Paris has got me spooked. I scroll up, scanning months-old conversation. An architect client, by the looks of things.

"Stella, are you still there?"

"I'm here," I say, straightening. "Let me ask you something, though. In your conversation with the prefect, did he mention anything about an investigation?"

"What kind of investigation?"

"Into Adam. His business. Because a policeman dropped by earlier today and said Adam was brokering the sale of stolen artifacts, which is ridiculous, and worse, I'm afraid an investigation will distract them from finding him. For the record, my husband sells reclaimed doors and shutters, not plundered goods. He's not a criminal."

"Does this policeman have a name?"

"Yes. Lieutenant Colonel Collomb."

There's a long pause, followed by a sigh. "Why does that not surprise me?"

"So you know him?"

"Yes, I know him."

Lucas doesn't say anything more, but he also doesn't have to. It's obvious from his tone that he's not a fan. It's a big part of why I keep going.

"The lieutenant colonel also said the bombing wasn't an accident, and that Adam was the target."

"The *target*? You're telling me that your husband, an American citizen, was the target of a bomb planted in a Parisian café, and I'm just now hearing this from you, his *wife*?"

"Yes, that's exactly what I'm saying."

"That's, that's…" There's a long pause while Lucas gets himself in check, three puffed breaths into the phone. "If even a sliver of that is true, then it's one hell of an egregious break in diplomatic protocol. The prefect should have alerted the ambassador immediately, and you should definitely not be hearing any of this from the French authorities while the embassy is still in the dark. It's not the way these things are done."

He's getting himself worked up, and as much as I appreciate his anger where the lieutenant colonel is concerned, it's not on my behalf and certainly not on Adam's. Lucas isn't offended by the thought that Adam might have been a target. He's offended because, by telling me first, Collomb broke the stupid rules.

"I don't know anything about protocol, and I really don't give a crap if it was followed or not. I'm telling you this because I need help and you said you'd give it to me. I need to know if any of what the lieutenant colonel said is true."

"I understand, and of course I'll do what I can. Give me a day or two to figure out what's going on. I'll call you as soon as I have answers."

"Thank you. I really appreciate it."

"And if the lieutenant colonel or anyone else from the French authorities shows up there before I call you back, let me know immediately. Do you have a pen and paper? I'll give you my cell."

I push off the window and step to the desk, pulling a notepad and pencil from the drawer. "Okay, I'm ready."

He rattles off a French number, and I jot it down, then read it back just to be sure. When he confirms it, I put down the pencil.

"Speaking of cell phones, the lieutenant colonel told me they found Adam's. He wanted the passcode."

"Did you give it to him?"

"No. But I would like the phone back."

"If your husband is the subject of a criminal investigation, his cell phone will be seen as evidence. But let me talk to the prefect, okay? And call me anytime, day or night. Whatever you need, whenever. I promise you I'll always pick up."

"Thank you. Truly."

"Talk to you soon," he says, and then he hangs up the phone.

I drop the phone on the cradle and sit back in the velvet chair, staring at a tiny smudge on the wallpaper and allowing myself the tiniest smidgen of hope. Because if anyone can sort out the truth from the lies, then surely it's someone from the American Embassy.

That night I dream of Adam. I open my eyes and there he is, bent over me in the bed. He presses a finger to his lips. *Shh.*

I breathe in his scent, the familiar combination of sandal-wood and leather and soap, and that tight knot around my heart loosens just a little.

"You're here," I whisper. "You're all right."

I'm here, he whispers. *I'm still with you. You have my heart, remember?*

My hand searches for it under the covers, the red glass pendant he gave me in Venice. I find it tangled in my hair.

"I have your heart."

He smiles, and he looks just like he did the last time I saw him, before he ran back for those stupid sunglasses. Strong. Happy. So handsome. A shiny chunk of dark hair falls over his forehead. I lift my hand to push it aside, but he straightens before I can get there. My hand falls back to the bed.

Time for you to go, Stella.

"Go where? No. I won't leave Paris without you."

He takes a step backward, shaking his head. *Go home. People are watching.*

"Who? What people?"

His body shimmers, undulating waves of dark and light.

"Adam, wait. Where are you going?"

He holds up a hand, holding me off. Or maybe it's a wave, because the ground beneath him shifts, tugging him back and away.

I lunge, my feet tangling in the covers. "Adam!" I scream, but it's too late.

The darkness swallows him whole.

ELEVEN

ADAM

Bilbao, Spain
Sixteen days earlier

> *The answers are all out there, we just need to ask the right questions.*
>
> —*Oscar Wilde*

"Would you like to take another look at the menu?" the waitress says in heavily accented English.

I look to Stella, who shakes her head. By now it's late, almost eleven, though relatively early for the dinner crowd here in Casco Viejo—Bilbao's old town. All around us on the balmy terrace, people are stuffing their faces with wine and *pintxos*, the Basque Country's version of tapas, while all that's left on our table is crumpled napkins and crumbs swimming on oily plates.

"Just the check, thanks," I say, and the waitress saunters off.

I lean back in my chair and search the square like I've been doing all night, like I've been doing ever since Capri. I scan the people seated at tables spilling out onto the terraces, lit up with strings of globe lights and flickering candles. The rows of shops with bright displays behind plate glass, T-shirts and candles and toys. Just above, the city's Gothic cathedrals rise into the night, black silhouettes against a deep purple sky. My gaze, though, sticks closer to the ground.

I turn back to Stella, and she laughs and rolls her eyes.

"What?"

"That waitress was hitting on you. The least you can do is flirt back."

"Really? Should I call her back? Or wait—here's an idea. Maybe when she comes back with the check, you can slip off to the bathroom. That way you won't see when I give her my number."

Stella laughs again, because Stella knows that there's not a waitress in all of Spain who could distract me from her. That day I first saw her, when she walked into Scott Markets and my stomach flipped, was the biggest surprise of my life. Ever since, there's never been anyone but her.

"What do you want to do now?"

I shrug. After two full days here in Bilbao, there isn't much left for us to see. The Guggenheim, La Ribera Market, long walks along the river—though no way in hell I'm doing that now. Too few people at night, too many dark corners where someone could hide.

"We could go back to the hotel for a siesta," I suggest.

She gives me a look over her glass of rioja, but she doesn't look particularly opposed to the idea. "We just had a siesta this afternoon. I still feel very well rested."

"This afternoon we didn't do much sleeping."

She grins. "I know. I was there, too, remember?"

Do I ever. I grin back. "Let's just sit here for a bit, then. Enjoy our last night in Bilbao."

The truth is, I'm trying to stretch these last few evenings out, to savor every last moment of this vacation. Things at work have been getting sticky for a while now, and this trip has felt like a welcome respite—all but the *Aphrodite IV* sighting, that is. Three whole days since we sailed past it in Capri, just long enough to convince myself it meant nothing. A random fluke.

Though that doesn't mean I've let down my guard.

I'm giving the square another sweep of my gaze when my phone chirps with my sister's ringtone. I wriggle my cell from my pocket, doing the math in my head. Just after three in the afternoon in Chicago. I scan the text. "Oh, shit. Babs had another fall."

In other words, Julia dropped her daughter. Again.

A familiar worry churns in my gut. Babs is my niece, a blond-haired, blue-eyed sweetheart with every congenital disorder you can think of. Physical, intellectual, developmental, too many issues to fit into one neat diagnosis. She doesn't talk. She can't walk and is doubly incontinent. She has a feeding tube and constant infections that have left her with only one kidney that functions at well below normal levels. The older she gets, the bigger and heavier her body becomes, the more strenuous it is for Julia to haul her from her bed to her wheelchair, and the more expensive her care becomes.

Stella frowns. "Oh, no. Is she okay?"

I scroll down, reading. "No broken bones, Julia says, but they're keeping Babs overnight just in case. Sounds like she got banged up pretty good."

"Do you need to go to her?"

"No. Julia says not to come home. Actually, her exact words are *come home and I'll kill you* in all caps."

"Still. This is the second time this year. Babs is getting too big for Julia to lift."

"Believe me, I know." What Babs needs is around-the-clock care, something that Julia and her husband, Ed, could never dream of affording on their own.

I bang out a text to my sister. Which hospital?

It better not be where the paramedics took her to last time, where Babs spent an entire night lying in a pool of her own blood on the floor. The nurses there were too busy to notice that she'd fallen out of bed and landed on her face hard enough to knock out a tooth. The second they were done cleaning Babs up, Julia got her the hell out of there.

But none of this fixes the problem, which is that Julia doesn't want to admit she can no longer handle Babs on her own.

"I know the goal is for Babs to stay at home," Stella says, choosing her words carefully like she does every time Babs is concerned, "but maybe it's time to talk to your sister about a facility? There must be some affordable ones nearby."

"No facility," I say, shaking my head. It's a subject that is off-limits, not just for Julia but for me, too. My sister and I know all too well what it's like to get shuffled from place to place, to be handed off to camps and nannies, leaving your fate in the hands of a constant stream of strangers. It's why she'd never place Babs somewhere, with caregivers who aren't her own mother, and why I would never let her.

I toss my phone to the table with a sigh. "When we get home, I'm going to need a couple days to catch up with things at the shop. But after that I need to fly up there. Arrange some in-home help for Babs."

"Can Julia afford that?"

No, but I can. I can afford everything Babs needs, and my sister is just desperate enough that she doesn't ask questions.

"I'll work something out with the insurance company, see if I can get them to at least pay for part of what Babs needs."

Stella plunks down her glass. "I can help. I want to help, too."

I shake my head because Stella's salary is crap. Barely enough for her share of the mortgage, which she insists on covering no matter how many times I tell her to spend that money on something else. She pays for groceries, too, and the cable and water bills and her own car loan. And I get it—honestly, I do. Stella spent her entire life giving in to the demands of her moocher mother, and now she swings hard the other way.

But what am I supposed to say, that Julia doesn't need Stella's money? That I've got more than enough to cover whatever Babs needs? Stella isn't anything like my sister. She'd demand to know where that money came from.

"I could ask for more hours," she says, "or find a job that has better pay. The airlines are desperate for flight attendants these days, especially experienced ones. They're emailing me constantly, and they pay a regular salary with benefits."

"I don't like the idea of you flying around the globe for days on end, sleeping in strange beds. I prefer it when you're in mine."

"I prefer that, too." She smiles, and I think she's going to drop it when she adds, "I have some savings we could dip into."

I shake my head again, the movement fast and final. "Savings are off-limits. Especially yours."

"We could take out a second mortgage. The shop does good business. I'm sure the bank—"

"Stella, stop." I soften my words by reaching across the table for her hand. "I love you for wanting to help—really, I do—but I don't want you spending your money." She begins to protest all over again, but I stop her with a squeeze of her fingers. "I'll figure something out. I've got this."

The waitress arrives with the credit card machine, and Stella snatches up the bill, fast as a snake. "Fine. But dinner's on me, and don't even *think* about arguing."

She's sliding her card into the machine when they come out of nowhere, a flood of teenagers pouring into the square from a side street, pushing past the tables on the terrace, streaming past us on all sides. A kid in expensive Nikes and a backward baseball cap runs smack into Stella's chair.

"*Barkatu,*" he says, something I'm guessing is an apology

from the way he holds up both hands. Behind me, one of his mates passes by close enough to brush against my chair.

Stella gives him a close-lipped smile. *"Esta bien."*

The waitress is not as polite. She yells at him in Basque, an angry rush of words that make the kid bust out laughing. A waiter in a black apron comes running out, shooing the kids away with a kitchen towel. By the time Stella is finished punching in her PIN, the teenagers are long gone.

It's a British woman on the far end of the terrace who figures it out first.

"My bag! Those thieves took my bag." She springs to a stand, gesturing to the back of her chair—empty. "It was hanging right here! They took it."

Stella gives me a look, one that says *rookie mistake*. Stella has stamps in her passport from countries on every continent, has set foot in more faraway places than a hundred average people combined, so she knows all the tricks. Who hangs their bag over a chair? Not in a foreign land. Not smack in the middle of a busy Spanish square. Any well-traveled person knows better.

The Brit's husband ducks his head under the table and searches the ground, but there's nothing but dirty cobblestones. Above him the woman wails on, ticking off all the things she lost along with the bag. When she gets to their passports, Stella wrinkles her nose. The first thing she does every time we arrive in a new hotel room is tuck both our passports in the safe.

One by one, people pop out of their chairs, their cries spreading like a virus. Wallets, phones, watches, bags—vanished just like the teens. A German man lumbers toward the road they disappeared down, and I want to tell him not to bother. Those kids were pros. By now they're safe at home, sorting through their loot.

Stella slides the card back into her wallet.

I pick up my phone and stand. "Guess it's a good thing I always make you carry all my shit, huh?"

Stella's bag, a crossbody she bought specifically for this trip, sits safe and snug crosswise across her chest, and holds as much of my stuff as hers.

She reaches in and produces it—the wallet some teenager just tried to nick from my empty back pocket.

"Good thing," she says, tucking her arm into mine. "Now take me back to the hotel and thank me properly."

TWELVE

STELLA

Paris

On Wednesday, I'm seated at the edge of a sunny terrace, sipping my second cup of café au lait, when the memory flashes in my mind: the roving band of teenagers, nicking bags and picking pockets on that terrace in Bilbao.

I put down my cup with a clatter. "No way."

The man at the table next to me glances at me over his copy of *Le Parisien*, but he doesn't respond. Maybe he thought I was referring to his breakfast, which a pretty waitress had just delivered: espresso and an ashtray. No wonder Parisians are so thin. As far as I can tell, they exist on breadcrumbs and nicotine.

Meanwhile my table is loaded down. Mini baguettes coated in flour, tiny pots of jams and chilled butter, croissants and *pain au chocolat* and other flaky pastries filled with who knows what. More food than I could eat in a week. I look at it and my stomach churns because I can't stop thinking of that last night in Bilbao.

There's no way.

I flip open the bag on my lap, staring at a jumble of my own junk. My wallet and two sunglasses cases, mine and Adam's, a cheap pleather thing with sloppy stitching to match the made-in-China plastic monstrosity that sat crooked on his nose. The pink velvet pouch I use as a makeup bag, a freebie from some Sephora sale. The leather billfold with both our passports, which I pulled from the safe along with Adam's vintage Cartier watch, now strapped to my wrist, and an envelope stuffed with three thousand euros.

I shove it all aside and there it is, sitting at the very bottom of my bag. A thick trifold made of well-worn, well-tanned leather. Adam's wallet. He must have dropped it in my bag at the café, right after paying for the galettes.

"No fucking way."

I flag down the waitress and ask her to clear my table, which she does without complaint or judgment. She piles everything onto a tray but my still half-full cup of coffee, the only thing she plunked on the table that I could contemplate choking down. I thank the waitress, then add in my best French, *"L'addition, s'il vous plaît." Check, please.*

As soon as she's gone, I flip Adam's wallet open on the empty table. Credit cards, personal and business. His Georgia driver's license and insurance card. A stack of dollars and euro bills. Some crumpled receipts and business cards, which, judging by the tattered corners, have been in his wallet for a while. I pull out the items one by one and spread them into neat rows on the table.

I begin with the receipts. Seven in total, one an ATM receipt for three hundred euros from a withdrawal in Italy, and the other six for food. Business expenses, judging by Adam's neat script noting the work-related activity for his bookkeeper. *Breakfast day four. Lunch at Saint-Ouen. Drinks with Antoine.*

The name pings me in the chest. *Antoine.* The name of the shop owner in the 18th, the one I couldn't remember. Adam's eyes and ears on the ground. I put this receipt on top of the pile, then pin it to the table with the empty wallet.

The business cards I organize into two groups: antique dealers here in Europe, and Stateside contacts I'm assuming are his clients. I flip through the hodgepodge of names and titles—architects and builders, a few business owners and CEOs—thinking that once I'm back at the hotel, I can cross-reference these contacts on Adam's laptop and see if any match up. Adam is meticulous in his recordkeeping, building files for each of his contacts that include dated correspondence, items his clients are trying to hunt down, the style of decor they prefer. If these people are on Adam's hard drive, I'll know exactly who they are, what kind of business they were doing.

Only one card doesn't belong in either pile. A plain white square of thick paper with no name, no logo, only a long string of digits written across three lines in blue ink, and in a handwriting I don't recognize. Too slanted to be Adam's, too many strange slashes on the ones and sevens for it to have been written by an American. I flip it over and check the back, but there's nothing there. I turn it back over and count the numbers once, then two more times to be sure. Forty-eight digits in total.

It's not a phone number, then. Far too many digits, and the first few—293—aren't any country code I've ever seen. Even if these three lines were for three phone numbers, it's still too many digits. I'm pretty sure the maximum length for any country is less than sixteen.

I sit back in my chair and twist the belt-buckle ring on my thumb, a hot pool of confusion bubbling in my stomach.

Some kind of code, then, or maybe a combination? Adam has a safe at the shop where he stores emergency cash, his backup drives and important paperwork. But what kind of safe uses a code this long? And who on earth could ever remember it?

"Excuse me. You're Stella Knox, right?"

I look up at a man standing on the sidewalk, one I'm pretty sure I've never seen before. He's a good head shorter than Adam but just as solid, with high cheekbones and bulked-up shoulders broad enough to span the width of a chair, but with an olive-skinned coloring that conjures up visions of lavender fields and crowded Mediterranean beaches. I take in his neat, wavy hair and dark suit, the paper coffee cup in his hand that matches the ones the café at my hotel hands out. I think back to the people I've seen there, the blur of strange faces as I've raced through the lobby. A guest? An employee? For the life of me, I can't place this one—and a face as handsome as this one would have lingered.

"Sorry, but do I know you?"

He smiles, faint lines fanning out from the sides of eyes so brown they're almost black. "Lucas Fournier from the US Embassy. We spoke yesterday on the phone." He sticks out his free hand and I drop mine in it, letting his big palm close firmly around mine.

"Oh, of course. Yes. Hi. Sorry I was so rude just now. After everything that's happened these past few days, I guess I'm just overly cautious."

A tourist bus lumbers behind him, rattling the dishes and burping a cloud of exhaust, and he waits for it to pass. "Understandable, I guess. I would be, too, in your shoes."

His gaze scans the mess on the table, the neat piles of credit cards and papers pinned down with Adam's empty wallet. I sweep everything, the business cards and square white card with the handwritten numbers, back into my bag before he can get a good look.

It's then that I start to wonder. "How did you find me here?"

I didn't tell anyone at the hotel where I was going. I didn't even know myself, other than *not* to the bombed-out square. I couldn't face more bodies being dragged from the wreckage who were not Adam, couldn't face the journalists and the gendarmerie and the hordes of people coming to pay their respects. I saw them this morning on the news, with their colorful bouquets and homemade signs and candles flickering in glass containers, and that was more than enough.

And so, I wandered aimlessly for a while until I spotted a waiter carrying a tray of pastries and decided to try to force some down my own throat. This terrace isn't all that far from the Hôtel Luxembourg Parc, but it's all the way on the other side of Boulevard Saint-Germain, in another arrondissement. There's no way Lucas could have known I was here, not unless he followed me.

"I just came from your hotel, actually." He wags the cup in the air as if to prove it. "I was hoping to find you there, but the receptionist said you were already gone." When he notices my expression, his pleasant smile bleeds away. "My next meeting is in the 4th and there's rain moving in later today, and I figured I'd soak up the sun while I still can." He shrugs. "The curse of living in Paris, I guess. You become a slave to the weather."

It's a lot of words, especially when I'm still hung up on the first ones. "You were coming to the hotel to talk to me?"

He nods, and my heart thuds. One lone boom that echoes in my ears. "Is Adam—"

"Still missing, I'm afraid. Sorry, I probably should have led with that. But I do have some answers for some of the other matters we talked about."

He glances at the tables surrounding me on all sides, their chairs pressed up close. Most of the people here are speaking French, but still. Just because Parisians refuse to speak English doesn't mean they don't understand at least a little, and what we have to discuss isn't exactly fit for strangers' ears.

The investigation.

The lieutenant colonel's accusations of Adam, his business.

Lucas must be thinking the same, because he looks up the sidewalk, squinting into a sky already going wispy with clouds. "Like I said, it's a beautiful morning for a walk."

THIRTEEN

"How did you know it was me?" Lucas and I are zigzagging the busy streets of Saint-Germain-des-Prés, an aimless stroll in the general direction of the river. "Back there on the terrace, I mean."

Just like everywhere else in this city, this neighborhood is unrelentingly gorgeous. Broad boulevards with neat apartment blocks and grand hotels, Gothic churches and cafés spilling out into the streets. A constant barrage of recognizable landmarks.

Lucas steps aside for a leashless Jack Russell terrier, his owner close on his heels. "I saw you on the news."

He saw me, clutching the picture of Adam on my phone, my cheeks covered in dirt and tears. The Paris Widow, wailing for the cameras and the world. The grief-stricken face of the Parisian bombing, of tragedy.

"Yeah, you and a million other people," I say. "Though so far, the only ones who've seen Adam are either psychics demanding ransom or they're aliens."

The Frenchwoman's words echo in my head—*he got what he deserved*—and I shudder.

Lucas slides his hands into his pants pockets, looking over

with a grimace. "Tragedies like this one bring out the kooks, unfortunately. We've had more than a few call the embassy, as well. Our experience is that for every hundred calls, there's maybe one decent tip."

One out of a hundred. I think of the thick stack of papers sitting on the desk in the suite, the dozens of new pages lined with names and numbers the receptionists downstairs have been recording for me. How many are there, a couple hundred? A thousand? All those callers, and only a handful of decent tips. The idea of working my way through any more exhausts me.

"Honestly, though," he says, glancing over, "I probably wouldn't have even noticed you sitting there if not for your hair. The curls. The color. It's rather…distinct."

I nod because I get that a lot. "Kids on the playground used to tease me about being a clown, but personally I prefer the comparison to Flamin' Hot Cheetos."

He laughs. "There is literally no way anyone could compare your hair to Flamin' Hot Cheetos. But now I'm craving some, so thanks, I guess? Another weird expat trait—we crave foods we'd never dream of eating in the US, purely out of nostalgia."

I summon up a stiff smile, not quite able to share in his joviality. I want Lucas to hurry up and tell me his news. Whatever he trekked all the way across town to tell me in person, so I can get back to the privacy of the hotel and the plain white card with those mysterious numbers. I stay silent, clasping my bag to my chest. Adam's wallet hums like a hunk of active plutonium.

Lucas takes the hint. "How much do you know about your husband's business?"

I make a breathy sound, a combination of a sarcastic *ha* and a sigh. This question again.

"Now you sound like the lieutenant colonel."

"He hasn't contacted you again, has he?"

I shake my head. "No, not yet. But to answer your question, I know a lot more about it than I used to."

"Do you know who Adam saw while he was in Paris? Where Adam does his sourcing?"

"I know there's a man who owns a shop in the 18th. I know Adam spent a lot of time at the Saint-Ouen market. Other than that, I have no idea. We don't really talk about our work in that much detail."

The boulevard opens up before us, a straight shot to the Pont Saint-Michel.

Lucas stops at the curb, pressing the button for the light. "Unfortunately, what the lieutenant colonel told you looks to be the truth. The police prefect confirmed that there is an active investigation into your husband's business activities, and there has been for a while now. He made it sound like whatever evidence he had was pretty airtight."

I lift my hands in frustration, letting them fall to my sides with a slap. "But how can that be? I've been on Adam's laptop. I've read every single one of his emails and texts, and there are a *lot*. But there is nothing that even remotely suggests what he's doing is illegal."

Lucas frowns. "I'm a little surprised the French police haven't confiscated Adam's laptop, honestly. Normally I'd think it meant they didn't have enough evidence for a warrant, but in this case, the prefect implied he has more than enough to charge him. I'm guessing *that's* why, because the police have already built a case. They don't need whatever is on Adam's hard drive."

The light flips to Walk and we step into the street, our soles tapping across the zebra path. A chocolate wrapper skitters across the pavement.

"Which is nothing," I say. "I've searched it. Multiple times."

Every inch, over and over until deep in the night. Every time I dozed off it was with the laptop on my chest, and it was the first thing I saw, sitting cool and dark next to me on the bed, every time a dream snatched me from my sleep. This morning I made myself a cup of Nespresso and went through it all over again, just to be sure. The only thing I didn't spot was the contact card for Antoine, but that's because I didn't remember his name until an hour ago, when I found it scribbled across one of Adam's receipts. *Drinks with Antoine.*

Lucas shrugs. "Or because whatever evidence they have, they found elsewhere."

"Like where? Not our house back in Atlanta. The lieutenant colonel said Atlanta police were going to search it, but my girlfriend who's watching it would have told me if they had. The only other place would be Adam's shop, and I can't imagine he would keep anything illegal there."

"The prefect is keeping a tight lid on this case. He revealed very little about the actual investigation, only that there was one and they had more evidence than they needed. Though Adam's cell phone in the wreckage complicates things."

"Why? Because I wouldn't give the lieutenant colonel the passcode?"

"Do you *know* the passcode?"

"That depends. Are you going to get me in trouble if I say yes?"

"For the record, I work for you. My job is to be your advocate, to support you and promote your interests to the French authorities."

I give him a tight smile, because that's not exactly an answer, is it? "You're quite the diplomat, but I plead the Fifth."

He arches a brow: *touché.* "Understood. But as I was saying, the complication is that while Adam's cell phone was found in the wreckage, there's still no sign of Adam."

"Yeah, the lieutenant colonel told me to prepare for the worst."

"Normally I would say that's good advice, except that's

not what I mean. The prefect told me they're still searching for evidence he was actually there when the bomb went off."

His words stop me dead, the rubber soles of my sneakers sticking to the sidewalk of Pont Saint-Michel. Lucas doesn't notice. He strolls onward, and so does the man on my heels, ramming me in the shoulder as he tosses a hasty *pardon* into the wind.

I aim my words at Lucas's back. "What are you suggesting, exactly?"

Now, finally, he notices the empty air next to him. He turns around, doubles back. "I'm not suggesting anything. I'm only relaying the information I got from the prefect. He sounded suspicious of the discrepancy."

"What is he thinking, that Adam disappeared on *purpose?* That he planted his cell phone to throw them off his trail?"

"I didn't say that. Only that he's considering it as a possibility."

I have to sit with that a minute. The French police think it's possible Adam faked his own disappearance. They think he might have left me here, in a strange city, to mourn his death when really he's alive and well and in hiding. They think this is all a ruse, orchestrated by Adam to escape the authorities.

I shake my head, wind from the traffic whipping the curls across my face. "Adam wouldn't do that. He wouldn't do that to *me.*"

I say it as much to convince Lucas as myself, at the same time the memories flash: those silly sunglasses he ran back to fetch, his warm, dry hand sliding around the heart necklace, tugging me in for a kiss. His deep voice before he disappeared down the alleyway, promising me: *See you in ten, back at the hotel.*

Why would he say that if he knew what was about to happen? Why fly me all the way over here? Why bring me to Paris only to leave me here alone?

I say it again, certain this time. "He *wouldn't.*"

Lucas shrugs, nodding like the matter is settled. "Okay."

"Do *you*?"

He frowns. "Do I what?"

"Do you think that Adam did this on purpose?" Suddenly, it's very important I know Lucas's answer. It's imperative. "That he planted his cell phone. That he knew to get out of there before the bomb went off."

Lucas sighs, a resigned sound that makes me brace. He looks over with a grimace. "I'm very sorry, Stella, but you have to see how this looks, right? Your husband is the subject of an active investigation, one that is airtight, but he vanishes before they can make an arrest."

All the hairs on my arms and the back of my neck rise. Adam was going to be arrested. The police were going to handcuff him and toss him in a jail cell. The sidewalk swims, the sparkling water of the river up ahead so bright it burns my eyes. A moped buzzes by, and I flinch at the sudden noise.

"But—but… They're still looking for him, right? The rescue workers are still looking for Adam." The last one's more a statement than a question, but I need to hear the answer. I hold my breath and wait for it. I need to hear the word come out of his mouth.

"Yes," he says, and the air leaves my lungs in a loud whoosh. "They're still looking for victims, but at this point they're assuming they are just that—victims. By now they've pretty much cleared the building of rubble. It's down to three people missing as of this morning, and if they don't find them soon, they'll be…"

He cuts his gaze away from me and to the river. Like he doesn't want to say the next part while looking at me. Like he can't.

"They'll be what?" I say, but my throat is closing up because I already know the answer.

"I'm sorry, Stella, but they'll be presumed dead. At some point very soon, the official search will be declared over and done because—and again, I'm very sorry to be so blunt, but I don't know how else to say it—there will be virtually nothing left of them to find. Traces of DNA, but that's about it." He pauses, another sign for me to brace for his next words. "They're looking extra hard for traces of Adam's."

The horror of his message crackles through me like a bolt of lightning, and I clasp the nearest solid thing, a street sign, to keep from falling over. I try not to think about what Lucas is telling me, but the truth has already lodged itself somewhere in my brain. What's worse—that Adam would fake his death to escape arrest, or that he was evaporated by a bomb? A bomb with Adam as a target.

A sudden surge of cars comes barreling through the green light on the bridge. Gently, Lucas nudges me forward. I take a step, then another. We're coming up on the Île de la Cité, normally one of my favorite views. Now I barely even notice.

"Do I...do I need a lawyer?"

"That depends. Did you know of your husband's illegal activities? Were you willfully involved in any of them?"

"No. On both counts. And I'm still having trouble reconciling all this. I know my husband, and I've not found anything in his things to make me think he's a criminal."

I say this while in my mind, a whisper: *Really? What about the gold ring on your thumb? What about the statues and artwork back home? What about the white card with the mysterious string of numbers? You haven't found anything?*

But Lucas must believe me, because he shakes his head. "Then no. You don't need a lawyer. And look, this is France. Wine lunches and red tape—that's what this country is best known for. Nothing here moves fast, especially when there are governmental agencies involved. The best thing to do now is wait for the DNA results."

"What about the lieutenant colonel? When you and I spoke on the phone, you didn't sound like a fan."

"Lieutenant Colonel Collomb is not the most diplomatic of agents, and I get that, as a diplomat myself, it's highly possible I'm holding him to excessively high standards, but still. Don't deal with him if you can avoid it. As soon as I hear anything from the French authorities, I'll make sure to pass it on to you." He smiles. "But it would be helpful to have your number."

I slide my cell from my bag, pull up his contact on WhatsApp and shoot him a text: Thank you. Truly.

His phone beeps, and he checks the screen, smiling again. "You're welcome."

By now we're in the middle of the bridge, and I suck in a breath because there she is—the twin columns of Notre Dame towering above the island. Even flanked by a maze of scaffolding and cranes, leftovers from the 2019 fire, she's majestic enough to stop me in my tracks. I stare at the colorful stained-glass windows, the gargoyles and flying buttresses, and suddenly I am back on the square with Adam's warm breath in my ear. His front pressed against my back, one arm hooked around my neck, the other wound around my waist. Holding me so tight there was no space between us.

"A thousand oaks were sourced from the ancient forest of Bercé to replace the spire," he said in my ear. "All of them somewhere between a hundred and fifty and two hundred years old, all straight, fifty to ninety centimeters in diameter and between eight and fourteen meters tall. They chopped them down before the spring, before they could start producing sap, and still they have to let them dry for another year before they can use the logs. The framers will work with medieval techniques and tools to re-create the spire, making it look exactly the same as it did before the fire took it. *La foret*, they called it. *The forest.*"

He said a lot more. That the restoration is a master class in

historical accuracy and precision, that the architects are ge-
niuses, that people will be studying this project for centuries—
all in a voice filled with wonder.

Which is exactly why I still can't square that Adam, a man
awestruck by the mending of an ancient church, with the one
pawning off contraband artifacts to corrupt billionaires, objects
he knew were plundered from ancient temples or stolen from
a museum.

Now I turn on the bridge to face Lucas. "You don't know
me or my husband, so you have zero reason to believe me
when I say that Adam respects history. All those antiques he
saves from old buildings, he doesn't add so much as a swirl
during restoration to honor the artist. The thought of him
selling goods he knew were ripped from a church... It just
doesn't make sense. Adam wouldn't. Not the Adam I know."

Lucas takes this in with a slow nod. "And what you said before, when I asked if you knew your husband's cell phone code."

He reaches into his jacket pocket and pulls it out—an
iPhone, the same size and color of Adam's.

"Is this—" I take it from him and tap the screen, and there
I am, sweaty and red-cheeked in front of a North Carolina
waterfall. I tick in Adam's passcode, and the lock screen dis-
solves into a page of colorful apps. Adam's apps. This is his
phone.

I look up, and Lucas is watching me. "How did you get this?"

"I have my ways." He smiles, pushes up his sleeve to check
the time on his watch. "Listen, I have to run, but you have
my number. Use it anytime, okay? I'll call you as soon as I
have something to report."

We say our goodbyes, and I watch him disappear up the
tree-lined street on Île de Cité, wondering what kind of sala-
ries they pay at the US Embassy.

Substantial ones, apparently, for Lucas to be able to afford
that Rolex.

FOURTEEN

It's almost closing time by the time I make it all the way up to the 18th arrondissement, clutching Adam's phone in one hand and the taxicab's door handle in another. The driver speaks a few words of French and exactly zero English, and he doesn't understand the concept of GPS. For the past ten minutes, he's been zigzagging around the same few blocks while the meter ticks higher and higher.

I scoot to the edge of the seat, tapping a finger to the Plexiglas divider. "No, go straight. *Tout droite.*"

He ignores me and takes a right into a narrow street, almost sideswiping a biker. The man shouts and waves a fist, and I toss him an apologetic wave through the rearview window. The taxi swerves, luring me off my seat as he narrowly misses a parked FedEx truck, and I beat a fist on the Plexiglas.

"You know what? I've had enough. Stop. *Arrêt.*"

The cabbie slams his brakes, screeching the cab to a stop, and I thread two twenties through the slot. A hell of a lot more than he deserves, but my stomach is about to revolt at his shitty driving, and besides, according to the map on Adam's phone, it's only a ten-minute walk from here.

The neighborhood is iffy at best, and I am more focused on the blue line on my iPhone than watching where I'm actually going, which is why I don't see him until he's already turning away. A man in all black, slim-fitting jeans and a T-shirt stretched tight across his broad back, hustling toward the corner. I can't see his face, but something about him stops me in my tracks. His build, maybe, or the set of his shoulders as he hurries away.

Or no—it's the way he breaks into a jog.

It comes to me in a flash of heat, the vision of a blond man with a crooked nose, covered in dust and other people's blood, running into the burned-out café. I watch his easy gait as he ducks into a side street, and now I'm certain. It's the British man I spotted in the square that first day, the one racing into the rubble to haul out the survivors. The Good Samaritan, except is he?

Is he *following* me?

I whirl around, taking in the other people mingling about on the street. An old man smoking a cigarette on a front stoop, a woman scrolling through her phone while her dog sniffs at a tiny patch of grass, two mothers speed walking down the sidewalk behind matching strollers. None of them seems to have noticed me, but still. My heart thuds so hard it's all I can hear.

I hustle to the corner, then stare down the dingy street where the Brit just disappeared. The sidewalks are mostly empty here, what few storefronts there are either closed or boarded up. At the far end, a stocky woman in a headscarf shuffles by.

But no Brit. Wherever he is, he's long gone.

A shiver travels down my spine and I half jog, half run the rest of the way, my eyes combing the streets until my phone dumps me, sweaty and stressed, at L'Objet Qui Parle. The Talking Object.

Antoine's shop.

I'm panting as I push through the door, and a brass bell on the glass announces my presence. I stand for a moment in the cool, dark space, letting my lungs settle and my eyes adjust— and not just to the dim light.

Antoine's shop is like one of our neighbors back in Atlanta, an eccentric old lady who wears feathers in her hair and talks to the slightly smashed mouse who lives in her pocket. The walls of his shop are the color of blood, hung with filmy mirrors and every kind of painting imaginable. A purple velour fainting couch piled high with embalmed and stuffed animals, foxes and boars and a cloud of mean-looking bats, dangling from the ceiling like a scary Halloween decoration. Yellowed globes and cracked boxing gloves arranged into towers. Plaster teeth molds like you'd see in a dentist's office, clenched around smoke-stained pipes. Suits of medieval armor sized for a child.

At the far wall, a giant sideboard is loaded with baskets of cards and buttons and balls, next to an old-school cash register. The pretty girl behind it smiles. *"Bonjour, madame. Avez-vous besoin d'aide?"* Can I help you?

I step around a mannequin wearing a fringed and jeweled dress that looks like it came from the set of *Moulin Rouge*. *"S'il vous plaît.* Do you speak English?"

"Oui. I do. A little."

"I'm looking for Antoine. I understand he's the owner? I'm hoping to speak to him about my husband, Adam Knox."

It's almost comical, the way her face changes at the mention of Adam's name. The pleasant smile drops off her cheeks like a guillotine, along with all the color. This woman knows Adam, and she knows what happened to him.

"You are Stella. Of course. I…I'm so sorry. Please, wait here."

She whirls around before I can agree, then disappears behind a plain wooden door. A few seconds later it's whisked open and an older man steps through it, looking like he time-traveled here from another century. Three-piece suit, bow tie, leather shoes polished to a high shine. Round spectacles sit low and slightly crooked on his nose, and a delicate golden watch chain dangles from one of the buttonholes of his tweed vest, disappearing into a pocket. I guess his age to be creeping toward seventy.

But it's his mustache I can't stop staring at, two long strips of silver hair wound into elaborate curls. They twitch when he speaks.

"Stella Knox. How lovely to finally meet you in person. I've heard so much about you, my dear." His English is impeccable. He takes my hand in both of his, clasping it tightly. His skin is dry but warm. "I feel like I already know you, even though we've just met."

I don't mention Adam only spoke of him once in passing, or that it was a combination of coincidence and detective work that brought me here. I only give him a tight smile. "Thank you. I'm sure you've heard the news."

"I have, and I can barely believe it. I take it there's still no word?"

I shake my head. "Nothing yet. That's what I'm here to talk to you about. Is there someplace we can talk?"

"Of course. Please. Follow me."

He gestures for me to follow him to the door, spouting off orders in rapid French to the pretty shopkeeper before leading me down a tiny hallway and into a room that could earn him a starring role on *Hoarders*. There's a desk parked in the middle—at least, I assume it's a desk, since it's drowning under piles of papers and teetering stacks of notepads and catalogs. There are piles lined up six feet high against every wall, too, heaped precariously on chairs. He heaves an armful from the chair across from his desk and drops it to the floor, sending up a cloud of dust.

"*S'il vous plaît.* Sit. Can I get you something to drink?"

I sink onto the edge of the chair, resisting the urge to brush off the upholstery. "No, thank you. I'm fine." My bag hangs on a hip, and I shift it to my lap, pressing it with both hands against my stomach. "When was the last time you spoke to Adam?"

Antoine unbuttons his jacket and takes a seat on a leather swivel chair, thinking. "It was the day the two of you arrived in Paris, I believe. You'd just come from…Luxembourg, I think?" He pauses for my nod, then flips the pages in a Filofax spread open on the desk. "So let's see. Ah, yes. Last week Friday. He wanted to know if I had any contacts at an international shipping company. It sounded like he was comparison shopping, looking for a better price."

"Did you give him any?"

"Just one, but he said it was the company he was already in discussion with. I'm afraid I wasn't very helpful."

"Has anyone else been here, asking these kinds of questions?"

Antoine frowns, tilting his head. "Anyone like who?"

"Like the police, maybe. They seem to think he might have been the reason for the bombing. A target someone was trying to have killed. I don't know who."

"That—" Antoine sits back in his chair with a huff of air. "Well, that just can't be right. This is not a dangerous profession Adam and I are in. Who would want to have him killed? Why?"

Everything I know about this man leads me to believe Adam trusted him, and maybe it's a mistake, but in that instant, I decide to, too.

"The French police say his Atlanta shop was a cover for his real business, dealing in looted and stolen artifacts."

Antoine laughs, a loud burst from deep in his belly, until he sees I'm not joining in. His smile bleeds away, and his eyebrows rise. "You can't be serious."

"I'm afraid I am."

"But—but that's *absurd*. People like Adam and me, we are in this business to earn money, *oui*, but it's a business that is driven by the artistry of the past. All those pieces you see out there in my shop, in his, they're selected because they are beautiful and special just like a Picasso is beautiful and special, or the parchments that make up the Dead Sea Scrolls. We sell them because we can't bear to let these treasures of history fade away, and we definitely don't come by these treasures illegally. We leave the looting to the pirates and thieves."

"That's what I said! Well, not word for word, but pretty close. I said Adam's business honors history and would never exploit it. But my contact at the US Embassy says the French police have built a pretty strong case. He used the word *airtight*."

I think about the other grisly *A* word that came out of Lucas's mouth—*arrest*—but something holds me back from mentioning it now. Pride, probably. Not because Adam's arrest was imminent—not a good look, certainly—but because of how it makes his disappearance seem. Like he ditched me to avoid it.

Antoine makes a face, hiking up his mustache on one side. "Airtight. I don't like the sound of that."

"Agreed. And there's nothing on his laptop or in his briefcase to corroborate their accusation, so now I don't know what to think. Like, maybe they got the wrong guy, or he got caught up in something by accident, without realizing the artifacts were stolen. I mean, that's possible, right?"

It's definitely what I would like to believe. That Adam is a pawn, manipulated by some powerful underworld people. That he made a deal with the devil unwittingly, and now the police have him on the hook for another person's sins. It would make this whole disaster, his disappearance, his fate… well, not easier to bear, exactly, but maybe a little less awful.

Antoine leans back in his chair, sending up a loud creak. "It's certainly possible. Some of the world's greatest auction houses and museums have been fooled by fraudulent export licenses or ownership papers. If it can happen to Sotheby's, it could happen to me or Adam." He pauses, frowning. "You said you still have his laptop?"

"Yes. I spent all last night combing through the hard drive. I read emails that went back *years*. There's nothing on there but corbels and herringbone flooring."

"That's a good sign, I suppose. Though I could take a look, if you'd like. If your theory is true, the emails might look innocent enough to someone with an untrained eye."

"Or the police have evidence that wasn't on his computer," I say, skating right over his offer. To hand over Adam's laptop to Antoine, to *anyone*, doesn't sit right, not until I know what's going on. "At least, that's how my contact from the embassy made it sound. He says the police have more than they need."

Antoine pulls a face, shaking his head. "This doesn't sound good, Stella. It doesn't sound good at all."

"I did find one thing." I say it before I can consider the consequences, the words flying out of me before I can think to snatch them back. Antoine waits for it, his eyes kind and curious, and I decide to keep going. "I found a card in his wallet, the size of a business card except there was nothing printed on it. No logo, no name, just some numbers written in blue ink. Not Adam's handwriting, by the way."

"May I see it?"

I shake my head, my fingers curling around my bag. "It's back at the hotel, I'm afraid. I locked it in the safe."

This part is a lie. No way in hell am I leaving that card behind anywhere, not even in a safe. It's in the bag pressed to my gut, which is telling me those numbers unlock an important mystery. And until I know what that mystery is, nobody is putting eyes on that card but me.

Antoine nods like it was the right answer. "A safe is the best

place for the card, at least for now. And there were only numbers on this card? No letters?"

Again, I shake my head. "Only numbers. Forty-eight of
them."

"I'm asking because sometimes auction houses will have
catalog numbers that long, but they almost always incorporate
letters as some sort of listing code. But forty-eight... Could it
be a phone number—or multiple numbers?"

"I don't think so. There are too many."

"Perhaps when you get back to the hotel, you could text
me a picture." He flips open a carved box on the desk, pushes
a business card toward me. "That is my mobile number at the
bottom."

Not a chance. Not until I know what those numbers mean,
and even then. Text messages get intercepted all the time. If
there's even the slightest whiff of truth to the lieutenant colonel's
words, if someone planted a bomb powerful enough to take out
Adam and half a Parisian block, then whatever those numbers
might lead me to is best kept quiet. In fact, I've probably said
too much already.

Still. I reach across the desk for his proffered business card,
but before I can get there, he snatches my hand out of the air.
The card flutters to the floor and his fingers clamp down on
my wrist, and the old man is strong, I'll give him that. He
gives my arm a good yank, pulling my hand to his face and
me a few inches off my chair.

His voice is sharp in the tiny room. "Where did you get this?"

The golden ring on my thumb, the one I found in the pocket
of Adam's jeans. He twists my wrist, turning my hand to get
a better look at the ring from all sides. The belt-buckle shape,
the inscription on the backside, and I don't like the new glint
in his eye.

A hum of warning starts up in my head.

"Where did you get it?" he says again. Demands it. "Tell me where you found this ring."

"Adam gave it to me."

Not an outright lie, exactly, but not the complete truth, either, and it occurs to me that I'm taking inspiration from my husband. If I'm to believe the police, Adam learned to keep his secrets hidden in plain sight. No over-explanations, no details that will only trip you up later. Provide only the barest of facts. It's the best kind of lie. The smartest.

And everything about Antoine's reaction—his scowl, his tone, the iron grip he's still got on my wrist—tells me to tread carefully. To hold back.

"When?" He gives my arm another tug, holding my thumb under the desk light, squinting at the ring. "When did he give it to you?"

"I don't know. Recently."

"May I see it? May I hold it in my hands?"

The metal is heating under the lamplight, turning hot against the skin of my thumb, and I try to tug my hand away but Antoine's hold is too strong. He's up off his chair, hunched over my hand, his nose ten inches from my thumb.

"Only if you let go of my arm."

He does, reluctantly, and I snatch my hand back. By now the metal is practically sizzling, and it's a relief to slide the ring off my thumb. He's far too eager when he takes it from my fingers, far too gleeful when he inspects it with the magnifying glass he pulls from a desk drawer. He squeezes one eye closed and peers at the ring with the other, taking in the belt buckle, the inscription engraved on the inside. Antoine studies the ring and I study Antoine, trying to glean what he's thinking from his expression. But the only change I can see is a light sheen of sweat that pops up on his brow.

"This is… This is an extraordinary piece." I don't miss the slightly higher pitch to his voice, the way he hasn't looked at me—not once—since he noticed the ring. "Did Adam tell you where he got it?"

"No."

"Did he tell you anything at all about it?" Antoine's face is still shiny and red. His mustache twitches at each of the corners.

"No. Why? What makes the ring extraordinary?"

"I'll give you ten thousand euros for it. I'll write you the check right now."

I shake my head. It's not exactly an answer, and besides. "Adam gave it to me."

He peers at it again through the magnifying glass, turning it every which way, and I turn and glance at the door. This was a mistake. Coming here. Trusting this man, even if not completely. In reality, I know nothing about Antoine, other than that he occasionally gave Adam tips about items coming up for sale here in Paris. I have no idea if Adam likes Antoine, if he trusts him. I consider Antoine's reaction to the numbers on the card, and the only thing I can think of is getting out of here.

But not without that ring.

With a flush of heat, I thrust my hand over the desk. "Can I have the ring back now, please?"

Antoine starts at the sound of my voice, looking up like he'd forgotten I was still here. His eyes are glazed over, his cheeks still pink like apples, and I could take him. I could leap over this desk between us, tackle this old man to the ground and pry the ring out of his arthritic fingers if I have to. He stares at me, and a few seconds elapse, then a few more.

I stab the air with my hand again. "It's mine. Give it to me."

Finally, begrudgingly, he hands over the ring.

I shove it up my thumb and lunge for the door.

He calls after me as I'm racing up the hall, something about keeping in touch, but I don't slow. I hurry through the crowded shop while the pretty girl behind the counter watches with confused eyes, the brass bell clanging as I push through the door to outside, where I take off running, down the sidewalk and away from Antoine.

FIFTEEN

ADAM

Luxembourg City, Luxembourg
Six days earlier

> *Good resolutions are simply checks that men draw on a bank where they have no account.*
>
> —*Oscar Wilde*

I stand on the edge of bustling Place d'Armes, my cell pressed to an ear, and watch Stella through the window of the restaurant where we've just had a late lunch. She's not happy—that much is clear. She shakes her head at something on her phone, and her thumbs move rapid-fire across the screen, stabbing at the glass. Something's up, but I can only handle one problem at a time.

I keep my gaze steady on her while I say to my client, "I'll be back in Paris in two days. Forty-eight hours. That's all I'm asking."

There's a loud huff of air into the phone, and I picture her vaping in her plush Parisian apartment, surrounded by all that art. "Where is the ring, Adam? I want it *now*."

"I already told you I have it. I'll deliver it myself."

On the other side of the glass, Stella tosses her phone to the table, those thick curls falling across her lovely face. She said she felt out of place, far too underdressed among all the bankers and business executives, but standing here on the sidewalk of the leafy square, Stella looks perfect.

"Yes, but when?" my client says in my ear, pulling my attention back to the phone. "*When* will you deliver the ring? And before you answer, I also want the Pinner Qing dynasty vase and the Greywacke statue. I'm sure I don't have to remind you that I've already paid you handsomely for both."

Sweat skates down the knobs of my spine, and I step into a slice of shade. It's hot as balls here in Luxembourg, the first day of what promises to be a brutal heat wave. Stella looks over, catching my eye through the window. I've been out here too long already. I smile and hold up a finger.

"I already gave you the—"

"*Tais-toi et écoute,*" the client barks into the phone, *shut up and listen*, and I do. At this point, what other choice do I have? "You have already betrayed me once, Adam. I suggest you don't do it a second time."

Automatically, my gaze tracks to Stella, taking a sip of icy bubbles, a bottle of rosé Ruinart I insisted on, even though she said it was too much of a splurge. I need to get back to Paris and placate this client with the ring and the vase and the statue. I need to do damage control before she blows me clear out of the water.

"Enjoy Luxembourg. Say hi to Stella." A fist clamps down on my heart. The line goes dead before I can respond.

I suck in a shaky breath, scrubbing my face with a hand. The day seems to be getting hotter, the crowd behind me louder. The client knows where I am. Worse, she knows my weak spot is Stella.

I flip over to the Signal app and fire off a text. We have a problem.

After it's gone, I delete the string from my phone and head back inside, taking my time as I wind my way through the tables, using the minutes before Stella spots me to regroup.

Stella, who thinks a two-hundred-dollar bottle of champagne is a splurge. Who wants to take out a loan and change jobs to help me pay for Babs's care. Stella, who can't know about any of this.

"Hey, gorgeous," I say, sinking into the chair across from her. "Crisis averted."

"Speak for yourself. Emily's late on her rent." She wags her phone in the air. The *again* is both silent and unnecessary.

Well, that explains the scowl I spotted through the window, at least, all that rapid-fire typing. Stella's mother flaked on her finances again and now she's hitting Stella up for a loan, which we all know is not technically a loan. It's charity.

I lift the bottle from the ice bucket and refill both our glasses. "How much does she need?"

"Who knows? I don't even know where she's living these days. Last time I asked, it was somewhere in the Panhandle, but she's not exactly a reliable tenant. More the kind who disappears in the dead of night."

The table next to us erupts with laughter, four men and one woman in business suits. Stella glances over, then drops her phone to the table with a sigh, exchanges it for her glass.

"Can we forget about the Emily Shit Show for a minute? I just want to drink champagne with my hot husband and listen to you tell me about your call. That wasn't Julia again, was it?"

"No, it was a client back home," I say as a pang of guilt stabs me between the ribs, trying not to dwell on how good I am at this. At coming up with lies on the fly, at coughing them up with such a smooth delivery.

Stella frowns, checking her watch. "Isn't it awfully early there?"

"It was that architect I sourced those eighteenth-century

marble tiles for, the octagonal ones. Apparently, what he had to say couldn't wait."

Stella puts down her glass. The architect is real. She knows him, and she knows he's a colossal pain in the ass. "Please tell me he didn't change his mind again."

First he wanted marble flooring, then Belgian soapstone, then wooden planks twenty centimeters wide—or actually, no, in a herringbone pattern. The octagonal marble tiles he finally settled on were outrageously expensive, but he said his client had no limits. It was the shop's largest order by far.

"*He* didn't, but his client did. She says she wants Burgundy flagstones now, a mix of gray and sand color, which is extremely rare and even pricier than the marble. I told him I was happy to source them for her, but I wasn't refunding the money for the marble. Not until we can sell it to someone else."

The best lies are the ones that stick close to the truth.

Her eyes run across my face, the way I'm relaxed and smiling, twirling the stem of my glass. She frowns. "How come you don't seem more upset? Why aren't you freaking out?"

"Because I'm in Luxembourg with the love of my life. Because we just had the perfect champagne lunch, and now you're going to show me the city. Did you know that Luxembourg is a grand duchy?" I lift the glass to my lips, then lower it again. "What's a *grand duchy* again?"

Stella laughs because she *does* know. Stella's the one who told me that factoid, which we've already discussed multiple times.

"A country ruled by a duke, you dork." And there it is, Stella's full, unrestrained smile. "So what do you want to do first?"

There's still so much Stella wants to show me. The warren of cobblestoned streets, the monarch's palace, the walkways high up on the Walls of the Corniche hanging like a balcony over the Alzette gorge. Luxembourg is a stunning city, a web of medieval fortifications set against dense forests and a bright blue sky.

"Up to you, but first..." I point to her phone, sitting dark and silent next to my fork. "First you text your mother and ask how much she needs."

"Really? Do I really do that? Because that would be opening a door I'm not sure I want opened."

"Yes, you really do. You open that door, and when she gives you a number, you tell her the money's on the way."

"Money I don't have. Money we'll never see again."

"We'll figure out a way if it means your mother has a roof over her head."

"Or maybe she's lying about the rent and wants money for booze and drugs."

"If that's the case, then we'll deal with that, too. But until you answer that text, you won't know anything for sure. And who knows? Maybe this time will be different. I believe people can change. Don't you?"

Stella goes silent for a moment, watching the table of suits gather up their things, say their loud goodbyes, head toward the door. As far as Stella is concerned, I could be talking about anyone. Emily, who only shows up in her daughter's life when she needs a favor. Stella, who's been burned by hope too many times to believe this time she might stick around. I lean in and wait for her answer.

"I do think some people can change," Stella says finally, her tone slow and even. "But only the people who really *want* to change, who regret their past choices and are committed to making better ones moving forward. I'd like to believe that they can change not just themselves but their whole entire circumstances."

My chest goes tingly, and I reach across the table for her hand, even though what I really want to do is shove the table aside, pull her on my lap and hug her tight enough to creak her bones. I repeat her answer in my head. Commit every single word to memory. Tuck it away in case one day in the not-so-distant future, I have to remind her of what she said, that she thinks people can change for the better.

The waiter drops by with the check, and I reach for the stack of papers pinned to the silver tray with a handful of mints. A handwritten tally on the restaurant's stationery and a white card with a long string of numbers. I glance up at the waiter—a stranger, but not the most discreet one. He stands there while I jimmy my Amex from my wallet.

"So why aren't you texting your mother?" I say, a distraction tactic.

"Because I'm not sure she's one of them. I don't think she wants to change."

"That may be so, but this is your mother we're talking about—the only one you've got. No matter how you feel about her in this moment, it's a bond that comes with an expiration date."

When she doesn't respond, I reach across the table for her phone and plop it in her hand.

She rolls her eyes, but she unlocks the screen, then turns her attention to tapping out a text. It only takes me a split second to slide the card into my palm, and she doesn't look up when I shove it in my wallet. Doesn't see how I tuck it deep in the pocket behind my insurance card or the way I triple the bill when the waiter returns, right before we gather up our things.

On the way out the door, he gives us a little bow. "*Merci beaucoup*, Mr. Knox. Madame Knox."

"See?" Stella says as soon as we step onto the cobblestoned sidewalk outside. "That's what happens when you order a bottle of Ruinart. The waiters kiss your ass."

I laugh and sling my arm around my wife, letting her lead me into the stunning medieval city of Luxembourg, spread out like a jewel on the other side of the square. Telling myself that everything that just happened—the card in my wallet, the ring and the statue and the vase, all the lies and betrayals—they're all forgivable, because people can change.

SIXTEEN

STELLA

Paris

The skies open up on the way back to the hotel, big, fat drops pounding the rooftop of the taxi like an animated drum line, pouring down the windows in solid sheets. Outside the cab, the sky is dark and dense, the promised storm Lucas mentioned when he spotted me on the terrace earlier this morning. Thunder booms overhead, the clouds shooting down water so fast the gutters can't keep up, forming deep pools in every dip in the road. The driver sloshes to a stop at the Hôtel Luxembourg Parc, smack in the middle of a puddle half a foot deep. I pay him and splash through it for the door.

I'm soaked to the bone by the time I make it inside, leaving a trail of dirty rainwater on my trek across the lobby. Vents high above my head blast down icy air, the temperature cranked to frigid—or at least it feels that way. By the time I make it upstairs, my teeth are chattering. I need a hot shower, room service and bed, in that order.

Upstairs, the lock gives three quick beeps, and I push inside the suite.

And stop dead.

The side table by the couch is the first thing I notice. The way it's out of place, turned a good forty-five degrees, one of its carved back feet gripping the carpet *behind* the couch, not beside it. Like someone rammed it as they were rushing by but didn't bother to straighten it. Not one of the maids, definitely not. I've been staying here long enough to know the cleaning staff always leaves the room impeccable.

Something shivers across my torso, and not from the cold. "Hello?"

One of the fringed pillows, which the maids always fluff and karate chop in a corner of the couch, lies belly-down on the floor.

I squish on wet sneakers farther into the room, clocking the lampshade—crooked—the puddle from a water bottle—empty—on the floor. My gaze lifts to where I'd left it, on the corner of the desk, and that's when I notice the other thing. Or the absence of it. There's nothing on the desk but Adam's laptop charger, the cable snaking across the polished wood to nowhere.

Adam's laptop is gone, and so is his backpack.

I race around the couch and into the bedroom.

The bed is pristine, which means the cleaning crew went through here sometime after I left for Antoine's shop, but they for sure wouldn't leave the room in this state. On the right side, my side of the bed, what were once neat piles of my books and papers lie scattered across the floor. I pick up the notepad, the top sheet filled with my scribbles.

Antoine.

White card—numbers?

What else?

Shit. Whoever was here saw my notes.

I step into the bathroom, where my makeup bag has been turned upside down, its contents dumped on the floor. My blushes and bronzers, my container of loose powder, the Chanel eye shadows I bought at duty-free, colorful dustings across the marble next to brushes and eyeliners flung into haphazard stacks like pickup sticks. Whoever did this was looking for something.

I think of Adam's Cartier watch, hanging on my wrist. The things in my bag, our phones and the passports and cash, now a couple hundred euros lighter, still strapped across my chest. The white card with the mysterious string of numbers. Because it now occurs to me that those numbers might be the key to a bank account, a secret one that's not listed to a name. Like the accounts in Switzerland, for example, though my bet is on Luxembourg. The landlocked banking capital of the world—almost a hundred and fifty of them in all, making it one of the richest cities on the planet—where Adam and I spent three glorious days, and where, despite global reform efforts, regulations are still fairly opaque and control is iffy at best.

I whirl around and that's when I spot the safe, its door hanging open.

I inspect the edges of the door, studying the surface for signs that someone might have pried open the steel, but there's no markings on the door, only a digital keypad. I know the hotel has access to the combination, which is how they transferred my things when I moved rooms. The thief would have to know it, would have to risk me or one of the maids walking in on them midtheft. It's a good thing I emptied it earlier.

Next I check the closet, an explosion of clothing tugged from the hangers, dumped from the drawers. I find my jewelry pouch on the floor under a stack of my underwear, freshly laundered by hotel staff. I rifle through the pouch, ticking off the items. A couple of golden rings, three interlocked circles on a chain, six pairs of earrings, none of them very valuable. The good stuff—a diamond-encrusted Cartier ring, a tennis bracelet too flashy for me to wear in my new life with Adam, dangly Alhambra earrings made of platinum and mother-of-pearl—is back home, hidden in a box at the back of the laundry closet. They're souvenirs from another man, from a very different me. But the point is, all my jewelry is here. They didn't take it, which means this wasn't a robbery.

I close the drawer and step to the phone, pressing 0 for reception.

Manon's friendly voice floats down the line. "*Bonsoir*, Madame Knox. What can I do for you?"

"There was someone in my room. They went through all my things and stole my husband's laptop. His backpack, too."

A long silence. "I'm sorry. You are accusing one of our cleaning staff of stealing your laptop?"

"No, I'm not accusing anyone. I am only reporting that it's been stolen."

"Oh, my. I am so very sorry, Madame Knox. I will send up the manager right away."

While I wait, I grab the notepad from the nightstand and flip to a fresh page, making a list of everything in Adam's backpack while it's still fresh in my mind. The notebook full of to-do lists and project reminders. Work receipts and business cards and his Delta SkyMiles card. Our house keys—shit. I fire off a text to Katie, telling her the house key has been stolen and asking her to make sure the alarm is armed when she brings in the mail. I make a note to have the locks changed, even though I'm pretty sure the key was the last thing the thieves were after.

I think they were after the white card—especially if my hypothesis is true. I remember Antoine's reaction to it, his barely suppressed eagerness when he suggested I text him a picture, and now I'm certain. A bank account stuffed with money would be worth the risk of getting spotted on hotel security cameras, worth breaking open a safe to try to recover.

But Antoine... There's no way he could have beaten me here.

I came straight from his shop, in a cab driven by a lead-footed Parisian who took the quickest, most direct route through rain-soaked traffic. It's possible Antoine could have sent someone to do the job for him, I suppose, someone who was closer to the hotel. I did tell him the card was in the safe. Or the Brit could have sneaked in while I was out. I picture him only a few blocks from Antoine's shop, and my skin prickles with warning.

Who is he? Why was he following me? Are he and Antoine working together?

There's a knock on the door, the manager arriving in a flurry of apologies. He bows in greeting, then looks up at me with big eyes, his chest heaving as if he took the stairs.

"Madame Knox. You reported a robbery." Mr. Laurent is tiny, a good half foot shorter than I am and with the build of a prepubescent child draped in a slim-cut three-piece suit.

I step back to let him in. "The first thing I noticed is that some things had been moved around."

I show him the table, the lampshade. "And look." I point to the spot on the floor where Adam's backpack used to be, the cable snaking across the desk. "The computer's gone. They took the backpack, too."

"Are you certain? Perhaps you moved it to another spot? Or perhaps the maid did, when she was vacuuming."

"Moved it where? I've looked everywhere. The laptop is not in the suite." I gesture for him to follow me into the bedroom.

He stops in the doorway, taking in the nightstands, the mess, the safe door yawning open, and sucks in a loud breath. "Oh, my. This is very unfortunate."

I don't respond. *Unfortunate* is not the word I would have chosen in this man's shoes. I realize that thanks to his generosity I'm basically staying here for free, but still. This is so much worse than unfortunate.

"Are you absolutely certain? Because I've already spoken to the staff, and no one has been in here since one of the maids cleaned it at just after 2:00 p.m. The key cards verify this. No other staff has been in the suite since."

"Your system tells you when an employee enters a room?"

"*Oui.* We see the name of the employee as well as the time. But only employees. We don't track guests' keys, nor can we see what time our employees leave. Only at what time they open the door with their key card."

"So it's possible someone got in as the maid was leaving. They could have slipped inside without the employee noticing."

Mr. Laurent looks surprised, like it's a prospect he hadn't thought of. "I assure you, Madame Knox. Our staff is well trained on how to maintain a safe environment in our hotel, and that includes making sure the guest rooms are secure. I can't imagine they'd miss someone entering as they were leaving. It's possible, I suppose, though it would be highly unusual."

Unfortunate. Unusual. Two words that are the understatements of the century.

"And the locks? Could someone have…I don't know…hacked the system?"

He shakes his head, a gesture that is both immediate and definitive. "Impossible. Our locks are the best, most advanced system on the market. The keypads cannot be manipulated by anything other than a key card, which we program downstairs at the reception desk. Every member of our staff has been through extensive background checks. I will check the computer records, but please, I assure you. We don't just hire anyone."

I think of the pretty women who work the desk downstairs, how helpful they've been in collecting all the messages from people who've seen my pleas on TV, highlighting the messages they think are of most importance. Would one of them program a key card for a thief? If so, then it's not far-fetched to think they would mess with me in other ways. Goose bumps sprout on my shoulders, and I shiver. Who can I trust?

"I assume you have security cameras," I say.

"*Oui, madame.* We have cameras monitoring the lobby, every hallway on every floor, the streets surrounding the hotel. So many cameras. It would take my security team hours to sort through the footage." I stare at him, unblinking and silent, waiting. He takes the hint and steps to the phone. "I will call the head of security now. *Excusez-moi.*"

He's deep in conversation when there's another knock on the door. I whisk it open without checking the peephole—a mistake. At least then I would have been prepared for the man standing on the other side.

Lieutenant Colonel Collomb.

I take in his solemn expression, the way he's wearing a plain white shirt and jeans instead of a uniform, and my heart beats double-time. This man is off the clock, which means whatever news has dragged him here, it can't be good.

"What are you doing here?"

The lieutenant colonel blinks, but he must be used to cool receptions, because he doesn't look offended. "I understand some objects that belong to Mr. Knox were stolen."

I frown. "How did you know? How did you get here so fast?"

His gaze flickers past me to Mr. Laurent, still yammering a flurry of French into the desk phone. "We received a call from the hotel. I am working your case. Forgive me—your *husband's* case."

He stands there on the hallway runner, watching me as Lucas's words flit through my mind: *if the lieutenant colonel shows up again, call me immediately.* I think of my cell, buried somewhere in the bag still strapped to my chest. The lieutenant colonel shifts on his feet, his gaze boring into mine.

"Lieutenant Colonel Collomb," Mr. Laurent says from behind me, dropping the phone back on the cradle. The rest of his greeting is in French, and I don't catch all of it, but their voices are both friendly and familiar. This isn't the first time the two men have met.

I stop them with a hand in the air. "Please, can we do this in English?"

"Of course," Mr. Laurent says with another bow. "My apologies."

"It's better for the police report if I hear it from you. Please tell me what happened."

I step back and let the lieutenant colonel in, then walk him through everything I just told Mr. Laurent: the out-of-place end table that alerted me to an intruder, the safe hanging open, my jewelry pouch sitting in a pile of clothing on the closet floor, the smashed cosmetics in the bathroom. The lieutenant colonel's eyes roam the room, the marble-and-tile walk-in shower, the stack of fluffy towels, the pillows three rows deep on the bed, the mint on the turned-down comforter.

His gaze sweeps over everything, then back to me. "Whoever it was, it seems they were looking for something. Any thoughts on what it could be?"

I lead him back into the sitting area, pointing to the empty spot on the floor. "My husband's laptop and backpack. They took both, and the laptop was valuable."

"But then why rifle through your clothes? Why ruin your makeup? The thief would have seen the laptop on the way into the bedroom."

"You're the police officer. Isn't that your job, to figure that out?" I'm being difficult on purpose, because I know what the thieves were looking for. My bag tingles against my hip.

Or no—it's my phone, buzzing in an inside pocket. I dig it out and check the screen: my boss. I shoot her a text that I'm in the middle of something and will call her back later.

And then it occurs to me, what else I can do with my

phone: track Adam's devices. I go to Settings and sign out of my iCloud, then try to sign back in as Adam. I type in his email and the password he always uses, LaBellaStella1601<3, but it doesn't work. It's the wrong password.

I drop the phone back into my bag as the lieutenant colonel fires off his next question. "Who has access to the room other than cleaning staff?"

Mr. Laurent tells him everything he just told me, about the key system, the cameras, the time it will take for his security team to comb through the footage. Lieutenant Colonel Collomb takes it all in with a series of nods, but he doesn't write a lick of it down. No notebook, no voice recorder, not even a quickly jotted note on his cell phone, and everything about it annoys me. Is he taking this theft seriously?

"Perhaps whoever was here used your husband's key card. I assume he had one, no? He probably kept it in his wallet."

"Yes." I nod, then shake my head no. "Except, this isn't our original room. Mr. Laurent moved me here the day of the bombing. If someone has Adam's key card, it wouldn't have worked here."

"Not true," Mr. Laurent says, holding up a finger. "Because of your delicate circumstances, we transferred the key code to work on this room. If you'll recall, we didn't issue you a new card."

I fall silent, my scalp tingling with realization. The manager is right. I've been so distressed that I didn't think of it before, but all this time I've been using the same key card. The original one the hotel issued when Adam and I checked in. Which means Lieutenant Colonel Collomb is also right. Adam's key card would have worked on the suite.

"Interesting," he says. "Whoever has possession of that key card could have followed you here. To this suite. This is possible, no?"

I glance at Mr. Laurent, whose cheeks are pink with urgency. He wrings his manicured hands. "Technically, yes. I will have the lock reprogrammed immediately and have the desk manager send up a new key card."

Lieutenant Colonel Collomb's gaze never leaves mine. "Who do you think it was? Who else besides you and your husband had a key card?"

"I feel like you're implying that Adam was the one who used that key card, but you can stop now, because it wasn't him. I haven't heard from him at all, and he wouldn't do that."

My tone is pissy because Lucas warned me of this, that the French police think Adam might still be alive and in hiding to avoid arrest. But I refuse to think he would do that—sneak past the hotel cameras and into the suite for something as trivial as a laptop. Especially since I've already combed the hard drive. There's nothing on there he couldn't pull up on his iCloud.

Also, everything about the lieutenant colonel annoys me. Even before Lucas's warning, there was something about him that sent up alarm bells. Something about him that makes me feel like a rabbit in a wolf's den. And not just because his reasons for searching for Adam are nowhere near mine. I only want Adam back. The lieutenant colonel wants to prove Adam is a thief. He doesn't trust me any more than I trust him.

"I don't think it was your husband who was here," he says at last.

I'm a little surprised by this revelation, but I don't let it show, because this could be a test. The lieutenant colonel could be bluffing, trying to frighten me into believing that he knows more than he does. I lock down on my expression, hold his stare without blinking.

"You don't?"

"No." He shakes his head, and his tone is decisive. But it's the look on his face that makes me brace. "Perhaps you should sit down."

I don't move. I barely even breathe. Suddenly, this conversation isn't about the missing laptop or Adam's key card. This is about something else entirely.

"Mrs. Knox, I am very sorry to inform you that earlier this morning, we recovered more remains from the blast site. Human remains, from a male. The height and clothing fit the description you provided."

I press a hand to my mouth, and I know how I look. Wide-eyed. Shoulders hunched around a pain in the center of my chest, a sharp spike straight through my heart. A male body, blasted into pieces. And the police think it's Adam.

I peel away my hand and shake my head, hard enough to rattle the thought from my brain, but it's still there. "So Adam… He's…dead?"

"The lab still needs to confirm it, but it certainly looks that way. My sincerest condolences."

I squeeze my eyes shut against a wave of despair, turning to the window because Mr. Laurent has already seen me fall apart once. I don't want to do it again, and definitely not in front of the lieutenant colonel. And maybe it's because the two men sense the waterworks coming, but they make a hasty retreat to the door.

As soon as they're gone, I crawl under the covers, soggy sneakers and all, and sob.

SEVENTEEN

Later, much later, I emerge from bed to find my phone, pulling up Lucas's number. It rings only once before his voice comes down the line.

"Stella. Is everything okay?"

"Sorry to call so late, but everything is not okay." I try to force up a laugh, but I choke on the sound. It comes out like a wet cough.

"Uh-oh. That doesn't sound good. Want to tell me what happened?"

"They found remains. The clothes and the size of the body match Adam's." My throat burns at the words, but surprisingly, there are no more tears. It seems I'm all cried out.

"Have they confirmed the remains are Adam's?"

"Not yet, but the lieutenant colonel gave his condolences, so it seems he's pretty certain. I guess I really am the Paris Widow now."

"I know this isn't the news you were looking to hear. I'm so sorry, Stella."

Me, too. I can't say the words, not without screaming, so instead I say nothing at all.

Lucas takes the hint, plugging the silence. "And I know this isn't your problem to solve, but by coming to you with this news before he reported it to the US ambassador, Collomb broke procedure yet again."

"Well, I'm no fan of the lieutenant colonel, but that's not the reason he came to the hotel, or at least not the only reason. Someone broke into my hotel room earlier today. The lieutenant colonel is the one who responded to the hotel's call."

Lucas pauses, a long breath sighed into the phone. "It does make sense, I suppose. Collomb is the lead on this investigation, and he would have been notified the second the report came in. Plus, like I said on our walk, he's got something to prove. What did the thieves get away with?"

"Adam's backpack, his laptop, a few of his personal things. They went through some drawers and my makeup bag, even managed to get in the safe."

"Sounds like they were looking for something. Any idea what?"

The ring on my finger. The white card in the side pocket of my messenger bag. It could be either or both, or some other item I haven't discovered yet.

I wring my free hand, twisting a knot in the duvet. "No clue. The only thing in the suite of any real value was Adam's computer."

I don't like lying to Lucas, not even by omission. But if the numbers on that card mean what I believe they do, I don't dare to mention it. Not after Antoine's reaction to it, not after a burglar tore through this room searching for it. Not even to the person claiming to be my advocate.

"Hotel safes are pretty easy to pop open," he says. "All you need is the override code, and you wouldn't believe how often hotels use the same ones. Something simple for staff to remember—2-4-6-8 or similar. What was in there?"

"Nothing. The passports are in my bag, and my jewelry isn't

worth the bother of locking up. The safe was empty." I settle into the bed, leaning my back against the headrest.

"Well, clearly they were looking for something, but it must be subtle. A note written in a book, maybe, or scribbled on the back of a receipt. Something you might see but wouldn't think much of if you didn't know what to look for. Maybe you should take another thorough look through Adam's things. See if there's anything you missed the first time."

"Good idea," I say, but I don't mean it because I was already thorough. I already found more than I wanted to, and honestly, the idea of dragging his suitcase out of the closet and going through it again exhausts me.

"Let me know what you find, okay? And be careful. If the person who came through there didn't find what they were looking for, it's a sure bet they'll be back."

There's a knock at the door, and I push off the bed and make my way there, spotting an envelope someone slipped under the door. I pick it up and lift the flap—new key cards. The hotel staff reprogrammed the locks.

"Thanks, Lucas. Truly. I'm really grateful to have someone in my corner."

"That's my job. I'll call as soon as I know more."

I thank him and hang up the phone.

But his words have me spooked. The thieves will be coming back. I check the locks for the hundredth time, but they're engaged, both on the handle and the dead bolt. The chain is flimsy, but I give it a good tug and it holds.

On the way back to the bedroom, I check the time and do the math. Just past three thirty in Chicago, which means Julia will be in the kitchen, cleaning the feeding tubes, getting things ready for dinner. I pull up her name on FaceTime and hit Send.

A few seconds later, her face fills my screen. "Stella! Oh, my God, I'm so glad you called. Any news?"

Like everybody else on the planet, Julia heard what happened on the news. It was an unintended result of that first interview, that people back home would hear what happened from someone other than me, from a journalist on their television or a headline in their paper, all of which makes me sad and relieved at the same time. The only thing worse than tragedy is telling people who love you that you are in the midst of one.

I open my mouth to tell her what I heard from the lieutenant colonel, about the male body that matches Adam's description, but at the last second, I chicken out. If it really is Adam they pulled from the rubble, his death is going to kill her. I can't do it, not until we know for sure.

Instead, I decide on, "Just that there are three people still missing, and your brother is one of them."

From the flurry of texts Julia and I have exchanged over these past two days, I understand that the Chicago news has really latched on to the tragedy. Local TV, radio, newspapers and magazines are beaming out Adam's story in a near-constant deluge. Chicago's very own hometown boy, tragic victim of a bombing in a foreign land. She says his face is everywhere, and so is mine.

"How's Babs?"

Julia frowns, the spot between her brows folding into two dark lines. She has Adam's coloring, but that's where the resemblance stops. Sagging skin, shadowy bruises under her eyes, her mouth perpetually turned down at the corners. Worry will do that to a person, I guess, age them by a couple of decades.

"Still bruised and sore, but she's back at home, at least. She's been extra grumpy, though. I swear she knows I'm the one who dropped her."

I don't miss the way her face twists in guilt—just a flash, but I recognize it. Once, in a particularly vulnerable moment, Julia told me that she didn't think she was particularly good at the one thing she's in charge of, care for her daughter. Her being responsible for Babs's fall is tearing her apart.

I shake my head. "I'm sure that's not true."

"Oh, it is. I'm already interviewing pediatric home health agencies. Adam is right. It's obvious I can no longer do this on my own."

"That's why I called, actually. I wanted to tell you not to worry."

"Well, of course I'm going to worry. Adam is my brother and—"

"I don't mean about Adam. I'm talking about the money. Adam and I were talking about it before the bombing, and I already told him I'd help. I don't know what's going to happen, exactly, and I hardly dare to say it out loud, but if heaven forbid he doesn't…come back, I want you to know I won't walk away from you and Babs. You're Adam's family, which means you're also mine. I'll make sure that you get whatever financial help you need. I'm not sure how I'll do that just yet, but I promise you I'll find a way."

Julia goes still. She stares unmoving into the phone, a stretch of dead air that lasts for so long, I tap the screen to make sure we're still connected. "Julia, did I lose you?"

"I'm here."

"Did you hear what I said?"

"I heard, and that's very kind. But…" Her mouth twists, and she looks away.

"But what?"

She looks back, clears her throat. "I don't need money. Adam already gives us plenty."

"He gave you *plenty*?"

"Oh, yes. He put it in a trust fund under Babs's name, one that pays for everything. Her medical care, maintenance on the house, the costs of running the household. Enough to care for Babs long after Ed and I are gone. Last time I looked, it was close to a couple million."

Now it's my turn to be stunned silent. I don't know much

about trust funds, but I've known plenty of people who've had one. Men, women, adults without real jobs but plenty of cash to burn because of their trust fund, this magical ATM that spits out money on demand. Lots and *lots* of money. Trust funds are how the obscenely wealthy pass down their cash.

What about all those things Adam told me? The money worries, the fretting over who would pay for Babs's in-home care? Babs has a trust. A *sizable* one. Funded by Adam.

Julia looks off to the left, her expression crumpling into one of worry. "Sorry, Stella, but that's Babs. I need to run. Keep me posted, okay?"

She ends the call, and I fall back on the bed, trying to breathe, trying to think. Trying to sort through everything Adam told me about his sister's finances, all these questions his absence has left swirling around my brain. The trust fund. The white card. The break-in. The bombing. His business—the one I knew about.

I think back over these past four years with Adam, searching for signs that he led another, secret life, combing my memories for clues that aren't there. Nothing that even hinted he had millions of dollars stashed away, money he never told me about. If anything, it was the complete opposite. He let me think Julia and her family were struggling *on purpose*, while in reality, they have millions and millions.

A giant bag of lies, a hit list of betrayals, and all this time I had no idea. His poor, blind fool of a wife. If Adam were here, I'd kill him myself.

EIGHTEEN

It's early afternoon, and I'm winding my way through the narrow strips of street in the Marais, searching for an address I scribbled onto the hotel notepad. I study every person I pass, scanning the people behind the windows of the pharmacies and shoe shops, watching the side streets and alleyways for a tall man with wheat-colored hair. If the Brit is here, following me again, I don't see him.

I find 11 Rue Barbette tucked between a row of bakeries and chocolatiers and butchers, and I peer through the windows into a dim room. A mirrored bar runs the length of the left side wall, looking out over a couple dozen tables pushed so close together that diners will be bumping elbows. The tables are empty now, but they're set for the dinner crowd, starched white tablecloths, crystal and silverware polished to a bright shine.

And there, seated on a leather bench all the way at the back, is a lone patron. Zoé, the pretty girl who works at Antoine's shop. She lifts her hand in a wave.

I step inside, and she stands, tucking a strip of shiny brown hair behind an ear.

"Thank you for coming. I hope the restaurant wasn't too much trouble to find."

She looks different outside the chaotic shop, less mismatched, much more Parisian in a flowy white top over light denim and sandals. Effortlessly chic in the way only women in this city can manage.

"Not at all," I say. "I found the place in one go."

She points me to the chair across from her, then pours two glasses of sparkling water from a sweaty bottle of Perrier.

"This restaurant belongs to my uncle. The chef is the only one here." She gestures to a corner of the dining room, where bossa nova music thumps from behind a plain wooden door. "He doesn't speak much English. Not much French, either."

Her accent is the kind that requires concentration, thick enough that there's a second or two lag between what she says and my comprehension of it. It's easier now, face-to-face, than it was when she called me earlier this morning on my cell. I wasn't expecting it, which is why it took a couple of tries for her to explain who she was and how she got my number—by sneaking it from Antoine's phone.

Which is strange, seeing as I never gave him my number.

But Zoé's message lands loud and clear. Whatever she has to say is sensitive enough that she called me here, to her uncle's empty restaurant, at a time of day when we will have total privacy.

I wrap my arms around my bag and watch her across the table, the white card pulsing through the leather. Zoé watches me with an open, friendly gaze, but I didn't miss the way her hands shook when she poured the water just now, or the way her smile is stiff around the edges. She's skittish, which means I am, too.

"I'm still not exactly sure why you wanted to see me."

She pushes one of the glasses across the table. "Believe me, I tried very hard not to call. You must understand. I have known Antoine since I was a child. My grandfather and he, they are friends from university. Antoine is like family to me. That is what makes all of this so difficult."

"Okay." The word is drawn out, more a question than anything else. I have no idea where this conversation is going, though I can tell from her mannerisms that it's somewhere bad. She can't sit still, her hands twisting under the table. "I'm sorry. All of what?"

"Telling you what I know. What I overheard when your husband was in Antoine's office. The fighting."

Fighting. It's one of those words that can have a million connotations, and in every language. Fighting can mean an argument. A little skirmish. A knock-down, drag-out brawl.

But I don't have to ask which one she means, because her right hand curls into a fist.

"They actually *hit* each other?"

She nods, her eyes wide, then shakes her head. "Well, I don't know for certain, but one of them hit *something*. It made an awful crashing sound. There was lots of shouting and yelling. They called each other horrible names. And your husband, Adam. I've met him many times. He was, how do you say? Kindly."

"Kind. Yes, he was." I nod, flinching a little at our use of the past tense. "Very much so."

Kind and, as I've recently discovered, also a liar.

She shifts on her chair. "Which is why it was so shocking. I've never seen him that angry before. Until that day, I never saw him angry at all."

"When was this? The fight you overheard, I mean."

"A few weeks ago—I don't remember exactly. I remember it was before you arrived in Paris. I know because we talked about all the places the two of you were planning to visit. I gave him a few recommendations. Then Antoine said they had business to discuss, and he asked me to run an errand. When I came back, I heard the shouting from the sidewalk."

In all the years I've known him, I've only seen Adam angry, *really* angry, a handful of times. When a contractor sent him a bill for eight times the price they'd agreed on. When a supplier switched out the antique knobs he'd ordered and tried to fool him with semi-decent replicas. There are very few things that get Adam worked up, but trying to fleece him is one of them. Of course, that's immediately where my mind goes. Did Antoine cheat Adam somehow?

"Do you know what they were fighting about?"

Zoé takes a delicate sip of her water, her gaze flitting past me like she's checking to make sure we're alone. I look, too, a quick glance over my shoulder to confirm it. We're the only two people in the dining room. When I turn back, she's leaning into the table.

She lowers her voice to just above a whisper. "*Le marché noir. The black market.* I heard them say the words many, many times."

Her words slither like snakes across my skin, and I sit here for a long moment, considering how to respond. This is twice now I've heard Adam's name mentioned in the same breath as the black market. Lieutenant Colonel Collomb didn't call it that, but I know how to read between the lines. *Stolen artifacts smuggled across international borders. Forged documents. Organized crime.* It's the same thing.

How is this possible? That Adam could be caught up in an underworld filled with dangerous characters, that he is being investigated for being one of them, that he was on the verge of an arrest but was the target of a bombing before the police could slap on the cuffs. Sweet, steady Adam, loving husband and brother. A man with millions to spare, apparently. This is so, so much bigger than I thought it would be.

Yet this can't be all to the story. The bombing, that Adam was the target, the ransacked room and the white card, the inscription on the ring that must mean something, but what?

I know more than I did, but there's got to be more. Maybe this makes me a fool, but I have to believe that there is more to this story than what I've learned these past few days.

"*Le marché noir*," Zoé says, interrupting my thoughts, "it is a very bad place. These antiquities come from countries where it is too dangerous to travel, countries that are at war or occupied. Syria, Iraq, South and Central America. ISIS is a big supplier. So is the Taliban, Al-Qaeda, the Italian mafia, the cartel. These are not people you want to do business with."

That's putting it mildly. According to the lieutenant colonel, the third-largest international criminal activity after drugs and arms dealing. Whenever there's that much money involved, of *course* there's danger.

I also can't forget Antoine's reaction when he spotted the ring on my thumb, the way he yanked me out of my chair to get a better look. Even now, I can feel his fingers clamping down on my wrist, can see his face light up with interest, with far too much eagerness to know where Adam got it. Stolen treasures. Secret codes. A dozen scary scenarios float around the murky swamp of my imagination.

Across from me, Zoé chews the inside of her cheek. "I heard Antoine say Adam had a death wish. These very bad people, they were calling him a thief. They were threatening to kill him."

"According to the police, they succeeded. What did they think he stole?"

The metal sizzles against my thumb. For a second or two, I consider showing the ring to Zoé. I could push back my hair, maybe, give her an opportunity to notice it. Antoine offered me ten thousand euros on the spot, his opening bid. If the ring is as valuable as I suspect, then maybe it would elicit a similar response from Zoé.

Or maybe it will bring *le marché noir* down on my head. A chill runs down my spine, and I bury my hands on my lap instead.

"I don't know," Zoé says, "but I heard Adam say something

about *collatérale*. He said he wasn't that stupid and of course he had *collatérale*."

Collateral could be anything—the ring, the white card, a trust fund stuffed with money no one can touch but his niece and sister. Whatever it is, it must be substantial if Adam thought it could save him from *le marché noir*.

"I'll be honest. I'm having a lot of trouble squaring all this with the Adam I know. He wasn't the type to throw punches, and he definitely wouldn't have done business with the mob."

She laughs, a nervous titter, and stops just short of rolling her eyes. "*Une telle naïveté.* That's what I used to think, too. It's why I studied art history, because I loved everything about preserving the most beautiful elements of the past. But that was before."

"Before…?"

"Before I realized who Antoine is working for. It's why I am looking for a new job, because these are not good people, Stella. They are dangerous. How do you say, *impitoyable*."

I shake my head. "My French is not that good, I'm afraid."

"*Impitoyable, sans merci.*" *Without mercy.*

"Ruthless?"

"Ruthless, yes. These people do not care about preserving the past. They don't respect anything but money, and these artifacts are worth so much. Money is the only thing they care about."

"And you think Adam is one of these people?"

"Not at first, but now…" She lifts both hands from the table, a silent shrug. "When I heard what happened to your husband, the bombing, it frightened me. You see now why I called you here, don't you? Do you understand what I'm telling you?"

I nod, the realization dawning with a sudden surge of chill bumps, spreading over my neck and chest like a rash. I think of Adam's ring on my thumb, the white card buried in my bag, and I shiver because Zoé is frightened for *me*. She called me here to warn me.

Her blue eyes drill into mine. "Be careful, Stella. Trust no one. Whatever debts Adam had, whatever he did to get himself killed, these people will not let them go unpunished. It doesn't matter that he's no longer here. You are connected to Adam, which makes you a target."

I suck in a noisy breath, but not loud enough to muffle her last words.

"These people who killed Adam, they will be coming for you next."

NINETEEN

Zoé's warning beats in my head the entire way back to the Hôtel Luxembourg Parc.

I take the long way, going far, far out of my way in order to stick to the busiest streets, the ones jammed with traffic and pedestrians. I size up every person I pass. Tourists. Parisians. The people whizzing by in their cars or waiting at the light. I search every face, watch for any sudden movements. I feel myself sinking deeper into contingencies, into panic.

Whoever's after Adam will be coming for you next.

Le marché noir. Adam is caught up in *le marché noir.* Which means now, suddenly, so am I.

Trust no one trust no one trust no one.

This is what I'm thinking when a text hits my phone, a message from an unknown number. I open it, and a sudden surge of anxiety stops me in the middle of the sidewalk.

Digging into Adam's business = digging your own grave.

Before I can stop myself, my thumbs tick out a reply: Who is this?

The answer lands two seconds later. A friend. I'm telling you now, stop.

A friend, my ass. Friends don't send threatening texts from an unknown number. They give their names instead of hiding behind a vague label. I'm not stupid enough to fall for that, *friend*.

I'm considering how to respond when a motor backfires a block or two away, and I flinch. I look around, eyeing the people passing by and leaning against a pair of immense wooden doors to catch my breath. German tourists in sandals and socks, a gaggle of Americans smothered in tattoos, petite Frenchmen in comically slim-cut suits. They barely notice me at all.

And then suddenly: eye contact.

It's a man coming toward me on the opposite side of the street, and there's something about him that turns the air solid in my lungs. The way he's walking too slowly, maybe, or the suit that doesn't quite fit his skinny frame. Or maybe it's those shoes, beat-up lace-ups that are too ugly, far too out of place among the hipsters here in the Marais. I press myself to the door and watch him pass, waiting until he's disappeared up the street and out of view.

The breath comes out of me in a loud whoosh, right as an elderly woman in an impeccable bouclé suit shuffles by, pushing a walker.

"Bonjour!" she says, at a volume that says she's more than a little deaf.

The sun beats down on my forehead, and I tell myself that this is ridiculous. I'm being ridiculous. I push off the doors and get moving.

I'm at the next corner when it happens again, another angry backfire, followed by the growl of a motorcycle gunning its engine. I stop in the center of the sidewalk, turning in a slow circle, and I think of the Brit, tailing me all the way up to the 18th. The motorcycle is louder now, moving closer.

I take a sharp right toward the Seine, where the boulevards are wide and more trafficked.

I spot him when I'm almost to the river, halfway across the zebra path to the busier side of the street. Black jeans. Black leather jacket. Black helmet with a visor shiny as a mirror. He's coming at me fast, tires squealing on the pavement as he swerves in and out of traffic.

I shove through the crowd and onto the sidewalk, packed with stalls selling posters and tourist trinkets. The motorcycle doesn't stop.

I turn and run in the opposite direction, racing up the sidewalk toward the bridge, but the crowd is too thick, making it hard to move. At the last second, I take a hard right, veering through three metal parking poles and onto a cobblestoned ramp leading down to the river. This is a pedestrian path, for running and strolling alongside the Seine. The bike can't reach me here.

At the bottom of the ramp, I turn and stare up the ancient stone wall. At the top, twenty or so feet above my head, I see the backs of the stalls, hear the hum of traffic and chatter from the pedestrians. I listen for the bike, telling myself I'm overreacting. That the conversation with Zoé has me spooked but there's no reason to believe that biker is coming for me. And even if he is, he'll never be able to fit his bulky bike between those parking poles. What's he going to do—jump the barrier?

Which is exactly what he does. I hear the screech of tires and the whirring of him downshifting gears, and then he pops a wheelie and squeezes right through. I stare up the ramp as he speeds down it, and I am literally frozen with indecision.

Now what? I can't outrun a motorcycle.

My head whips around, looking up and down the path, searching for backup, for witnesses, but there's no one around. A couple of empty houseboats, a pair of runners fifty feet up the path. That's it.

I press myself to the stone wall and brace.

The biker is less than ten feet away when he slams the brakes, screeching to a stop so sudden and so spectacular that my feet leave the pavement. I rear back, but there's nowhere for me to go. My entire backside is already pressed to the stone. Cement crumbles against my scapula.

I'm about to scream when he reaches into the pocket of his jacket with a gloved hand, and I freeze. I can't move. Can't run, can't yell for help, can't even breathe. Panic flashes like my body has been dipped in hot oil like the falafels they fry at the street stalls. I stare at his hand and think, *This is it. This is how you die.*

But the object he pulls out is not a gun, not a knife. It's small. Rectangular. Dark and shiny.

A cell phone.

He extends his arm, holding it out to me, and I frown, dragging my gaze upward to where his face should be, but all I can see is myself, reflected in the shiny expanse of visor. Wide-eyed and terrified, mouth open in a silent scream.

He juts his hand in my direction, a wordless order. I take the cell phone from his fingers.

After that, everything happens so fast I don't have time to think. The smell of burning rubber and exhaust as he peels out and whirls the bike around, scattering a gaggle of pedestrians coming down the ramp. The sound of screeching tires and roaring engine, the gears shifting as he guns it back up to the street. I'm watching him lift into another wheelie to get past the poles when it occurs to me.

I didn't think to check for a license plate.

I look at the phone in my hand, right as it rings.

TWENTY

With shaking hands, I hit Accept and press the phone to my ear. "Hello?"

"Hey, gorgeous. It's me."

Four little words, only four, but they hit me like a high-speed train. The pathway spins, the words thrumming in my chest like a drum line. *It's me it's me it's me it's me.* I collapse against the stone wall, grabbing on in order to stay upright.

"Adam? Oh, my God. Is it really you? Are you all right?"

"Yes. It's me. I'm...okay."

His voice is confirmation enough that it's him—real, flesh-and-blood Adam—on the other end of the line. He's not missing. He didn't die in the bombing. None of this is real.

I'm trembling now, my body caught in the cross fire of a million overpowering emotions. I whip my head around, searching the joggers farther up the river, the pedestrians now passing the row of houseboats.

"Where are you? What is happening?"

"Babe, I need you to listen carefully. Your iPhone. Throw it in the Seine."

My gaze skitters to the water, less than twenty feet away. "What? How do you know—"

"*Stella*. I don't have time to explain. Throw your cell phone in the water, *now*. Tell me when it's done."

I dig my iPhone out of my pocket, race across the running path and chuck it in the Seine. Just like that. No pushback. No questions. If Adam has been tracking me on this device, then so could anyone else. It hits the surface of the murky water with a splat, and two seconds later, it's gone.

"Okay, it's done."

"Thank you. I installed an app on this phone called Signal. You can use it to communicate with me, but only Signal. No texts, no WhatsApp. Don't contact me any other way, and it's imperative nobody else gets this number. If you need to call home, use the hotel phone. Understood?"

"Yes. I understand."

"And don't panic if I don't respond right away. I'm moving around a lot, and I can't always stop to answer the phone. Send me a Signal message, and I'll get back to you as soon as I can, I promise."

"Okay, but tell me what the hell is going on! The police say the bomb was for you, that whoever planted it wanted to kill *you*. They say you're brokering in stolen and looted artifacts."

There's a long stretch of silence on the line, and I know what it means. It means there's truth in what I just said. He sighs, a long puff of air into the phone. "It's not—it isn't what you think."

But I can tell from his tone that it is. It's exactly what I think.

"Why? How?"

"I can't tell you that."

"Why not?"

"Because the less you know, the better."

"It's too late! I already found the white card in your wallet, Adam. I found the ring. The one that looks like a belt buckle."

"Take care of that ring. It's very valuable, and it doesn't belong to me. A woman named Katrijntje will be coming to get it from you. She'll return it to its rightful owner."

"Which is who? How do you know this person?" I don't repeat the woman's name because I can't, not without murdering the pronunciation. It's a mishmash of unfamiliar sounds, strange vowels and throaty consonants. German, maybe.

"Kat is a friend. She'll contact you on this phone, but don't give anything away. Agree to a time and place to meet and nothing more. The less you say to her, the better, until you're face-to-face, and even then, make sure no one else is listening. But you can trust her. Who else have you talked to?"

"Antoine. His assistant, Zoé. A million cops. Some guy from the embassy. He gave me back your cell phone."

Adam's voice turns low and urgent. "Stella. Where is that phone right now? What did you do with it?"

"It's here with me. In my bag."

"Toss it in the river, now. *Shit.* Toss it and then I need you to get out of there."

I dig it out of the side pocket and throw it as far as I can. I watch it hit the Seine and disappear, and then I turn west and start speed walking. "Okay. The phone's gone, but now what? Where do I go?"

"Just keep moving. What do you see? Who's there?"

Farther up the path, a pair of runners in black gear come down the ramp and turn my way.

"Just some joggers. Adam, you're scaring me. Who's after you? What did you do?"

"Where are the joggers now?"

"Less than a hundred feet. They're moving my way."

"Has anyone else reached out to you?"

"No, but somebody was in the hotel suite. They took your laptop and your backpack."

"That's it? That's all they took? Nothing else?"

"Just your backpack." I pause, thinking back to the lieutenant colonel's questions, his observation that Adam's old key card would have worked. "So, that wasn't you?"

"Definitely not. I haven't been anywhere near the hotel. It's not safe for me there."

"But it is for me?"

"Yes. As long as they think I'm dead, it is. Tell me about the joggers."

They're closer now, thirty feet and closing in fast. Two women, dark ponytails bouncing, their voices drifting along the water. "They're speaking French. Something about children. It seems like they're friends."

I keep a careful eye on them as they jog past. Neither woman so much as glances my way.

"Okay, they're gone."

"Keep moving, and did you hear what I said just now? It's important—no, it's *essential*—that everybody thinks I died in that explosion. Play the grieving widow. Talk about me in past tense. Better yet, go back to Atlanta and put on a funeral. Get on with your life."

I lurch to a stop on the walking path, crushed under the weight of the words he didn't say: *without him*. Adam wants me to get on with my life *without him*.

"No. *No.* I'm not leaving Paris without you."

"Stella, please. I don't have time to argue about this. You're in danger if you stay here."

"In danger from who, *le marché noir*? Because there's a British man following me, and Zoé said that Antoine was involved with *le marché noir*. Are you? And those numbers on the white card—are they for a bank account?"

"Burn the card. If they find it on you, they'll kill you for it."

"Who's they?"

"This is not up for discussion. Whatever you're doing, whatever you've found. Stop."

"Adam! You...you can't do this to me. If you love me at all, if you've *ever* loved me, you'll tell me what's going on. Tell me where you are and who's after you."

"These people blew up an entire Parisian block. They killed more than a dozen people in an attempt to get to me, and they won't hesitate to hurt you, too. They know you are my weakness. I need you to remove yourself from this situation. Play dumb. Go home. I can't keep you safe when you're here."

I'm shaking my head, but I don't speak. I can't. The questions I want to ask him are too awful.

What about you? What about us?

Adam seems to be having trouble, too. I hear him on the other end of the phone, breathing. Struggling.

"You know I love you, right? That I would do anything for you. *Anything.*"

Three days ago, my answer would have been immediate: yes. Of *course* I know that. Now, though, after these past few days, I don't know what to say. My head swirls, because I don't know *anything.*

"What are you saying, that you're…you're faking your death for me? Because I don't want this." I pause for a sob I can't contain. It's too much. I can't hold it in any longer. "I want *you.* I want our old life back."

"God. You have no idea how much I want that. How much I wish I could go back and change every decision I ever made that led us to right here. I'm sorrier than I will ever be able to say. I never wanted this to happen."

"Didn't want *what* to happen?" My words echo around the pathway, bouncing off the stone, carrying over the water. "I want to see you. I want to have this conversation in person. Tell me where you are and I'll come there."

"You don't know how much I want that."

"Then tell me!"

"Go home, Stella. Trust no one."

The same words Zoé said, only coming from Adam, they sound suspiciously like a goodbye.

"Adam!" The word explodes out of me, but it's too late. I'm screaming into a dead line.

TWENTY-ONE

ADAM

Amsterdam, The Netherlands
Eleven days earlier

> *The truth is rarely pure and never simple.*
>
> —*Oscar Wilde*

"Pretty sure it's this way." Stella gives a tug on my hand, dragging me down yet another tiny alleyway—the fourth, though I'm smart enough not to mention I've been keeping count. Or that the first three attempts to find the hidden courtyard were all duds, the crooked alleys either dead-ending into a locked door or looping back around to the Kalverstraat with its crowds and shop fronts blaring music. But Stella has only been here once, and it was ages ago.

I stop in front of a sign for the Amsterdam Museum, a bald woman in an elaborate catsuit. "This looks interesting. Should we check it out?"

As far as museums go, a fashion exhibition is pretty low on my list. We've already seen all the big ones, Rijksmuseum and Van Gogh and Hermitage, along with a string of historic sites, the Anne Frank House and the Six Museum and, my personal favorite, a hidden church smack in the middle of the Red Light District.

But my phone is buzzing away in my pocket. Something is going on, and I need to get away from Stella for a minute or two to check. I need to do damage control.

"I promise you the courtyard is better," she says.

Secret and medieval, apparently, and the oldest courtyard in all of Amsterdam. Bordered by long rows of private homes and bookended by two ancient churches, anchored by a perfectly tended patch of raised grass in the center. According to Stella, the most charming and quaint oasis nestled in the busiest part of the city.

"Lead the way," I say, following her through an iron gate. My phone buzzes again, and I dig it out of my pocket. Seeing that boat in Capri spooked me more than I'd care to admit. "Sorry, just need to make sure there's no crisis for one of my projects."

It wouldn't be the first during this trip. A shipment held up at customs, a builder back home losing his shit at yet another delay. I joked that was the problem with having moneyed, demanding clients, that they gave exactly zero fucks that I'm on vacation. Unfortunately for me, that part is true.

But this text is from closer by, my Dutch contact, Kat.

I must see you. This cannot wait.

It's going to have to. I slide the phone into my pocket without answering and let Stella drag me down a cobblestoned path that's more tunnel than street. Two-story buildings rise up on either side of us, crooked facades with big doors and tiny windows. Houses, I'm guessing from the plants and lacy curtains behind the glass.

She stops to admire one, and I fish out my phone. Not now. I'm with Stella.

Where? I will come to you.

"This is it! I found it." Stella points to a pair of heavy wooden doors next to a small, simple sign screwed into the brick: the Begijnhof. No wonder she had trouble finding this place. The sign is subtle enough that if she hadn't been watching for it, we would have breezed right on by.

Some hidden courtyard IDK. I'll call as soon as I get the chance.

I flip the switch to Silent and drop the phone in my pocket, peering through the ancient portal, past doorways and a couple of wandering tourists, to the raised field of grass at the end. "Pretty."

"Mister, you just wait."

With a grin, Stella winds her arm through mine and leads me through the double doors, and the city noise falls away like someone hit the mute button, a dead silence that amplifies my own urgent thoughts. Kat needs to see me—why? She says it's urgent, that it can't wait. Urgent enough she doesn't care that I'm with my wife.

These are the twisted thoughts swirling in my mind as Stella leads me around the courtyard, no bigger than a city block. She points out the gingerbread facades, an old water fountain, a wooden house from 1528 with a doorway half my size, the big linden trees rising like soldiers from the grass, their leaves combing the sky. I barely see any of it.

"How about I just go wait over there," she says, pointing to a bench pressed up against one of the churches, "while you deal with whatever is going on at work."

"That obvious?"

She gives me a look. "Babe."

I run a hand down my face, trying to shake it off. The stress is getting to me. It's literally making me crazy. My mind churns with all the things I should have done back when Stella and I first met, all the truths I should have laid out right away, but then I wouldn't be here, standing in this quiet courtyard in the middle of noisy Amsterdam with Stella, the love of my life, my anchor.

And now it's too late to tell her the truth. It's too late for a lot of things. She looks at me with lovely, trusting eyes that make it hard to breathe.

"Things at work are just a little stressful, that's all. But it's nothing I can't handle." My forehead is shiny with sweat, I just know it. I can feel the dampness creeping into my hairline. "I need some shade. Can we sit for a bit?"

I take her by the hand and drag her over to the bench, the one she just pointed to. We settle in, and she threads her arm through mine.

"Do you want to talk about it?"

"What I really want is to *not* talk about it. I want to forget everything but this lovely little courtyard and you." I wipe away a line of sweat at my temple. "Tell me about this place."

Stella grins, satisfied. She loves playing tour guide, and I love letting her. I swing my arm around her shoulders and settle into the bench.

"Okay. This courtyard is the most famous in all of Amsterdam. It's named after the Beguines, a female Catholic order of women who didn't take vows but still lived like nuns." She points to the building in front of us, a house with a covered portico jutting out into the sidewalk. "This is one of many hidden churches in this city, a Catholic church that was allowed to remain open when the Calvinists took over Holland, the only stipulation being that it didn't look like a chapel. The last Beguine died in the seventies, I think."

"So a hidden church in a hidden courtyard. I like it."

I'm not a religious person, but maybe being here with Stella is proof of a greater power, the universe throwing me a bone. Telling me that the yacht off the coast of Capri was a crazy, random fluke. For the first time since seeing it, I draw in a deep breath, let my shoulders relax. Maybe those two churches at the far end, with their bell towers rising like exclamation points into a perfect blue sky, are a sign of good things to come.

"It gets better," she says, "because once upon a time, the Beguine Chapel contained the holy relic of the Miracle of Amsterdam. A puked-up communion cracker of a dying man, which the maid tossed in the fireplace. But the next morning, sitting in a pile of ashes, was the cracker in pristine condition. One of the women who lived here once told me that, a sweet lady who lived in that house up there." Her gaze wanders to one of the bigger houses halfway up the courtyard, four stories of dark brick topped with a gable of elaborate white piping.

"Okay, I admit it. This place is pretty amazing."

I want to say more, but I can't because that's when a bomb goes off—or that's the way it feels. I stare across the square at the woman, tall and blonde, in jeans and a tank top. Her fists are full of heavy shopping bags, her hair windblown like she ran here. It's Kat. She found me, and she's headed our way.

I catch her gaze and shake my head. Subtle, barely perceptible, and her eyes flash with understanding, but she doesn't slow down. Just continues her march across the square. The moment stretches out, tense and sizzling. Kat is almost to the bench and *shit*.

Suddenly, the bottom drops out of one of the bags. Dozens of books rain to the ground, falling in messy heaps at her feet.

Stella springs off the bench, because that's the kind of person she is. She rushes to Kat and bends at the knees, snatching the closest books up, shaking dirt out of the pages.

Kat gives my wife a friendly smile. "That's very kind. Thank you."

Like most Dutch people, Kat's English is effortless, accented with a trace of something Germanic. She doesn't look at me, but I can feel her scrutiny.

I sit here on the bench, sweating, mind spinning while Stella stacks the books into the crook of an elbow, flipping through the top one. The books are old, leather bound with gold accents, the paper yellowed and frayed around the edges.

"These are beautiful. Adam, come see."

Silently, I push off the bench.

"My husband and I met because of a book," Stella says with a bright smile. "A first-edition *Winnie-the-Pooh*. He tried to play it cool, but he was like a kid in a candy store when he saw it."

I look down at the books in Stella's arms, a few still scattered on the ground around Kat's feet. I clear my throat. "You have a good eye."

Kat's lips quirk, just a flash and then it's gone. Her eye is better than mine, better than most people in this business, and everybody knows it.

"If you like old books, then you should take a look at this one." She shoves a small, leather-bound book in my hand and takes Stella by the arm, pointing her to an arched doorway at the end of a small tunnel—a different entrance from the one Stella and I came through. "And you should take your husband to the market just outside. He'll have to dig through a lot of junk, but occasionally there are some decent finds. I once got a signed Dali there for five euros."

I flip open the book cover, read the words slashed in black ink on the front page. Stella pivots, and I snap it closed, handing it back to Kat. "A signed Dali, huh? I'm impressed."

She gives me a meaningful nod and gestures to the end of the bench we just came off of. "I need to reorganize. Do you mind?"

"Go for it," Stella says with a wave of her arm. "I hope you don't have far to go. These are heavy."

"Only to my bike, parked around the corner. I thought I was being smart by taking the shortcut through the *hof*, but I probably should have put the heaviest ones in my backpack." Kat shrugs it off and drops it to the bench, working the zipper open. "I'm just so unsettled by the news that I wasn't thinking. All of Amsterdam is unsettled by it, actually."

And here it comes, I think. The danger Kat came here to warn me of.

Stella looks at me, and I can tell her mind is going big. Plane crashes, bridge collapses, shootings. The kinds of tragedies that would warrant an entire city being disturbed.

I shove my hands in my pockets as she turns back to Kat. "What did we miss?"

"A famous Dutch journalist was assassinated, just this morning. Right around the corner from here, on a very busy street in the middle of the day. A man drove up on a scooter, shot him in the head three times, then sped away. The assassin is probably halfway to Eastern Europe by now."

Stella presses a hand to her chest. "Oh, my God."

"I know." Kat bends down, stuffing as many books as will fit into her backpack, stacking them in like Jenga blocks. "A few years ago, I would have said this is not the kind of thing that happens in my country, but unfortunately, this is the kind of thing that happens in my country now. Pim Fortuyn, Theo van Gogh, Peter R. de Vries. They were all murdered in public, too."

"But why? Murdered by who?"

"It used to be because of politics or religious beliefs, but now..." Kat doesn't look at me as she says it. She keeps her gaze locked on Stella, who waits for her to continue with a frown. "Now it's the underworld."

In other words, the mob.

Stella gives a slow shake of her head. "I guess I didn't realize the mob operated in Holland. It just seems like such a peaceful country."

"The mob is everywhere, and Holland has one of the biggest airports plus the major sea harbor for all of Europe. We are one of the wealthiest countries in the EU, which means we attract many criminals." Kat zips up the backpack, then begins distributing the lighter books into the remaining bags. "Like the Moroccan man who assassinated this journalist. They call him Aljazaar, Arabic for The Butcher, because he tortures his victims in shipping containers. That's one of the crimes this journalist exposed, that these containers were basically murder chambers."

"Jesus," Stella says, and I have to sit. I sink onto the bench with a thump hard enough to shake my bones, because first Capri, now Holland. The land of tulips and cheese wheels, of windmills and wooden shoes. Aljazaar is here, too. He's following us.

Kat's gaze flits between us, sticking when it lands on mine. "I'm very sorry. I didn't mean to scare your wife, but this mobster, Aljazaar, he is very, very dangerous. His enemies all either disappear or are killed in the most gruesome way. Every single one."

"Then I guess it's a good thing we're not Aljazaar's enemies, huh?" Stella laughs, but she's the only one.

Kat's expression doesn't change. The pinched lines of warning in her forehead don't smooth out, and I'm pretty sure my face matches hers. She hoists the backpack onto her shoulders with a grunt, then bends to pick up the rest of her bags. "Anyway, thanks for your help. Enjoy the rest of your vacation."

She leaves, and Stella turns to me with a frown. "Okay, that was weird."

I don't contradict her. Aljazaar, the torture chambers, the assassination in the middle of a busy Amsterdam street. It wasn't a random anecdote. Kat told us this story for a reason.

It was a warning, as was the message Kat wrote in the book. *Leave Amsterdam. You are in danger here—both of you.*

TWENTY-TWO

STELLA

Paris

I recognize her the second she steps through the doorway of the Galerie d'Anatomie Comparée. A woman, blonde and tall, with light eyes and a face that has never seen a Botox needle. Pretty, but in that natural, windblown way that Dutch women have down to a science. She stands on the other side of a swarm of kids gawking at the skeletons and lifts a hand in a wave.

It's the same woman Adam and I met in Amsterdam, the one with the bags full of books. A Dutch woman with an unpronounceable name. The one Adam told me to call Kat.

She's prettier than I remember, though that could be the jealousy talking. When she wandered through the courtyard that day, Adam knew her but pretended she was a stranger. Unbeknownst to me, the two of them had some sort of relationship, even if it was only a working one. I take in her blond curls and fat lips, her floral silk blouse over faded jeans and ankle boots, the brown leather bag slung over a shoulder, and I feel it then, a cold, slippery spite for this woman, for her secret history with my husband.

She steps up beside me, and I catch a whiff of expensive perfume.

"I'm very sorry for the subterfuge the first time we met. It was the only way I knew to get the message to your husband," she says, staring out into the crowd.

The place is packed with what seems like every elementary school in Paris, and the excited shrieks and squeals in what's essentially a giant greenhouse are deafening. It's why I asked Kat to meet me here, at the tail end of a rhinoceros skeleton that once belonged to Louis XV, because Adam told me to make sure no one was listening, and no one will ever be able to hear us over the racket.

I think back to that day in Amsterdam, our interaction that I found weird. That story about the Moroccan mobster who'd had a journalist executed in broad daylight. How all his enemies either disappeared or died, but only after being tortured in a shipping container, gaining the mobster his moniker, The Butcher. Is that what's happening now? Adam is running from the mobster?

"The books were a neat little trick. How did you make the bag rip at the exact right time?"

She puffs a laugh. "The bag was a lucky coincidence, as was finding the two of you in the Begijnhof. He said 'hidden courtyard' and that's the most famous one. I was planning to trip or maybe stop to tie a shoe, but then the bag fell apart and I didn't have to."

I hear her explanation and I think I even believe her—who could even plan such a thing?—but my mind is snagged on one thing she said. *Lucky.* The word doesn't sit right.

A little boy races by shouting a steady stream of animated French, his cheeks cherry pink with excitement, and I wait for him to pass. "Nothing about this situation feels lucky."

"I imagine it doesn't, but it would feel even worse if that

bomb had hit its intended target. Adam and I were supposed to die in that square."

I fall silent for a long moment, latching on to everything she didn't say. This woman not only knows Adam, she seems to know that he wasn't killed, and my heart gives a little flutter, because that phone call was real. Adam is alive. No one can take that away from me. No one can tell me otherwise.

But the relief is short-lived, followed by a sharp whiplash of resentment. If Kat knows about Adam, it means she's important enough that he reached out to her, too.

Another kid goes whizzing by, trailed by what looks to be his entire class, and already this place is getting to me. The heat from the sun blaring down on the glass above our heads, the hundreds of overactive bodies and their high-pitched shrieks, all the commotion and clamor. How little humans can make this much noise is beyond me.

"How do you know my husband?"

I don't look at her as I say it, and the *my husband* is intentional. A proverbial lifted leg on the man I married, because I can and I don't like how this woman makes me feel.

She lets a couple of beats pass. "Honestly, I'd rather not say."

My gaze whips to hers, and she winces. "For the record, there's nothing inappropriate going on between Adam and me, and there never has been. Our relationship is and has only ever been professional. In fact, I'm not sure I even like your husband all that much. At the very least, I really, really hate his business."

"Which business are we talking about?"

She sighs. "Come on, Stella. You seem smarter than that. Surely by now you must know that Adam's hands are far from clean."

"And yours are?"

"I'm not the one selling stolen pieces, pieces that belong to a culture and its people, not on a wealthy client's wall. Do you know how many people died smuggling those artifacts over international borders? They call them 'blood antiquities' for a reason. This is how your husband makes his money. You know this, right? He's been doing it for years."

I fall silent because Kat's right. By now I *do* know, and I don't need any more convincing that the man I married is a liar. A smuggler with blood on his hands. I stand here and wait for the familiar flash of heat, the fury at his betrayal, but it doesn't come. The only thing I feel is a heavy cloud of disappointment and regret.

In Adam.

In myself.

Because how could I sleep next to this man for four whole years and have no idea? How could he keep this from me? Does he not trust me enough to tell me the truth?

Or maybe it's worse than that. Maybe I played a hand in this. After all, my own history is why I chose Adam, because he didn't have any interest in peering into the dark corners of my past, didn't want to know who else I'd been with, what other versions of me existed. He doesn't know about the part of me that is more like him than I care to admit, because I never told him, just like he never told me about the other versions of him. We both simply projected what we thought the other wanted to see: that we're normal, respectable, unassuming and mainstream. It's so much easier to blame Adam for his lies of omission than to take a hard look at my own.

I turn to Kat. "So if you and Adam are on opposite sides of the law, then why are we here? Does it have something to do with the Moroccan man you told us about? The Butcher who's part of the underworld."

It's the word she used that day in the courtyard, even though I could have said any other to her now. The mob, organized crime, *le marché noir*. Tomato, tomahto. But it feels like the crux of all of this. Adam is running from something bigger than all of us.

Kat confirms it with a brisk nod. "They call him Aljazaar, but that's all I am willing to say. Defining the danger would put your life at risk, too."

Too. Which means she's not just referring to Adam. "What about you? Is your life at risk?"

"I told you that day in the Begijnhof. Aljazaar's enemies all either disappear or are killed."

"And you're one of them." She doesn't nod, but fear flashes in her expression. She is this man's enemy, too. "Adam said I could trust you."

"Then he's wrong. You cannot trust anyone, Stella. Not even me. Especially not me. Adam's client is out for vengeance, and you are their next target. If you want to stay alive, then you must leave Paris—*now.*"

"Who's his client? If it's not Aljazaar, who else is after me?"

She puffs an ironic laugh through her nose, rolls her eyes. "I cannot tell you. I promised Adam I wouldn't. And believe me, it's safer if you don't know."

I believe her. I believe the way her face went three shades paler at the mention of Aljazaar's name, believe the tremble in her voice that says she's terrified. I line up the puzzle pieces in my mind: Aljazaar, the police investigation, the fight Zoé overheard, yesterday's phone call with Adam. All these people coming to me with vague warnings to watch my back for surprise attacks from a nameless, faceless man. I'm getting really tired of all the ambiguity.

"If you're not going to tell me, then why are we here?"

"Because of that." Without looking over, she gestures to the ring on my thumb. "There are many people looking for this ring, who will not hesitate to kill you just for having it on your finger. It's very valuable."

I stuff my hand into my jeans pocket. "And I'm just supposed to hand it over to you."

"Yes. Adam was going to give it to me before the two of

you left Paris." She glances over with a small smile. "You didn't see me at the café, did you? I was sitting in the square."

I think of how Adam was on his phone when I returned from ordering the food, the pictures he showed me without missing a beat, his calm reaction. He was completely unfazed by this woman watching from a bench nearby, by the danger. Could he have faked that so well? And what does it say about him if he did? It makes me wonder what else I might have missed.

"So that day at the café, our last day in Paris, why didn't he give you the ring then?"

It's a question and a test in one. Adam didn't have the ring with him that day. I found it much later tucked in a pocket of his jeans, already packed in his suitcase for the trip home. If Kat lies to me now, if she tells me the plan was for Adam to hand over the ring at the café, I'll leave. Walk out of this place with this thing still on my thumb.

"Adam didn't bring the ring to the square. He said it was too dangerous. By then Aljazaar was already following me."

"But why? What did you do to make Aljazaar your enemy?"

"Aljazaar works for Adam's client, a woman who wanted us dead and didn't care about all the innocent people who would die in the crosshairs. But Adam knew that something was coming. That's why he returned to the square, to tell me to run. The explosion happened a few seconds later." Kat shakes her head, but it's half-hearted at best. "I already said too much. It's better you don't know the details."

"Isn't it better if I know who's coming after me?"

"No. It's better if you give me the ring and then forget you knew anything about it. Get on a plane, Stella. Go home before you're killed."

Now she sounds just like Adam. For a second or two, I consider telling her what I told Adam, that I'm not leaving this city without him, but I already know what she'll say and I'm tired of arguing this point. Instead, I decide to change gears.

"Adam said you are going to return the ring to its rightful owner." Behind the denim of my pocket, the metal zings on my hand. "Who does it belong to? Not Antoine. Do you know him?" I glance over as she nods, her mouth curling down at the corners. She knows Antoine, and she doesn't like him. "He didn't like that I was wearing it."

She smiles, though it's one without the slightest trace of humor. "That's because Adam stole it from him."

"Answer my question, Kat. Who does this ring belong to?" She shakes her head, clamping down on her perfectly lush lips, and I turn back to the slew of screaming kids with a sigh. "Suit yourself. But for the record, if you can't be bothered to tell me whose ring this is, then I can't be bothered to give it to you."

"It's not that I *can't* tell you, Stella. It's that I don't *want* to, and you shouldn't want that, either. You should also know that wearing it is a sign that you were involved in the theft. With that thing on your finger, you might as well be wearing a bull's-eye."

"Fine. Then I'll stop wearing it. I'll hide it somewhere no one will ever find it, like the bottom of the Seine. The ring means nothing to me."

It's a lie. It means something to Adam, obviously, and thus it means something to me. Wherever I hide it, it won't be on the garbage-strewn bed of a city river.

But Kat doesn't know this, and I didn't miss the flash of panic when I mentioned the Seine, the way she's chewing on the inside of her bottom lip. This ring is worth more to her than the gold it's made of—that much is obvious. I wriggle my hand out of my pocket, the buckle glinting in the overhead lights.

"Fine." It comes out on the tail end of a sigh, and she lifts her gaze to mine.

"Once upon a time, that ring belonged to Oscar Wilde. You know, the Irish playwright."

"I know who Oscar Wilde is." I roll my eyes, even though,

apparently, I *don't* know—or at least my memory has fudged on some of the details. I thought he was British, and wasn't Oscar Wilde a poet? Not that it matters for the purposes of this conversation, and not that I'd ever dream of giving Kat an edge. For all she knows, I could tick off every play he ever wrote, and maybe even quote some of the best lines.

"He and a friend named Reginald Harding gifted the ring to William Ward in 1876," she says. "That's what the initials engraved inside the ring mean. *OFOFWW + RRH to WWW.* Oscar's full name was Oscar Fingal O'Flahertie Wills Wilde. The inscription on the outside is Greek, loosely translated to *gift of love, to one who wishes love.*"

She got the inscription right, at least. I nod. "Go on."

"The ring was on display at Oxford University when it was stolen in 2002, along with a couple of Wilde's other belongings. The thief sold them to a gold scrap dealer, so everybody just assumed it had been melted down for the value of the gold, which wouldn't be all that much and the world would have lost a precious piece of our history. We all thought the ring was lost until, suddenly, there was chatter in London's underground market. Adam and I went after it, but Antoine got there first."

"So Adam took it from him?"

"It's more complicated than that, but yes. Essentially."

"And you intend to return it to Oxford and Oscar Wilde? Because I'm pretty sure he's dead."

"I plan to return it to its owner, yes. The Oscar Wilde Society."

I pause, letting a few more seconds tick by while I try to figure out whether I believe her, whether I can take her promise at face value. Why would I? Why should I believe anyone at this point?

"How do I know you'll do that?"

She shrugs. "You don't. But I can promise you, I don't want

that ring on my person for one second longer than absolutely necessary. And you shouldn't, either. As soon as you give it to me, I'm on the next flight to London."

If it were only her saying these things, I wouldn't even consider it. *The ring is very valuable. It doesn't belong to me. Kat will return it to its rightful owner.* It's not her words but Adam's that make me wiggle the ring from my thumb.

But I don't hand it to her, not yet.

"Will this be it?"

She looks over with a frown. "What do you mean?"

"If I give you this ring, will The Butcher leave Adam alone? Will he be safe enough to come out of hiding? Can we go home, go back to our happily-ever-after?"

Kat gives me a sad smile. "I think you and I both know there's no such thing."

TWENTY-THREE

I'm back at the hotel, stabbing the button for the elevator, when Manon comes jogging around the corner. *"Madame Knox, un moment, s'il vous plaît."*

"It's Stella," I remind her, and for what must be the hundredth time. If I'm allowed to call her Manon, she can call me Stella—as a matter of fact, *please* call me Stella. *Madame Knox* makes me feel ancient.

"This man was here for you today." She shoves a business card at my chest. It's white and cheap, the paper thin and glossy, with a printed seal at the top right corner. United States of America Embassy. I scan the name and title, Benjamin Marshall from the Department of Citizens Services. "He would like very much for you to call him."

"I've already talked to someone from the embassy."

And that was *before* I talked to Adam, before his voice on the other end of the line sucked away the urgency to have an American with pull in my corner.

Manon hands me another paper, a handwritten list of phone messages, all of them timed and dated to today, all of them from Katie. Some of them barely five minutes apart. "Your friend made me promise I would give this to you the second you arrived back at the hotel, and that I tell you to call her back immediately. She was very insistent."

"Yes, she usually is," I say with a smile. The elevator dings, and the doors slide open.

"She says you haven't been answering your phone."

She's right. How can I, now that it's at the bottom of the Seine? I drop the messages in my bag and thank her with a smile. "I'll call her as soon as I'm upstairs."

Manon shifts from foot to foot, wringing her hands. "I do want to mention, though… I didn't tell her the news. I thought you should be the one to do that."

For a second, just for an instant, I think she's referring to the news that Adam is alive. But of course Manon doesn't know that, and I can't let her find out. I catch myself just in time.

"I'm sorry. What news?"

The elevator doors slide into motion, and I shove a foot inside before they close. The sensor dings, and the doors glide back open.

"That there are no more names on the missing persons list," Manon says, her eyes blinking wildly. "They say Monsieur Knox… I'm so very sorry."

"So it's official, then. Adam is…" I don't finish. Now that I know he's holed up somewhere nearby, I can't make myself say that terrible word out loud.

And neither, for that matter, can Manon. She gives me a hesitant nod. "Please let us know if there's anything at all I can do."

I don't have to fake my emotions here, as the tears come up hot and fast. Tears of what, exactly? Frustration. Exhaustion. Despair. Take your pick. I feel them all and more.

Also, there's this: Now that Adam's officially been declared dead, how much longer will Manon's boss allow me to stay without charge? I can't afford the penthouse suite, and now that the search through the rubble has ended, now that police have moved Adam's name from the missing to the dead column, how soon before Monsieur Laurent assumes there's no good reason to keep funding my stay?

And yet I also can't contemplate leaving. Despite Adam's pleas. Despite Kat's dire warning. I'm nowhere near ready to leave this city, and it's not just because I want to see Adam, to see with my own eyes that he's okay. It's not even to learn the truth about what he's done and who's chasing him.

I want to hear it from *him*. I want Adam to stand in front of me, look me in the eyes and tell me why he let me walk around for *three whole days* thinking he's dead. I want him to say it to my face. After all these years together, he owes me that much. I'm not leaving here before I hear it from him.

I thank Manon and duck into the elevator.

I find my center on the ride upstairs, the tears drying into something that feels a lot like resolve. I think of Kat, watching us eat galettes from her perch in the square, of Adam sneaking away to warn her of the danger. The way he used those stupid sunglasses as an excuse. That required some quick thinking on Adam's part, which I suppose shouldn't surprise me. If nothing else, I've learned Adam was excellent at hiding the parts of himself he didn't want me to see—and I should know, since I've done the same with him. My husband isn't the person he pretended to be, but neither am I.

In the penthouse, I dump my stuff on the couch, sink onto the chair at the desk and pick up the phone, then drop it back onto the cradle. As much as I want to talk to Katie, as much as I want her take on what I should do next, I can't call her—and not just because her number is programmed into my Seine-soaked cell and not in my head. Katie is the type of friend I tell everything to, and she'll hear from my voice that I'm holding back, because this is the kind of news I can't say over the phone. Someone was in this room. What if it was this Aljazaar person? What if he planted a bug? Katie will kill me for it, but it's safest to ignore her calls for now.

Instead, I dig a pad of paper and pen out of the drawer. I need to make a list, to write everything down before I forget.

What do I know? Adam had a ring that once upon a time belonged to Oscar Wilde, one he stole from Antoine. He was going to give the ring to Kat, but couldn't find a safe moment. The Moroccan hit man who works for Adam's client planted a bomb intended for them both, but Adam and Kat got out just in time. Did someone warn them? A British man was there at the scene, and now he's following me. It's a lot more than I knew yesterday, but it feels like less. It's so confusing.

And then there's the white card. The one I found in his wallet, the one he told me to burn. Adam didn't confirm those numbers were for a bank account, but he didn't deny it, either. It would explain why Antoine was so eager to see them, why someone ransacked the suite.

And what about the sailing skills I didn't know my husband had, his knowledge of all those big yachts in the bay off of Capri? I think back to the other stops we made these past three weeks while crisscrossing our way through Europe. What else have I missed when I didn't know I should be paying attention?

When I'm done, I stand up and stare at my list, thinking. Kat's name was short for something. I don't have her last name, not even an initial.

I dig the Android cell phone from my bag and look up the number she called me from. It's a French number, and I'm guessing a burner. I plug the number into the browser of the Android and hit Search, but the listing that comes up is for a local home cleaning business. I dial it from the hotel phone just in case.

"Bonjour. Vous avez rejoint la messagerie vocale de Domicile Services qui s'occupe du menage et de l'entretien de votre maison."

Something about cleaning my house, which means it's a legit number.

I hang up and plug "Kat nickname Netherlands" into the browser, but what I find is way too much. According to Google, Kat could be short for dozens of names, Cato or Catharina or Katherine. I go down the list, hitting the speaker icon to hear how the name is pronounced, then finally hit the jackpot at Katrijntje. That's it, the name Adam had said earlier. It's common enough in Holland that there are pages and pages of them in Amsterdam alone. I try a sub search with Amsterdam and Paris, but nothing that matches up with the woman I met in the museum. Without a last name, she might as well be a ghost.

I put a pin in it and keep going, surfing to icloud.com. It's a risk, logging in to my account on this phone, but I'm on Wi-Fi and trusting that the Android is a burner, which means no one knows about it but me and Adam. If anyone's watching my iCloud account, they'll see someone logging in from the hotel's IP address. Ever since the lieutenant colonel made his awful accusations, a memory has burned feverish in my mind. I have to know for sure.

I log in, then click on the icon for Photos, scrolling backward past weeks and weeks of vacation shots, on beaches and in restaurants and trains, silly selfies in front of world-famous landmarks, until I find the ones I'm looking for.

Capri.

Our afternoon on the boat in Marina Piccola.

I sift through the pictures one by one, zooming in to study every detail. Adam's phone lying in the boat's cockpit, its screen lit up with a notification—from Delta, time to check in. A woman in a red one-piece hanging above the water in a swan dive from a nearby boat, smiling faces on the heads bobbing in the water all around her. The big yachts we passed by that day, the people sunning on the decks or polishing the handrails, climbing aboard from tenders bigger than the boat we were on.

I stop on the last one, the massive yacht looming dark and sleek in the turquoise water. Adam didn't think I noticed, but the yacht was kind of hard to miss. The grandest of the bunch in all of Marina Piccola, even more impressive than the *Flying Fox*.

I zoom in on the name, hung in decorative brass letters high on the hull. The *Aphrodite IV*. I noticed that, too, but I brushed it off as a fluke. I lay under that perfectly blue sky and pretended that my blood wasn't humming. Capri is a popular vacation spot, I told myself at the time, and summer is high season. It's not so crazy to think we might cross paths. I sipped rosé and nibbled on Italian cheese and sunned on the deck with my husband and pretended that name didn't ring a bell. The perfect caricature of a relaxed woman on vacation.

But.

I log out of iCloud and type the boat's name in the Google field, but I don't spend much time scrolling through the hits. What Adam said that day was true, about how mega yacht owners tend to hide their identities under multiple layers of trusts and LLCs. The *Aphrodite IV*'s owner is no different. After a few minutes of scrolling, I give up and back out of the browser. Besides, I already know who the owner is.

A woman I haven't thought of in ages. One I'd hoped never to have to think about again.

And now here she is, back in my head after all this time. Margot Fazzari was on a tiny island off the coast of Italy at the same time as Adam and me. Bobbing on a boat in the same slice of ocean fifty yards away from ours, in the same cove Adam and I just happened to be sailing through.

After everything that's happened these past few days, the bomb and the warnings and the little trinkets Adam left for me to sort through, surely, *surely*, that can't be a coincidence.

TWENTY-FOUR

I spot him as I'm turning onto the Rue Dauphine, a plastic bag with a brand-new burner dangling from my finger. I see his wheat-blond hair bobbing in a cluster of people, the way he's keeping an eye on me. He's trying hard not to be obvious about it, but he doesn't turn and run this time. He just stands there, trying to blend into the crowd.

The British man, on a tiny shopping street in the 6th arrondissement, in a city of eleven million people. He's found me. Again.

I stop at a souvenir shop, pretending to study a display of berets while I watch him on the other side of the street. He's standing amid a bunch of everyday people enjoying a blessedly normal day, tourists and businessmen and a dog walker with a half-dozen dogs and the Brit. Like the *Aphrodite IV* parked in the same cove off of Capri, it's too much of a coincidence for it to be one.

I set off at a fast clip up the sidewalk.

Pont Neuf is straight ahead, and I pick up the pace to make it across the street before the light changes. But the bridges of Paris are busy places, the sidewalks jammed with tourists here for the view. A herd of bodies blocking my way, none of them in any sort of hurry. I shove my way through the crowd, daring a glance over my shoulder. The Brit is still on the opposite side of the street, but he's keeping pace.

And then it occurs to me: if he knew to find me here, if he's been following me around this city for who knows how long, then he knows everything. Where I'm staying, who I've talked to, where I've been, what's sitting at the bottom of this shopping bag. And where am I going to run? It's not safe at the hotel, where there's already been someone in my suite—maybe it was him. The best place for me to be right now is here—on a crowded bridge full of people.

I step to the edge of the sidewalk and shout across the traffic. "Who are you? Why are you following me?"

The Brit stops, giving me that same lopsided smile he did on the grass in the square, when I told him the old lady wanted him to find her cat. Surprise mixed with amusement at the audacity.

He cups a hand around one ear. "What's that?"

The Brit heard me just fine. Despite the cars and scooters whizzing by, his answer floats across the street loud and clear, and he wasn't even really shouting.

With my free hand, I point farther up the bridge. "Meet me at the corner."

He shrugs, then nods, and the two of us take off. Like before, he lets me set the pace, but this time I don't hurry. Now I walk slowly through the milling crowd and force myself to take deep breaths. I'm trying to slow my heartbeat, trying to think back to that day in the square. The bombed-out café, the dust and debris, the bloody bodies he was carting out onto the grass. I showed him the picture of Adam, begged him to help me find him. I don't remember what he was wearing or if we ever exchanged names. I only remember thinking he was a Good Samaritan.

At the corner, he waits for the light to change, then comes

across the zebra path with a herd of tourists. He steps up on the sidewalk, that half smile still on his face, but he doesn't say a word, not even hello. He's waiting for me to start.

"Are you even British?"

He nods. "Want to see my passport?"

"I do, actually. Yes."

He barks a laugh, one that says *fat chance*. "You're just going to have to take my word on this one, sorry."

"Okay, then. Who are you to Adam? Why are you following me?"

"I'm a friend. One who's been watching both your backs."

Now it's my turn to laugh. "Sure you are."

The Brit shrugs. "Just because you don't believe me doesn't make it untrue."

"You were in the square! I talked to you right after the bombing. Did you have something to do with it? Are you the one who lit the fuse?"

He gives me another one of his amused grins. "Where do you get your bomb knowledge from, the Road Runner? The kind of bomb that blew up that restaurant doesn't have a fuse. It has a timer. Switches. Power sources. This one was very sophisticated."

"And you know because you planted it."

"For the record, Stella, I'm not the bad guy here. And I don't think Adam is, either."

It was the exact right thing to say, that Adam is not a bad guy. He's not a thief. He's not a looter or plunderer or a black-market operator of some kind. *Finally*, someone is telling me what I want to hear. But is it the truth?

I fold my arms across my chest, the plastic bag bouncing off my rib cage. "Okay, I'm listening."

"Look, that's not to say that Adam hasn't done bad things, but doing bad things doesn't necessarily make you a bad person. I'm sure you understand the nuance."

Indignation zips up my spine, and I stand a good three inches taller. "What the hell's that supposed to mean?"

"It means exactly what you think it means. Adam may be guilty of many things, but in this particular case, he's a victim. And I'm a friendly. Someone on Adam's side. On yours, too."

I don't respond, mostly because I'm hung up on the part about Adam being a victim. A victim of what, exactly? The bombing or something else? I can't tell if the Brit means it literally or not, if he knows Adam survived.

"This lieutenant colonel the French police have assigned to the case, Collomb—he's a decent cop, but he's looking for someone to take the fall, and he's banking on that person being Adam. Collomb is so sure, he's staking his entire career on it. He needs a win, which means he's not likely to back down anytime soon. That's the good news."

That doesn't sound like good news. That news doesn't sound good at all.

"I hardly dare to ask, but what's the bad?"

"The bad news is Collomb is betting on you, too." The Brit pauses, waiting for a pair of tourists to finish snapping their selfie and move on. "He knows who you are. He's seen your files."

His words make my knees go weak and watery. I look past the Brit into the busy street, the cars and the mopeds whizzing by, the pedestrians waiting at the crosswalk, but none of it's there because suddenly I'm back in that airport in Nice, watching a pimply customs agent pull a fourteenth-century book of Persian poetry out of the lining of an empty backpack.

"My files are clean."

That's what the slick French attorney told me, that it would be like it never happened. Like I never got led out of the airport in handcuffs, never spent twenty-six nights shivering in a French prison with a constant flow of drug smugglers and common criminals, never went hoarse from answering question after question with *I don't know*. I didn't know the book was sewn in the lining of my bag. I didn't know the French-woman on the yacht I was supposed to be delivering it to. Those *I don't knows* are the only reason I'm still alive.

But that day outside the prison, the attorney handed me a bag with a hundred thousand euros in cash and told me to forget the past twenty-six nights ever happened. It was insulting, that the Turkish man I'd loved for two whole years thought he could buy my forgiveness with a pile of unmarked bills, but what other choice did I have? I took the money and high-tailed it home, determined to leave the whole episode behind me—a period Katie calls my Era of Bad Decisions. I locked all those memories away in a box at the back of my mind. Or at least, I tried to.

And now here he is—the Turkish man, worming his way back into my thoughts. My past, popping up like a weed in my present. My record still exists. I look up the street to the Seine sparkling in the early evening sun, the facades of the building rising up on the other side. Collomb is here, some-where in Paris, and he's closer than I would like him to be.

"Then maybe you should stop believing everything you see on TV," the Brit says, "because nobody's files are wiped clean. Files get buried, and often not all that deep. Every-body's past can be dug up and dusted off. You just have to know where to look."

"But—but I don't have anything to do with Adam's busi-ness! I work for a caterer. I serve lunch to actors and produc-tion crews."

If nothing else, my years as a flight attendant taught me how to cater to demanding people, but the real lure of the job was that it would keep my feet firmly planted in Atlanta. De-spite everything, I still loved that Turkish man. I loved him and I didn't trust myself not to go racing back. A new job. A new life. Adam.

"*Now* you do. But you have to see how it looks, right? Your husband is accused of moving stolen artifacts across international borders, something you were caught doing during your time as a flight attendant. Why wouldn't Collomb think you were involved?"

"Because I'm not! Okay, yes, I did that one time, and I've done other things I am not proud of. But that's nothing compared to what Adam's done. If I'm to believe what everyone is telling me, he's been moving priceless artifacts for a decade."

The Brit doesn't respond, and maybe it's because I'm looking for it, but I see something in his eyes—sympathy. It doesn't make me like him any more, this Brit with the cockney drawl. But at least sympathy implies that he might believe me when I say it was a onetime mistake.

He pulls a Sharpie from his back pocket, shoves the cap between his molars and gives a hard tug, spitting the top onto the street. With his other hand, he grabs my wrist and scribbles across my palm. "Tell Adam I can help him if he'll let me. I can help you, too."

"Do you have a name?"

He nods, dropping the pen into my bag. "Yes, but Adam will know me as Finn."

I pull back my hand, the skin tingling under the black ink. "Why should I believe anything you say? You won't even tell me your real name."

He laughs. "Really? You're really going to get hung up on my name? Okay, fine. My name is Alexander Finneas Pearson, but my father is a Finn and so was his father and the father before him, so that's what I go by, too. A little confusing at Christmastime, but a hell of a lot better than being the only Alex. Do you believe me now?"

I shake my head.

"Your husband is not who he claims to be, Stella. I know

that's not what you want to hear, but it's the truth. Tell him to call me."

And then, with a two-fingered salute, he turns and disappears into the crowd.

Finn's words pound through my head all the way back to the hotel. The French police are poking around in my past and have found a record that could incriminate me. A *criminal* record, one that I was assured wouldn't exist.

Except it does. Collomb knows what I did. No wonder he treats me like an adversary, because he thinks I *am* one. He thinks I'm in cahoots with Adam because he's seen my record.

More importantly, though, I can't stop thinking about all the parts Finn left out. About how he knows so much about bombs, the French police and Lieutenant Colonel Collomb, what they know about me. And the way he talked about Adam made it clear he knows Adam is still alive.

And maybe he's not the only one.

What if someone from the underworld thinks so, too? What if it's Aljazaar? What if he's been following me, too, because he wants me to lead him to Adam?

The thoughts chase me through the lobby and into the elevator, new urgency bouncing in my toes as it carries me upstairs, where I pack at the speed of light. I tug clothes from the hangers. Empty out drawers. Shove my makeup into my cosmetics bag and everything into the suitcase. And then I roll Adam's suitcase from the back of the closet and steer both to the elevator.

In the lobby, I say a demonstrative goodbye to the women staffing the reception desk. I offer up a credit card that they wave off, and I don't have to pretend to be touched by the gesture. I dole out hugs and ask them to please extend my thanks to Monsieur Laurent and the cleaning staff, and I make a point of mentioning, loudly and more than once, that I will miss their welcoming smiles. That there's nothing else left for me here in Paris, and that I'm ready to go home.

The bellhops load the luggage into the trunk of a cab and direct the driver to Charles de Gaulle. I sink onto the back seat, clutching my passport.

For anyone watching or listening, I am a tourist at the end of my trip. On the way to board a jet that will whisk me across the Atlantic and deposit me back home. By the time anyone bothers to look for me on a passenger manifest, I'll have disappeared into the streets of Paris.

As soon as we round the corner, I lean into the glass partition and give the driver an address for a place I found on the burner's browser, in the northeastern-most outskirts of the city. A hotel on a street pushed all the way up against the Boulevard Périphérique. About as far as you can go without actually leaving the city.

The driver frowns, catching my eye in the rearview mirror. *"Êtes-vous sûr? C'est un endroit dangereux."*

The last word rings in my ears—*dangerous*—and just in case I didn't catch his meaning, he holds up a hand, forming a gun with his thumb and forefinger.

"Pew pew," he says, shooting at the sky.

"Oui. Je suis sûr." Yes. As a matter of fact, I'm *very* sure.

Google already told me it was a dangerous neighborhood. One of the worst in all of Paris, apparently, a dingy place filled with drug dealers, thieves and hardworking laborers who can't afford anywhere better. They live in the tall apartment buildings that hang over the Périphérique, looming large and ugly and, most of all, cheap. Paris's version of a ghetto— not a place you end up by choice, not unless you want to buy drugs or other black-market garbage from the gangs who run the streets.

Dangereux, indeed.

But also, a place where I can be anonymous—or at least that's the plan.

I clock the cars trailing behind the cab as we zigzag our way north. I'm watching to make sure we're not being followed, and I'm pretty certain we're not. Though, honestly, how the hell would I know? This isn't something I normally worry about, and Finn was right. Most of my spy knowledge I've gotten from TV.

I stare out the window as the pretty shops of the 1st and 2nd arrondissements make way for discount stores of the 10th as we wind into the 19th. Here the streets are narrow, the sidewalks cluttered with litter. Trash. Needles. Piles of abandoned junk.

Suddenly, the cabdriver screeches to a stop, pointing up a dim one-way street with a stream of rapid French. I catch enough of it to get the gist. This is as far as he's going.

I twist around to look out the rear window, up the empty road. No cars. No Brit or Moroccan butcher lingering at the corner. I hand the driver some cash and he pops the trunk just long enough for me to haul the suitcases out. The second I close it, he's off, gunning the engine for safer streets.

I stand here for a moment, pretending to rummage around in my bag while getting my bearings. This neighborhood looks nothing like the Paris you see in the pictures and guidebooks. Boxy buildings rising up on all sides, seventies cuboid slabs of concrete painted in bright colors, cheery reds and yellows and blues that somehow make the place look even more depressing. Maybe it's all the graffiti, or the gutters lined with trash and dog shit. With one last look around, I duck up the one-way street.

The Hôtel Charme is anything but charming, a single door leading into a lobby barely big enough for me and my two American-sized suitcases. I step around a rickety chair to a window of bulletproof glass. The man sitting behind it doesn't smile, but when he asks me for my passport, a requirement here in the EU, I slide two hundred-euro bills from Adam's stash of cash under the window, and he doesn't ask a second time. He just shrugs and passes me a key for a room on the fourth floor.

There's no bellhop waiting with a cart, no elevator to whisk me up to my room, and it takes me two trips to lug the suitcases up the cramped stairwell. The room is just as tiny, a square box with a banged-up dresser and a single bed shoved up against the wall. I wedge Adam's suitcase into a corner, then wheel mine in beside it. I won't be here long enough to unpack, and besides, spreading my things around the room will only slow a speedy exit down—and even then, there's nothing in either suitcase I'm so attached to that I won't leave it behind. The really important items are in my bag, which is pretty much permanently strapped across my shoulder.

I sink onto the bed with my phone and tap the Signal icon, opening the text string between me and Adam, pounding out a message.

I have an update, but I'm not telling unless it's face to face.

Two seconds later, the Android beeps with a flurry of texts.

What happened? Are you okay?

Talk to me, Stella. I need to know what's going on.

Why are you in the 19th?

The last one gives me pause, though I probably should have known Adam would be tracking me. It's how he followed me to the Seine, how he knew where to steer that motorcycle.

I lean back on the bed to peer out the window, where two men down on the street are talking to a man on a scooter. They shake hands, money in exchange for a small plastic bag. A drug deal in broad daylight.

My thumbs fly over the screen.

I mean it Adam. I'm not saying another word until I see you in person.

It takes him a full three minutes to respond.

Meet me tonight at the southern base of the Eiffel Tower, 10 pm. Make sure you're not followed.

TWENTY-FIVE

I leave at dinnertime.

I head north, stepping over a drunk asleep on the street to catch a southward-bound train at the Rosa Parks station. At the third stop, I linger by the doors until a chime announces they're about to close, then lurch onto the platform right before the doors can slam me in the shoulder. I choose a train at random, one that carries me to the western fringes of the city, where I step out and head north, then east, then south again. I do this a handful of times, ping-ponging my way around Paris while studying the faces of everyone I see on the trains and platforms. If my gut is right, if someone is following me, I'm not going to make it easy for him.

The sun is setting by the time I emerge from the Commerce station in the 15th, still a hike to the tower but in the general vicinity. I take a roundabout route, and I'm so hyped up on adrenaline and nerves that I don't think about how many miles my legs have carried me, or how my shoes are pinching my feet, or that I'm operating on caffeine and nowhere near enough sleep. I don't think about anything but Adam, seeing him again. All these answers I've been searching for, I'm finally getting them tonight.

I stop at the edge of the Parc du Champ de Mars, a long stretch of grass between the Eiffel Tower and the École Militaire, and take in the packed crowd. Vendors selling trinkets and waters and Nutella crepes, tourists with their phones at the ready, waiting for the infamous sparkle that happens every hour on the hour after dark. I check my phone: two minutes to ten. My heart gives an excited flutter.

The southern base of the tower is massive, and I move through the throngs of people standing around in clusters, searching for Adam among the many faces, but the crowd is too big. Too many people and trees he could be hiding behind, too many shadows for him to disappear into. And then it occurs to me that he'll never find me like this, with me constantly on the move. I stop at a well-lit bench at the edge of the cordoned-off road and ping him my coordinates on Signal.

While I wait, the questions roll through my head on repeat, so many questions I barely know where to start.

Why did you have Oscar Wilde's ring?

How much treasure do the numbers on the white card unlock?

Where did all that money, the money for Babs's trust fund, come from?

How much more is there?

Who is Finn to you?

Who's Kat?

How do they both know you're alive?

Why does Finn tell me you're a good guy when everyone else tells me you're a criminal?

Who are you, really?

Earlier this afternoon at the Hôtel Charme, I did a bit of Googling on Alexander Finneas Pearson. I plugged in everything he told me about himself during our brief conversation, but the UK is too big and there were far too many hits. An analyst at a cryptocurrency trader in London, the husband to an Ethiopian fashion model, a sophomore soccer player at

University of Liverpool FC. My search coughed up plenty of Finns, but no one who looks or sounds even remotely like the one I met. The Good Samaritan in the square, my stalker in the 18th and on the bridge, the one with the crooked nose and the cockney accent. Google's never heard of him.

Suddenly, a hum goes through the crowd, and I look up as the air around me lights up in a bright flood. The Eiffel Tower as dazzling as any Christmas tree, its pillars and beams lit up with a million twinkling lights. It's one thing to see it from the other side of the Seine, another thing entirely to be standing at the base when it lights up. The crowd erupts in a loud cheer, pointing their cell phones at a tower so bright, I have to shade my eyes.

And then I feel it, someone slipping behind me, passing by close enough to rustle my hair. I whirl around, but the crowd is still so thick. I scan the bodies, the profiles, the smiles tipped up to the sky. If anyone looks familiar, I'm not seeing it.

My gaze snags on a face and holds. A man in shorts and a gray sweatshirt, a battered baseball cap slapped backward on his head. Have I seen him before? The only thing I know is that he's definitely watching me, looking at me with some kind of question in his eye. He smiles, and I think it might be a come-on.

Still, the episode makes me uncomfortable. I twist back around on the bench and keep looking for Adam in the crush of bodies, and it occurs to me that maybe sitting was a mistake. Maybe I'm too close to the ground for Adam to pick me out of the crowd, so I stand and take a few steps to my left, to a clear spot closer to the road. I check the time on my cell. Three minutes past ten.

I fire off a message to Adam in Signal. I'm here. Where are you?

The message lands, marked as Delivered. I stare at the screen and wait for it to change to Read, but there are no dancing dots, nothing at all to indicate Adam has seen it. I watch my phone until the screen goes dark, then tap it with a finger to keep it awake. I do this for a good ten minutes. No response.

By now the twinkle lights have fizzled out, and so has the crowd. People are wandering off, trampling across the grass in the direction of the river, the city. I watch them disappear into the darkness as a breeze kicks up, spinning a clump of trash across the road like a tumbleweed. I sit here for thirty minutes, then forty-five, trying not to think about where Adam might be, what kind of disaster might make him stand me up. The Adam I know would have kept his word.

Then again, if there's one thing I've learned these past few days, it's that I don't really know Adam. The lieutenant colonel. Kat. Zoé and her boss, Antoine. Finn's words whisper through my head: *your husband is not who he claims to be.*

Or maybe a truer thing to say is that I've been too trusting, too eager after my last disastrous relationship to choose someone *good* that I took him for his word. I never looked too hard, never probed too deep. Never thought to question what he was really shopping for during all those buying trips to Europe.

"You know this continent so much better than I do," he said when we planned this trip, a nod to my time as a flight attendant. "I want to see Europe through your eyes."

But a man who's been smuggling artifacts across international borders for a decade will know this continent, too.

A memory bubbles up from nowhere, in the months after we splurged on a fixer-upper ranch in Peachtree Hills. I was happy to let Adam take the lead on the renovation—his department, after all, and Adam has exceptional taste—happy to let him fill it with French floors and antique doors and reclaimed carved wood paneling he got for a "steal." Except it wasn't. I found one of the bills by accident, and I told him we would *never* earn our investment back, not on a three-bedroom ranch on a tiny lot, no matter how gorgeous the finishes. He told me the vendor made a mistake, said he'd charged us retail by accident and that our price was much, much lower. And I believed him, just like that.

The park spins, and I plant my feet into the pavement, working to hold my center.

And okay, fine. Some might say I'm not one to talk, but my lies feel different because I'm a different person now. I learned from my many mistakes and corrected course, promised myself I would never again let myself get so taken in by a man that I blow past every one of my moral codes. And yet here I am, so taken in by Adam that I let him lie to me for years.

I check the time on the Android—by now, well past eleven—and the only thing I can think is fuck it. Fuck him and fuck this. I pull up his number and hit Call.

The phone rings and rings and rings. I hang up and try again, but either Signal doesn't have voicemail, or Adam never set his up.

I'm trying for the third time when a message hits my phone.

Check your Delta app. You're booked on the 10:40 flight tomorrow morning. Please go. I love you, Stella, and I'm so sorry.

I put my hands over my eyes and take deep belly breaths, letting myself give in to the tears, suddenly feeling more alone than I ever have. I'm supposed to be getting answers tonight, but instead I only have more questions. Because what about all the words he didn't say? He's sorry for what? For standing me up? For getting me involved in this mess? For running off and leaving me to deal with his shit all alone, with no one to talk to, no one on my side?

And suddenly, my mind fills with another man. The one from the embassy, the man who called himself my advocate. Who said his job is to support me and promote my interests with the French authorities. I haven't heard from Lucas since I called him Wednesday night, and I wonder about the results of the DNA on the male body they pulled from the rubble. I wonder if he knows about my wiped file that's been excavated by Lieutenant Colonel Collomb, if he knows Finn.

I'm reaching for the Android when I remember I saved his number into my iPhone, now wedged in the sludge at the bottom of the Seine. Shit. Now what?

I pull up the embassy's website and spend a few minutes searching for a list of staff, but the site is massive, and I don't find anything beyond a list of key staff members, none of them Lucas. I move on, surfing to the contact page instead, then tap the number at the bottom of the page. The line connects to a recorded greeting, short and to the point—the embassy is currently closed, but if this is an emergency, please dial zero. I do, and a woman with an American accent picks up.

"American Embassy. What's your emergency?"

"My name is Stella Knox. I am an American citizen currently in Paris. My husband, Adam, is one of the missing, presumed dead from the bombing at Place Carlou Aubert." My voice is surprisingly calm, considering I'm still shaking.

"I'm so glad you called, Mrs. Knox. Mr. Marshall has been waiting to hear from you."

"That's why I'm calling, actually. I've already been in contact with someone from the embassy. Lucas Fournier from the Department of Citizens Services. But I recently changed phones and I seem to have lost his cell phone number. I realize it's late, but is there any way you can put me in touch with him?"

"Of course. I will get him a message right away. Can you repeat the name one more time?"

"Lucas Fournier."

A pause while she clicks around on a computer keyboard. "And Mr. Fournier also works in the Department of Citizens Services, you said?"

"Yes, correct." But it's here that I start to have doubts. The past few days have been so hectic. Maybe I'm remembering the department name wrong, or maybe I misheard him. Did he say Citizens Services? Now I'm not so sure. "At least, I *think* that's the department. But his name is definitely Lucas Fournier. That much I'm positive of."

There's a long stretch of silence while she rustles papers in the background, clicks around some more on her keyboard. I think of Lucas, sound asleep in a bed somewhere nearby, and I feel a twinge of guilt for calling so late. But I am in desperate need of an ally, and unfortunately for both of us, Lucas is the only one I've got.

The woman on the other end of the line clears her throat. "Mrs. Knox, I'm very sorry, but I'm not finding Mr. Fournier in my system."

"Okay." I wait for her to brush it off with some kind of excuse, something about the system being out of whack, or to ask me to call back in the morning, but she doesn't continue. She doesn't say anything else at all. A tingling starts up on the top of my head, creeping downward over my scalp. "I don't understand. What does that mean?"

"It means no one works at the embassy by the name of Lucas Fournier."

TWENTY-SIX

ADAM

Venice
Seventeen days earlier

> *The heart was made to be broken.*
>
> —*Oscar Wilde*

I'm so screwed.

It's the only thing I can think as I stare blindly into a shop window filled with papier-mâché masks. Roaring lions sitting next to elephants with big, floppy ears, rainbow-colored fish heads above birds with dead eyes and foot-long beaks and edges dipped in glitter. Stella and I are on a tiny street smack in the middle of Venice, and all I can think is *I am so fucking screwed.*

"Are these for kids or adults?" she says, tapping the glass at a white ghoul's face. His mouth gapes open in a silent scream under a complicated black-and-silver hood. "Because that one's super creepy."

All day long my mind has been spinning, trying to work things out. Thinking through options, doing damage control.

When Aljazaar slid into Stella's chair at the breakfast table this morning, I almost fell out of mine.

"Your wife's a beauty," he said as he swiped a strawberry from my plate, his accent a weird mix of sharp and soft, of Arabic and French. "Would be such a shame if something happens to her."

I tried not to let on that my entire body pulsed with panic. Stella was still dodging tables on the way to the bathroom less than twenty feet away. What if he went after her? What if she turned around? How the hell was I supposed to explain the strange man sitting in her chair?

She glances over now, her eyes bright with delight while I stand here like an idiot, my arm hooked around her neck and sweating bullets. It's a hundred and fifty degrees in the shade, and Aljazaar didn't come all the way to Venice just to poach my breakfast fruit.

"Adults," I say, my voice hoarse. "Or at least I hope these are for adults."

I look up the busy shopping street, no bigger than an alley-way. Throngs of tourists, a couple of shopkeepers standing, arms crossed, in the doorway. If Aljazaar is here, if he's watching, he's well hidden in the crowd.

Stella gestures to a gold-fringed woman, her hair a jumble of pink and orange feathers. "Look at that one. It's giving me *Eyes Wide Shut* vibes."

I lean into the glass and pretend to study the stupid mask. "I can't tell if I'm turned on or not."

"You're such a freak."

"No, pretty sure the freaks are the Venetians. Who actually wears these things?"

She looks over with a smile, slow and happy, and a bead of sweat drips down my temple. I drag my free hand through my hair and look at my gorgeous wife. I want to scream, but I can't.

She tugs me away from the display, and we wander aimlessly

for a bit, winding up and down the maze of tiny streets, crossing ancient footbridges and coming up on charming *piazzettas*
with their lines of people snaking into the square. The most
gorgeous city in the world, and all I can think about is how
I've endangered Stella.

Stella, who thinks I spent the days before she arrived scour-
ing French markets for architectural antiques.

Stella, who once told me that she didn't know who she was
waiting for until she met me.

Stella, who works in catering, even though the only thing
she can manage to heat up is a can of soup, whose red hair is
shiny and spreads across the pillow like a mermaid's tail when
she sleeps, whose body fits mine like a puzzle piece I didn't
know I was missing.

Stella, the love of my life Stella, who, no matter what happens to me, I have to keep safe.

When she slips inside a store to buy us both a water, I duck
into the nearest alleyway and break into a sprint.

It's almost an hour later when I find her sitting outside the
convenience store, on the rim of a dry fountain in the middle
of the square. She's chatting with a man—stocky, short, bald-
ing head he tries to disguise with a generous comb-over. An
American man, judging from his outfit, a plaid shirt stretched
over a giant potbelly, shorts and dingy white sneakers. I see
them sitting together, and my heart gives a hard thud.

"There you are," she says, looking up with a smile. "Where'd
you go?"

I hook a thumb over my shoulder, gesturing in the opposite
direction from where I came. "Over there, looking for you.
You told me to meet you at the corner, remember?"

She twists around on the fountain, pointing at the far end
of the square. "No. I told you to meet me at *that* corner. No
wonder we couldn't find each other."

My gaze slides to the man, and I study his features, comparing them to the ones I've seen these past two days in Venice. At the hotel, at the pizzeria last night, on the water taxis that shuttle us back and forth across the Canal Grande, sipping espresso from a miniature cup at the edge of the San Marco Square. Have I seen him before? I'm not sure.

"Who's this?" If Stella notices the edge in my voice, she doesn't let on.

"This is Eric. He's an insurance salesman from Texas. Eric, this is my husband, Adam."

Eric stands and thrusts out a hand, his twang flaring. "Howdy, Adam. Nice to meetcha. Your wife here's been keeping me company."

His grasp is firm, but mine's firmer, an iron squeeze that'll probably leave a bruise. If this guy really sells insurance in Texas, then it's a dick move. If not, it's a clear warning.

Either way, he takes the hint. Eric sinks back onto the fountain rim next to Stella, just long enough to gather up his bags. "Well, better go find my wife before she buys up every stitch of lace this fine city has to offer. Why on earth anyone needs twenty-seven tablecloths, I'll never understand, but I've been married long enough to know when to keep my mouth shut. Happy wife, happy life." He wags a fistful of bags in the air and turns to go. "You got a good one here, sir. Y'all have a nice day."

Eric trudges across the square, disappearing into a lace store.

"Nice talking to you," Stella calls out to his retreating back, then looks up at me, squinting into the sun. "You weren't very friendly. Is everything okay?"

"I'm fine. Just hot."

"I know. You told me that a hundred times, which is why I bought you this." She hands me the bottle of water she bought, now lukewarm at best. And then she sees it, the small, white bag dangling from my other hand. "You went shopping?"

I hold it up so she can read the gold lettering across the front: *gioielleria*.

Her brows rise in delighted surprise. "*Jewelry* shopping?"

I nod.

"But why? What's the occasion?"

"We're in Venice. Who needs an occasion?"

A few feet to our right, two women are gathering up their things at a terrace table. I grab Stella's hand and drag her over, and we sit. I shove empty glasses and crumpled napkins aside and place the bag on the table between us.

"Go on. Open it."

She tugs on the ribbon and reaches into the bag, and I watch her face as she pulls out a white box. The way she bites her lip when she peels the box open, the way her eyes light up when she sees the necklace tucked inside.

"Oh, Adam." She picks it up by the chain, paper-clip links of shiny platinum. At the bottom, a ruby-red heart sits inside a diamond-encrusted cage.

"It's Venetian glass. Handblown by a designer here in Venice." The necklace is heavy, the heart fat and solid. The diamonds sparkle in the Italian sun. "Do you like it?"

She looks up, her eyes fuzzy with tears. "I love it. It's *perfect*."

"Good. Because I can't return it. I'd never find the shop again."

It's the joke we'd been making for two full days now. Venice is a labyrinth of crooked streets that all look the same, of pretty *piazzettas* that are each a copy-paste of the one before it. They say there's no such thing as a wrong turn in Venice, but for Stella and me there were *lots* of wrong turns. It's a miracle when we find our hotel at the end of each day.

She laughs. "But glass… What if it breaks?"

I take the necklace from her fingers and drape the chain over her head. The heart sits only an inch or two away from her own, the glass cool and heavy between her breasts.

"That's what the cage is for, to protect the glass. The jeweler says it's strong enough to protect the heart if it bumps up against something hard. You can even drop it and it'll be fine. Apparently, the only way to break it is to hit it with a hammer."

"Well, I definitely won't be doing that." She runs a finger across a curved line of diamonds. There are lots of them, set into swirling bands that hold the heart like claws. She leans in and gives me a long, lingering kiss. "Seriously, though. Why?"

I pick it up off her chest, holding it in a palm. "Because you are my heart, and my heart is yours."

"You're just saying that because you want to get laid."

I laugh. "One hundred percent I want that. But I'm also saying it because it's true. In case I've never told you before, Stella Knox, you were the biggest surprise of my life. My most precious treasure. I knew it the second you walked into that booth. I fell for you that day, and it was the best thing I've ever done." I give a gentle tug on the heart, pulling her face closer to mine, willing her to understand. "If anything ever happens to me, just remember you always have my heart."

TWENTY-SEVEN

STELLA

Paris

I don't know what it is, exactly, that pops my eyes open, but whatever it is, it lurches me upright on a gasp, instantly awake. I blink into the dreary room, listening to the shouting coming from the other side of the wall behind my head, an angry woman screaming at someone in a language I don't understand. Not French. A toilet flushes above my head, the water gushing so hard through the pipes, it sounds like they're in the same room.

I kick the scratchy blanket off my legs and reach for the Android, checking for messages I might have missed during the night. Nothing, not so much as a peep from Adam, and I picture him holed up in a hotel room somewhere in this city, in a neighborhood much like this one. I think of him, and a panicky longing presses against my breastbone. He made it sound like he was close, but the truth is, my husband has never felt further away.

Now what? What do I do now that Adam has gone further underground, now that Lucas has turned out to be a liar and a con artist? I can't believe I fell for his act so easily, for only seeing what he wanted me to see. That he works for the American Em-

bassy. That, like his fellow American expats, he craves Flamin'
Hot Cheetos and chases the sun.

And for what? To gain my trust? To get me to tell him things
I might otherwise not say? For me to lead him to Adam? Is that
why he gave me Adam's iPhone, so he could track my movements all over Paris? I think about the phone, now sitting at
the bottom of the Seine, and I wonder how he got his hands on
it, when Lieutenant Colonel Collomb told me it was in police
custody. Is Lucas a cop? Did he steal it from the evidence room?

Also, Lucas knew about the override codes for the hotel safe.
He told me hotels often use the same ones, codes that are easy
for the staff to remember. I picture him ticking it in only to
find the safe empty. No ring. No white card.

Zoé's warning comes to me with a sharp chill. *Trust no one*,
she said, but I already had. I trusted Lucas when he said he was
on my side. I was so desperate for an ally that it didn't even
occur to me that Lucas might be lying about who he was, that
he was playing me. I'm such a fucking idiot.

I pick up the Android and fire off a text to Adam.

If you ever loved me, you'll tell me the truth.

Two seconds later, his reply hits my phone.

Goddamn it, Stella. You're supposed to be on a plane right
now. I can't protect you if you stay.

Protect me from what? Where were you last night? Why did
you stand me up?

Get on a plane. I'm begging you.

And I'm begging you, tell me what's going on. Tell me the
truth, Adam, all of it. I'm not leaving until you say it to my face.

His reply is a link, nothing else, and I tap it with a fingertip. The screen flips to the browser, a video with multiple warnings in all caps. Horrific footage. View at own discretion.

The video is short, ten seconds at most, and it's just as shocking as promised. A woman's body tumbling from a tall building, arms flailing, blond hair floating around her face. I count the windows on the way down, five stories at least, before she lands with a sickening thud, smack on a line of metal parking poles. She hovers there for a second or two, and then...

And then it's like a punch to my chest, like the wind has been knocked from my lungs. I gasp and drop the phone onto the bed, blinking hard, pressing a palm to my mouth, breathing into my fingers. Oh, my God. *Oh, my God.* I lean over on the bed, trying to shake the image from my head. That poor woman was *impaled.*

The video reloads, and I can't watch it again. I give the screen a quick swipe with a finger, scrolling me down to a thick chunk of text. My gaze snags on a word, one that pops a bubble in my chest.

Katrijntje.

A name that, according to Google, is not all that uncommon. Thousands of hits in the Netherlands alone. What are the chances? Surely this can't be the same Kat that knows Adam.

I scroll some more, and there she is, the blonde with the bag of books in the hidden courtyard in Amsterdam. The same one I met yesterday in a museum filled with screaming kids. It's definitely her.

I go back to the top of the page and read.

A woman was found dead after falling from an upper-story window of a hotel in Paris's 12th arrondissement. The victim was identified as Katrijntje Ryskamp, a Dutch art detective known as "the female Indiana Jones of the Art World" for her remarkable recoveries of looted artifacts.

Two words ring in my ears. *Looted artifacts.* I return to the screen and check the date. The footage is from last night, only hours after we met at the Galerie d'Anatomie. I think of the ring I slid from my thumb so she could return it to its rightful owner, the Oscar Wilde Society. I wonder where it is right now, if it's in a plastic evidence bag at the morgue or in somebody's pocket. My money's on the latter.

I return to the screen and keep reading.

At 34, Katrijntje was one of the most famous art sleuths in the world, trusted by both thieves and police for her unprecedented access to the criminal trade in stolen artifacts. Her recoveries include a stolen Henri Matisse painting, a pair of bronze statues once owned by Adolf Hitler, and a bracelet that once belonged to Marie Antoinette. French police did not provide many details on the circumstances leading to Ryskamp's death but say it was likely a suicide.

Suicide, my ass. Kat told me her life was in danger, too. She said *too*, as in also. In the hidden courtyard in Amsterdam, she told me and Adam about the Moroccan man who made all his enemies either die or disappear. She was obviously afraid of him. Is that who did this to her?

You cannot trust anyone, Stella. Not even me. Especially not me.

Trust no one. Got it. Message fucking received. I think about the people I've relied on these past few days—Lucas, the Hôtel Luxembourg Parc staff, Adam. He knows I've ditched the Luxembourg Parc for this shitty place, which means this cell phone must be tracking me. I flip through the apps, looking for one that might be spyware, but I don't know what I'm looking for. I also don't see anything unusual.

But still. Cell phones can be traced, and if Adam can find me through this thing, then so could anyone else. The Android is a weakness, and so is the burner I bought so I could call my mother, which I haven't done. Even worse, I haven't even *thought* about calling her. The burner is still buried somewhere in my suitcase, still sitting in the store's shrink-wrapped packaging.

I swing my legs out of bed and slide them into my awaiting flip-flops, digging the phone out and plugging it into an outlet by the bed. While the burner charges, I turn off location services on the Android. Adam might know where I'm staying, but at least now he won't be able to track me around the city. He won't know where I'm going, and I won't have to explain what I'm about to do next.

I pick up the burner and pretend I need to work hard to remember a number I haven't used in years. Pretend that it's not right there, floating just beneath the surface of my memory, waiting for me to call it again after all this time. To call *him*, the Turkish man, the one person on the planet who, despite how things ended between us, I know will help me now. With information. With protection. Pretend that when the call flips to voicemail, that my heart doesn't give an excited flurry at the sound of his voice, speaking in his native tongue.

"*Ben Sully. Ne yapacağını biliyorsun.*" This is Sully. *You know what to do.*

There are a few more Turkish words in my vocabulary, too, words that push to the tip of my tongue now, as eagerly as when I was saying them to him all the time. I wait for the beep, and then I can't help myself. I smile into the phone.

"*Merhaba aşkım, benim.*"

Hi, my love. It's me.

TWENTY-EIGHT

Sully and I met while hurtling through the sky at 35,000 feet, somewhere above the Indian Ocean.

He was like something straight off a movie set, dark almond eyes and jet-black hair, sculpted body draped in cashmere and designer denim. I spotted him the second he boarded, and I wasn't the only one. There was something alluring about him, something that sizzled deep in my stomach. When I brought him his drink, a glass of top-shelf bourbon, he thanked me with a long, lingering look. From that moment on, I was a goner.

While the rest of the first-class cabin dozed or watched movies, Sully and I talked and talked. He told me that he grew up on the European side of the river in Istanbul, the only son in a family of seven. That he worked in international finance, a job he loved enough to leave his loud but beloved sisters and move to Dubai, where he lived on the top floor of a glass-lined condo with a view of the iconic Burj Khalifa Tower. That he didn't usually fly commercial but had loaned his jet to a friend for one last visit to a dying father. That his name was Suleiman but all his friends called him Sully, and he was positive we were destined to become good friends. By the time the captain announced the descent into the greater Dubai area, we had plans for dinner.

The next two years with Sully were one endless dopamine rush, a painfully blissful time when I thought about nothing else but him. The little freckle on his right earlobe. The way his eyes crinkled when he smiled. The sound of his laugh and the smell of his skin. The way being in the same room with him set my blood on fire.

"Stella, come," he'd say, and off I'd go to meet him in Dubai, Amsterdam, Madrid. I molded my work schedule around his, swapped legs with other flight attendants so I could be anywhere he was. Quickie trips to New York, London, Paris, Milan. Long layovers where I saw nothing of Dubai but his bed. He was hypnotic, and I was completely under his spell.

Back home in Atlanta, the longing was sharp and desperate. Every love song on the radio reminded me of him. Every text that pinged my phone made me miss him even more. Somewhere in the back of my head I knew love wasn't supposed to feel like this, like an obsession that left a throbbing ache in the center of my chest that only Sully could fill. But then he'd call again—*Stella, come*—and off I'd go, chasing another euphoric hit. The effect he had on me, I can't explain it.

With Sully there were a lot of firsts. My first time taking a private jet to dinner, to a concert, to a private box at the World Cup. My first time in a Pagani Huayra, an Italian car with a 1.3-million-dollar price tag. My first time being tailed by bodyguards, big men with guns and earpieces scanning the shadows for danger.

Because that job Sully had in international finance? The one that made him so obscenely wealthy? As it turns out, it was also highly illegal.

Not that Sully saw it that way. He saw it as working the system, using every available loophole, bending the rules to his will to hide his clients' money. He hid it in undisclosed accounts at offshore banks, in shell companies he stuffed with secret trusts and holdings, in hard-to-trace assets like real estate and yachts and jets. Complex financial engineering to avoid taxes and launder money, buckets and buckets of it. By the time I found all this out, it was too late. I was already in too deep to care.

But I didn't have to look very hard to see that that kind of money came with a dark and dangerous underbelly. Why else surround yourself with bodyguards driving bulletproof cars? Why live in a condo building with so many layers of security it was basically a bunker? It wasn't only the police Sully was sheltering himself from. It was the scarier of his clients.

Thugs. Crooks. Members of the cartel. Heads of corrupt regimes. Arms dealers. That was the type of people Sully served. Those were the people financing his lifestyle. The only reason to live in a bunker is when you're at war.

But I consoled myself with the fact that Sully's crimes were financial ones. He moved money around. He didn't trade drugs or traffic in humans. He didn't murder innocent people. Not Sully, who was so sweet and kind and generous. Love is blind, but I was willfully so.

And so, when he asked me to do him an occasional favor and carry a thumb drive across international borders to deliver to one of his clients, of course I agreed. After all, I was a flight attendant, always on the move just like his jet-setting clients. If our schedules happened to match up, I could save Sully the trip, save more of his precious time for myself, which of course I was happy to do.

This went on for two whole years, and each time I breezed through customs with a smile and a wave, I felt more and more sure of my place in Sully's life. These little favors made me just as dangerous and exciting as he was, and they entwined our lives in a way that made me feel necessary in his. Sully *needed* me to run his business, and that pleased me more than I'd care to admit.

And all these little favors, I did them gladly. Sully was always so generous, always financing our getaways, buying me expensive gifts. He never asked for anything more than my time and affection. Finally, finally, there was a way for me to give back. A gift that I could give *him*.

And then one day he asked me to deliver something more substantial than a thumb drive. A rare book of Persian poems Sully had purchased from an art collector as a gift for a client he'd been courting, a priceless piece that would bring in this woman's business and cement Sully as her financial adviser forever and ever. I had to work a flight leaving two days later out of London, and her yacht was anchored off the coast of France—practically on my way. It never even occurred to me to say no.

It also didn't occur to me to ask a single question. Not even when he had his assistant sew the book into the lining of a bag. I just let him hang it over my shoulder and gave him a loving kiss goodbye.

Later, much later, Sully tried his best to make things right, but by then the bubble had already burst. Twenty-six nights in a French jail cell will do that, I suppose. Make a girl come to her senses. Give her some clarity. Despite how much I loved that man—and, God, how I loved him—I wished him the best and walked away.

Until now.

TWENTY-NINE

At 11:00 a.m., the hotel bar is hopping.

I sit on a stool at the far corner, sipping a freshly squeezed orange juice, while all around me, tourists toss back morning cocktails. Mimosas and Bloody Marys, fizzy flutes of champagne. Spread out on the bar in front of me is a copy of yesterday's *New York Times*, bought from a newsstand on the walk over, partly because of a headline about the bombing, but mostly to have something to do. In all the years I've known him, Sully has never been on time.

"I'm in trouble." It was all I needed to say.

Immediately, Sully began barking orders in Turkish—to fire up the jet, to drag the pilot out of the bar and sober him up. Molding everyone's time to fit his own mercurial wishes, a change of plans to fly to Paris for a girl he once loved, because she is in trouble. This morning he texted me this address, a slightly shabby three-star hotel near the Opéra in the 2nd arrondissement. Not exactly Sully's style, but that's precisely the point. No one would ever look for him here.

Also, it's not Sully who walks through the door.

It's Mustafa, a tall, beefy Turk who is just as capable of killing you with his bare hands as he is of whipping you up a five-course meal while belting out an aria from *La Bohème*. A cross between a trained assassin and a teddy bear, and the sweetest guy you'll ever meet. I slide off the bar stool just in time for him to wrap me in a bear hug so tight it creaks my ribs.

"Stella, *gülüm*. Where have you been all this time?"

Gülüm—my rose. And the question was rhetorical. Mustafa knows exactly where I've been. Sully, too. I haven't spoken to either of them, but I'm certain they've been keeping tabs.

"Good to see you, too, Mustafa. I've missed you. How's Haleh?"

Haleh is his daughter, last time I saw her an adorable toddler with inky black hair. She must be six or seven by now.

His hands slide down my back and around my sides to my hips, where he holds me with two giant paws. For everyone else in the place, it looks like two old friends at the tail end of an embrace, but I know what this is. Mustafa just gave me a subtle pat-down.

"A real troublemaker. She says she will be a butterfly when she grows up." He releases me with a roll of his eyes. "I hope she marries well."

I smile. "There are two cell phones in the bag hanging from a hook under the bar. Both have their location services off, and both are powered down."

"I still have to take them. You understand."

I nod, because I do. Cell phones can take pictures and make recordings. They can be traced even if they're not connected to Wi-Fi or GPS. Even during the height of our relationship, I got used to slapping my cell in Mustafa's hand before he'd usher me to wherever Sully was. His penthouse. His jet. The VIP room of some club or a restaurant's private dining room. Sully wasn't big on public places, and he has a strict no-cell-phone policy, which he enforces with everyone but his bodyguards.

Mustafa slides a twenty on the bar, then grabs my bag from

the hook and me by the hand. "Come. Everyone's waiting out-side."

By everyone, he means two more beefy bodyguards in head-to-toe black—one stationed to the right of the hotel's double doors and the other watching from across the street. Mustafa bypasses them both as he leads me to a black Mercedes-Maybach idling at the curb, its windows tinted so dark it's impossible to see whoever's seated inside.

But I know who it is, and my heart, that old fickle traitor, gives an excited flutter.

Mustafa whisks open the back door, blasting my bare legs with icy air. Nineteen and a half degrees Celsius, which trans-lates to a frigid sixty-seven, just the way Sully likes it. I slide onto the back seat, and Mustafa pushes the door shut, the sound not unlike the closing of a bank vault. The inside of the car smells like spices and money.

I take a deep, bracing lungful and look at Sully for the first time in more than four years.

Full head of perfectly tousled jet-black hair over almond eyes with a bit more crinkle around the edges. Just the right amount of facial hair, a neat mustache that dips down into an immaculately trimmed beard. I try not to remember the feel of it against my skin, but my pulse tells a different story. This is the man I once called the love of my life, the one whose touch could set my body on fire, and now I feel that old, fa-miliar pull. I've been here two seconds, and already I feel my-self falling back under his spell.

He smiles, genuine and generous, and suddenly, I'm think-ing all the same things I used to whenever I looked at this man—that he has to be a good guy. Otherwise, how could he smile at me like that? How could he be so sweet and tender with me if he wasn't deep in his heart a good man?

He leans forward and says something to the driver in his native tongue—no partition, as anyone who Sully employs is well practiced in the art of discretion. The driver dips his chin and slides into traffic.

As soon as we're moving, Sully sits back, taking me in. "Why do you have a French number?"

Four-plus years since Sully and I last spoke, and these are his first words to me. Not *what are you doing in Paris?* Not *what's wrong?* Not *are you still angry at me?* He barrels right over the most important part of my message—that I'm in trouble and need his help—and zeroes in on the strange, foreign number.

"Because the phone I called you from is a burner."

One dark brow quirks at the last two words—*a burner*—and he doesn't have to say what he's thinking. That burners are for immigrants and criminals. That there are better ways to hide your identity than prepaid minutes on some cheap flip phone. Even after all this time, I can still read this man's thoughts, and I hate that I still love it.

I also hate that I feel pinpricks when he looks at me like that, like he's missed me, too. That all these years later, he still has this effect on me.

His gaze dips to my arms, the way I'm clutching them. "You're shivering."

"Because I forgot that you're basically a polar bear. I should have brought a sweater."

"I suppose I should congratulate you," Sully says, and I don't have to ask for what, because his gaze is glued to my ring. I also don't have to ask what he thinks about it. There are a million things I don't know about this man, but I've always known how he felt. It's one of the traits I loved most about Sully, that he's so openly emotional. It's also the trait I most feared.

Now his eyes narrow, and his lips seem to frown, and his expression kind of breaks my heart. Sully and I never talked about marriage. We barely talked about the future unless it was to plan my next flight to wherever business or pleasure would take him. And yet he doesn't hide that he's crushed by mine.

"His name is Adam. I wasn't expecting it, to fall for somebody so soon after we…well, you know. But I was just so sad and lonely… Weren't you?"

He gives me a slow, sad smile. "I thought of you constantly. I still do. It hurt to see you move on so quickly."

Two weeks to the day after I walked out of the French prison and away from Sully, I walked into that booth at the Scott Markets. The very definition of a rebound relationship.

And it's not like I ever thought Adam would stick. Adam was too nice, too good, too available for me to use him as a distraction from my broken, stomped-on heart. He was temporary… until one day, suddenly, he wasn't. Suddenly, he was the man I thought of when I first opened my eyes, the one I was counting the seconds to see. It helped that he was the direct opposite of the man sitting next to me now, a safe spot to land after the heartbreak of dazzling, dangerous Sully. I always thought falling in love with Adam healed me, but maybe it was more complicated than that. Maybe it was also time and distance away from this man.

I look away, staring out the side window at the buildings passing by on the other side of the glass. We're somewhere near the Louvre, the sidewalks crammed with tourist shops. At the corner, a performer painted in head-to-toe gold tips his top hat at a cluster of kids.

"Where is this Adam of yours now?"

"I don't know. He won't tell me, and he's stopped answering my texts." I turn away from the window, meeting Sully's gaze. "He says it's too dangerous."

Too dangerous. Sully gives a sarcastic puff. With men like Mustafa and the other two guarding the street, with measures like private jets and bulletproof Maybachs, for Sully there's no such thing as too dangerous.

"What did your husband do?"

I open my mouth to tell him the story—all the parts I couldn't say to him last night over the phone. About the bombing and Adam moving from the missing to presumed dead list, even though he's alive and well and holed up somewhere in Paris. That we were supposed to meet last night but he didn't show, and now he's trying to get me to go home because he says this city is not safe. That I'm not leaving without him, and I can't let this go until I see him with my own eyes and make him explain everything.

But instead, I tell Sully the very worst thing. "He lied."

"And you? Were you truthful with him?"

I know what Sully is asking. He's asking if I told Adam about him, even though he should already know the answer.

"I didn't tell him about you. I never told anyone."

For twenty-six days, the French police peppered me with questions about Sully. What he did, how he made his money. It didn't matter that I pled ignorance, or that I exercised my God-given American right to remain silent. They slid pictures of the two of us across the table—sunning on his yacht, boarding his plane, kissing on the terrace of his penthouse. They said I was in bed with the enemy, a dangerous man and a wanted criminal. They knew about the thumb drives, and they waved around the precious book like a dime-store paperback. They didn't care that it was one of a kind and irreplaceable. They only cared about its power to make me talk.

I didn't then, which is why he believes me now.

While his driver makes aimless loops through the Parisian streets, I tell Sully about the bombing, and the French detective who claims Adam was the target. About his Atlanta shop being a cover for his real hustle, selling looted artifacts to the world's 1 percent. About the British Good Samaritan and the Dutch art detective and the French shopkeeper's ominous warning about *le marché noir*. About the yacht anchored off the coast of Capri that Adam and I sailed by close enough for me to see a bouquet of pink-and-white irises through the window.

"It was Margot's boat, Sully," I say now. "The *Aphrodite IV*."

Margot Fazzari, whose Italian grandmother founded one of Europe's most famous multinationals, the Fazzari Corporation. After L'Oréal and Estée Lauder, the third-largest cosmetics company in the world. Margot is the client Sully was courting, a woman with an art collection almost as vast as the fortune he wants to help her hide from the authorities. The rare book was intended for her.

Now Sully frowns. "That feels like too much of a coincidence."

"Exactly." I twist toward him on the back seat, shifting to better face him. "And now that I know what I know about Adam, all these crimes he's being accused of, seeing her boat that day can't be random. These things have to be connected."

"I agree."

A million bucks a foot, Adam said, but Sully told me Margot's yacht is worth a lot more than that. The Florentine mosaic hanging on a wall in the dining room, one of four from the Amber Room of Charlottenburg Palace in Russia, is priceless. Literally. The palace was looted during World War II, and the entire Amber Room disappeared. The Eighth Wonder of the World was thought to be destroyed and lost forever. Sully said Margot loves to brag that she paid fifty million for it.

And apparently, the Amber Room mosaic isn't her most valuable treasure. The *Aphrodite IV* is loaded down with pieces just like it, hundreds of millions of dollars of ancient artifacts on her yacht alone. It's why the boat is so heavily guarded.

"Perhaps she is a client. Maybe she came to Capri to do a transaction," Sully says. "Did he slip away when you were there?"

I think back to those three blissful days on the island, zipping around on rented scooters, sipping on Aperol spritzes in the *piazzetta*, long dinners under lemon trees and hikes to the top of Monte Solaro. One afternoon I fell asleep at the hotel pool, and when I woke up, he was gone. I found him in the room a few minutes later, sweaty and red-faced from a run.

"It's possible, I guess. Our hotel wasn't that far from the marina."

Sully pauses, thinking. "Let's back up a little. How did you and Adam meet?"

"Through a friend. She was selling some stuff that belonged to her ex. Family heirlooms, mostly. Adam bought them."

"I thought his business was antique architecture."

"He was filling in for a colleague."

I don't remember his name—Doug? Dave?—but I remember the discussion and why he was absent: food poisoning after eating airport sushi. Adam said his friend wanted that *Winnie-the-Pooh* book.

"A coincidence," Sully says. "Another one."

"What about serendipity? Do you believe in that? Because people meet and fall in love all the time—and not just in the movies. You meet a stranger and you discover you have a connection. That's what happened with you and me, and it's what happened with me and Adam. And my friend contacted *him*, by the way, not the other way around."

"Are you sure about that?"

"Yes," I say, even as doubts start to niggle. Katie never told me how she'd found Adam's colleague, only that they had an appointment. Did she Google "antique buyers Atlanta"? Or did Doug/Dave somehow search her out? And if that's the case, how would he know she was looking for a buyer for Pete's heirlooms?

And also, there's this: I remember being surprised when Adam called later that day. He'd slid me his card at the market. He gave me *his* number. I never gave him mine. I'd always just kind of assumed that Katie did.

"You just learned your husband is doing business with a

woman whom you once gave a gift. A very illegal gift. Doesn't that strike you as strange?"

"The gift was from *you*, remember? And it never got there. I was arrested before I could deliver it."

Sully concedes the point with a tilt of his head, but he's still right. It looks likely that Adam knows Margot. We met two weeks after I deleted Sully from my phone. The coincidence is far too neat.

My mind whirs with questions. Not about whether or not Adam is a criminal, as I'm pretty sure we sailed past that station days ago, but about our origin story, the way we met and fell in love. Did Adam lure me there on purpose? Is it because...? Because what? Because of my connection to Margot, or maybe Sully?

Evidently, Sully has come to the same conclusion.

"You are lovely, Stella. I think of you fondly and often." He turns to me with an expression I've seen him use many times before, on employees and business associates, but not on me. Never on me. "But if you or your husband implicate me in any way, I will not hesitate to silence you both."

I nod, animated and immediate, because I believe him. If I betrayed Sully, even accidentally, I believe he would follow up on that threat.

"I think you know me better than that, Sully."

"True. But I don't know your husband."

"Adam's not the one asking for your help. I am. I need intel. I need to know what Adam's connection is with Margot, what she wants from him. From me. I need to know how to protect myself."

Sully stares at me for a long moment, then dips his chin. "That burner, you still have it, no?"

I nod, then shake my head. "Mustafa has it."

"Go back to the hotel bar where I picked you up. Mustafa will be waiting there for you. I'll reach out as soon as I know more."

Sully taps the driver on the shoulder, and the car swings into the far right lane, pulling to a smooth stop. This is how Sully ends all his business negotiations, abruptly and absolutely, no strings or open issues. Conversation over, time to get out. Apparently, after four years apart, I have become a business negotiation.

I'm reaching for the handle when he catches my other hand, the one with Adam's ring. He looks at me as his fingertips search it out, then gives a gentle twist to the band.

"This Adam of yours. I hope he's worth it."

I think about how to respond to that. Sully isn't wrong to have doubts about Adam, or to have planted all these new ones in my head. These past few days have opened my eyes to all sorts of new truths about my husband, truths I can never unknow. Adam is not who I thought he was. He lied about a lot of important details.

Suddenly, though, I'm thinking of the pink tulips Adam planted under the living room window because I once said tulips were pretty. The claw-foot tub he installed in our bathroom because it was big enough for two. His boyish excitement when he showed me those pictures of antique wall panels while we waited for galettes on a Parisian terrace. That was all real. What we have is real. I know it is.

And I have to believe that these new truths are not the whole of his story. It's what I keep telling myself, that this isn't everything. There's more, and I intend to find it.

I smile at Sully, tell him the God's honest truth. "I hope so, too."

THIRTY

It's five short blocks from where the Maybach dropped me to the hotel bar in the 2nd, where Mustafa is seated at a table by the back wall, nursing a double espresso. He plants a kiss on my cheek and drops the bag over my shoulder. Then, with a wink, he's gone.

I head through the lobby for the door, rooting around in the bag until I find the burner. But here's the problem with throwaway phones: there's nothing on them. No contacts, no email addresses or phone numbers. Without my old iPhone, I have no idea how to reach Katie. I haven't memorized a phone number since sometime last century.

"Shit."

I need to log on to my iCloud again, but I don't dare, not even from the burner. I already did that once, but that was before my conversation with the Brit on the bridge, before Kat fell from the sky and onto a parking pole, before Sully told me what he'd do if Adam or I implicated him in any way—even accidentally. I may not know yet who or what I'm up against, but I know enough not to fuck with Sully.

I drop the phone back into my bag and turn back, breezing through the hotel lobby without so much as a nod to the reception staff. The trick to getting access to anywhere is looking like you belong. A harried tourist on an economy budget—that's what I am.

Once I'm past the desk, I pause, digging around in my bag, pretending to search for my key card while I surreptitiously take stock.

A seating area with couches and chairs. A cluster of loud Germans around a table. Bookshelves and bathrooms and a low-slung counter with the word *Internet* painted above it on the wall. And just below, a pair of stools before two ancient but unmanned desktops.

I hurry over and pull up the browser, navigating to iCloud. I work as quickly as possible—sign in, plug Katie's number into the burner, sign out. Boom. A span of ten seconds, max. Fast enough that if anyone is keeping an eye on my iCloud account, watching for me to log in so they can track my location, then hopefully I didn't give them enough time. I delete my history from the browser and head back outside.

Other than the 2nd arrondissement, I have no idea where I am, so I turn in the direction where most traffic seems to be headed, hoping it'll take me toward a taxi stand. While I walk, I pound out a quick text.

Hi Katie, this is Stella. I know you're furious at me for going silent on you, and I promise to tell you everything as soon as I can, but for now I need to know how that first meeting with Adam unfolded. How did you find the dealer at Scott Markets? The guy Adam was filling in for—Doug? Dave? Also, how did Adam get my number? Did you give it to him? Love you xx S

I hit Send, then think of one more thing.

p.s. Please don't give anyone this number. If anybody asks, you haven't heard from me at all. XX

I look up as the Rue d'Amboise dumps me onto the Rue de Richelieu, a busier street where there's a cab waiting on the corner. I slide onto the back seat and direct the driver to the Hôtel Charme, and his face is much like the first at the address—*dangereux, pew pew*. He plugs it into his GPS and hits the gas.

The Android beeps from deep inside my bag, and I dig it out and check the screen. A Signal message from Adam.

Why have you gone dark? Does this mean you're on a plane?

I tap out a quick reply.

Nope. Still here. I already told you, I'm not leaving until you tell me what's going on. You owe me the truth, Adam, and you owe it to me to say it to my face.

The little dots dance around, but I already know what he's going to say. He's going to hedge, warn me of the dangers, beg me to leave Paris. And sure enough, seconds later the text hits my phone.

The truth is that these people are not playing around, Stella. They will kill you just like they killed Kat, like they tried to kill me. Go home. I'll come as soon as it's safe. And then I'll explain everything face to face, I swear.

I drop the phone into the side pocket and stare out the window at the scenery whizzing by, the people and the parks and buildings that only a week ago would have stopped me in my tracks. He wants to wait until it's safe to tell me the truth, but who knows how long that will be?

What I do know is that I won't get any answers by leaving Paris now. I know Adam won't fly all the way home to tell me the truth, and even worse, I know that the second I board a plane, I can forget ever seeing him again. That is the reality of our situation, and this feels like emotional blackmail, like trying to manipulate me with empty promises of things that'll never happen.

But there's another side of me Adam doesn't know, a stubborn side that does daring, dangerous things for the man I love. And I'm not stupid. I know how to protect myself. No, I don't have a team of beefy bodyguards or a bulletproof car, but I spent two years loving a man who was skilled in outsmarting danger. I like to think I've learned a few things.

The cab dumps me at the mouth of the one-way street, and I trudge the half block to the hotel, dragging myself up the four flights of stairs to my room. I'm exhausted and hungry, and I can't remember the last time I washed my hair. I strip and turn on the shower, wishing I was back in the fancy suite with its thick towels and rows of perfumed shampoos and soaps. I take in the scratchy towel hanging from a plastic hook, the wrapped bar of soap on the sink, and tell myself not to be such a diva.

I unwrap the soap and line up the two cell phones in its place, on the top edge of the porcelain. I unwind the crystal heart from my neck and place it on top, then step inside the steam.

I'm working the soap into a lather when one of the cells buzzes with an incoming message. Adam and Katie and Sully. It must be one of them. They're the only people with these numbers.

I shove the curtain aside, just in time to see the vibration send the phone wobbling across the sink. The heart slips off the screen, and for one horrifying second, I watch it teeter on the edge of the porcelain before it settles. I blow out a sigh of relief, right before the chain slides off the side of the sink, tugging the heart over the edge. I lunge for it, but I don't get there fast enough. The necklace plunges to the floor.

And bounces on the hard tile. Twice. But it doesn't break.

Huh. Adam was right. The diamond cage really is designed

to protect the glass heart, because there's not so much as the faintest of cracks.

Soapy water dripping down my nose, I hold the necklace up to the light to be sure, but there's…

I lean closer, frowning. There's something in there, something that doesn't belong. A smudge of something dark, a shadow of an object that is not part of the glass.

I hold it up to my ear, give the heart a little shake. There's the faintest of sounds, a dull rattling.

You are my heart, and my heart is yours, Adam said when he gave it to me. *The biggest surprise of my life. My most precious treasure.*

I think back to that scorching afternoon in Venice, how Adam slipped away when I was inside the shop picking up a couple of waters. How he'd seemed distracted and on edge all day, and the way he looked at that Texan when he'd returned from his little errand was odd. I'd brushed it off to the heat at the time, but now I wonder if this heart necklace has something to do with it.

And then I think of the other words he said. *If anything ever happens to me, just remember you always have my heart.*

I shut off the water and snatch a towel from the rack, wrapping it around me as I step into the bedroom. I stand at the edge and look around the sad room, but there's not much here but furniture and a bulky clock radio on the nightstand. Not a hammer, but it's hard and heavy and it'll have to do. I pull the plug from the wall and carry the radio back into the bathroom.

I place the heart on the tile floor and start whacking. The diamond claws bend but they do their job, and it takes me a good dozen tries to smash the glass. And then, finally, I hit it just right, with a corner of the radio between the misshapen claws, and I hear the telltale crunch. One more good *thwack* and the glass shatters, shooting red shards over the cheap white tile.

My neighbor bangs against the wall, shouting at me to shut up.

I ignore him, digging a finger through the messy mound. Pulling out a tiny piece of plastic with a golden chip. It's a SIM card. The kind used to store data on cell phones.

I have so many questions, I barely know where to start. What was Adam's plan? Did he want me to find the SIM when he hung the heart around my neck, or for me to just wear the heart, completely oblivious? Was he planning to come back and retrieve it at some point? Surely, *surely*, he understands the danger of slipping me the SIM.

I pick up the Android, thinking I'll pop in the SIM, but then I drop the phone back into the sink. The Android is my only connection to Adam, and I have no idea if anyone besides Adam has been tracking this thing. I also don't know what will happen if I plug a new SIM card into an old phone. Does it delete the files? Reset the phone data? Send some kind of alert into the ether? I have no idea, and I'm not about to take that chance.

I copy Katie's number into the Android and then remove the old SIM from the burner, sliding the new one in. And then, heart thudding, I power up the phone.

The screen lights up with the prompt for a PIN. Automatically, my thumbs type in 4-0-4-8. It's the PIN on Adam's phone, the one on all his ATM cards, the security code on our alarm. The screen shimmies, and then…nothing.

I think about what else the passcode could be. His birthday. Mine. Our house number. I tick all of them in, all with the same result. I'm still locked out.

And then I remember something else Adam said to me that afternoon in Venice when he hung the heart around my neck. *I knew it the second you walked into that booth. I fell for you that day, and it was the best thing I've ever done.*

I try the date, 0-2-2-0, and *voilà*—I'm in.

The home screen looks like any other cell phone, with apps for texts, email and phone, except there's no service. This cell phone isn't connected to a mobile network. There's no way to send messages or make calls, not unless I hop on the hotel's Wi-Fi, which no way in hell am I planning to do. Being online also means that I am discoverable, and until I figure out why Adam went to all the trouble to hide this SIM card in plain sight, it seems like the smartest tactic is to fly under the radar.

The email app is empty, as are both text messages and WhatsApp. Looks like whatever Adam was doing with this thing, it was offline, as well.

I tap the apps for contacts and hit the jackpot. There are 347 contact cards. Cards with names, phone numbers, private emails and physical addresses of people all over the world. The US. South America. Europe and Asia. I click on one at random, a Nancy Davenforth of Newport Beach, and scroll down to the notes section.

Statue of Varaha depicting Hindu god Vishnu's boar avatar, from Temple Complex in Atru, Rajasthan, India $486,000

2 homo erectus fossils $534,000 ea.

Green stone mask depicting sun god Kinichi Ahua from Classic Mayan Río Azul site in Guatemala $572,000

Inscribed stone tablet of alabaster, from floor of Awam Temple in Marib, Yemen $779,000

Wish list: strong interest in ancient religions of Middle East, Asia, South America in particular. Looking for Ganesh statue from Koh Ker temple complex in Cambodia; painted icon of Jesus Christ crowned with thorns from Emperor Tewodros' Mountain Fortress in Maqdala, Ethiopia, Mesopotamian ivory relief from Iraq Museum in Baghdad

There's more. Lots more.

I find photographs of the artifacts, hundreds and hundreds of them, filed neatly into individual categories. Collectors' names, names of sacred sites and temples, brokers like Adam with looted goods for sale. I click on one of them and scroll through the pictures—to my untrained eye, piles of old, dusty junk. But for Adam or a collector, they'd be worth millions. I check the dates, and they go back almost a decade.

A decade. The timeline matches up with what the lieutenant colonel said, that Adam has been in this business for that long. I think of his shop back home in Atlanta, the architects and the clients and the dozen or so staff who restore the eighteenth-century floorboards and ceiling garlands that Adam finds in some old château to their former glory. How does Adam do both? How does he run a real business and a criminal one? Where does he find the time?

The burner beeps, alerting me that the battery is down to 5 percent. I move into the bedroom and plug in the phone, backing out of the photo app, moving on.

The notes section takes me the longest to sort through, as it's the biggest of the bunch. Copies of emails tying Adam to sellers and collectors. Names and past business transactions, meticulous lists of banks and numbered accounts. Research on criminal networks responsible for ransacking sacred sites. Lists of looted items and their potential buyers. Names of the shell companies and trusts his buyers used to hide their purchased items and disguise the ownership. I do a quick search for Sully, and I let out a sigh of relief when I don't find him.

But it's true. The SIM card is black-and-white proof that Adam did all those things the lieutenant colonel accused him of. He sells illegal artifacts to the world's 1 percent, and even worse, he's keeping score. Adam is a spider in a vast web of criminal transactions that he's tracked and recorded onto a secret SIM card with his usual obsessive orderliness. And then, when someone came after him for what he'd done, he hid the evidence in a crystal heart and hung it over my head.

I feel it then, as physical as a breeze blowing up my neck, as real as if I'm standing at the edge of a hurricane. All those things he said about the crystal heart, about his heart being mine and remember if something happens that I have it, was that some kind of code? Did he *want* me to find the SIM card?

I go back to the list of contacts and hit *F*, and there she is, right at the very top. Margot Fazzari. One of Adam's clients. According to the long list of transactions in the notes section, a big one.

Sully's words pound through my head.

"You just learned your husband is doing business with a woman whom you once gave a gift. A very illegal gift. Doesn't that strike you as strange?"

Yes, Sully. Yes, it sure as hell does.

I scroll through the list of transactions, scanning the items she purchased from Adam, and my gaze snags on one I recognize. A golden ring shaped like a belt buckle that once belonged to Oscar Wilde. Apparently, she paid eighty-five thousand euros for it. Kat was the last person who had it on her finger, and now she's dead.

If after all this I still had any lingering doubts, I don't anymore. Not after the red pin I spot on the map underneath her name, on a street only a few miles away.

Margot owns a home in Paris. And I'd bet a million dollars she knows that I'm here.

THIRTY-ONE

I get dressed at the speed of sound, tugging on yesterday's shorts and a fresh T-shirt from the top of my suitcase, shoving my feet in my tennis shoes. I toss the burner and the Android to the bed and dig through my bag for Adam's emergency cash. The envelope is a lot lighter than it used to be, and I do a quick count of the bills. Eighteen hundred euros and some change. I drop it back in the envelope and stuff it back in the bag, then pull up the browser on the Android.

There has to be a reason Adam gave me this SIM card. Beyond the information stored on it, beyond the powerful people it could take down. *If anything happens to me, remember you always have my heart.* He said that to me for a reason.

I follow Google Maps directions to a sketchy electronics shop three blocks from here, the kind of shop without a sign or so much as a name, with a dirty front window lined with steel bars and reinforced with roll-down steel shutters for night. I push on the door but it's locked. There's movement inside. A tall man in a Sikh head wrap points to my right. A button underneath a handwritten note: *Sonnez SVP.*

Ring, please.

I press the bell, and the man buzzes me in.

The shop is tiny and crammed with enough tech products to stock a store ten times its size. Boxes piled in teetering towers on shelves and on the floor, stacks of crates containing messy knots of wires of every length and color, smaller packages hanging twenty deep from long hooks on the wall. The door falls shut behind me with a sharp click, and I step around a display of remote controls to the counter at the back of the shop.

"Do you speak English?"

The man nods. "I do. How can I help you?"

British English, apparently, with a heavy Indian accent.

"I'm hoping you can tell me how to copy data from a SIM card onto an external drive."

"So you want to clone the SIM?"

"Not exactly. I don't need the actual calling data, only the contacts and pictures, things like that."

"Ah. That makes things a lot simpler, then." The man rounds the counter, stepping around the end into the messy store. On his way, he pulls a slim box from a hook on the wall. "You need one of these."

A thumb drive, according to the picture on the box, a flat black device with a slot at the end for the SIM card. On the other end, a USB plug.

"Looks like I'll also need a computer."

His dark brows creep together in a frown. "You do not have a computer?"

It's a valid question. Any American who can afford to travel to Paris will also own a computer, and probably more than one. I think about the MacBook Pro Adam gave me for Valentine's Day on the kitchen counter back home, the old Dell I shoved to the back of a drawer, and I'm glad I didn't bring either. Anyone who's been tracking Adam has probably been tracking me, too. Better to start with a fresh system, one that's not connected to the internet.

"I don't have my laptop with me. Isn't there any way to by-pass the computer?"

"There is, but you'll need another device, and they're pricey. You're better off finding a computer to borrow. Your hotel will probably have one, or you could go to an internet café. Or if you have the SIM card with you, I'm happy to allow you to use one of mine."

The SIM card is tucked into a fold in my bra, but no way am I admitting that to anyone, least of all a stranger. This man seems nice, but still. *Trust no one.* The files on the SIM are what sent Adam underground. The fewer people who know what's on it, the better.

"I'll take a laptop, a cheap one, the SIM reader, all the wires and a thumb drive. Actually, give me two."

Two thumb drives. Two backups, just in case.

The man's brows lift, first in surprise and then pleasure, and he gives me a little bow. "My name is Harbhajan, madame. At your service."

Twenty minutes later I'm back out on the sidewalk, eight hundred euros lighter but a heavy bag of electronics hanging from a fist. I do a quick sweep of the sidewalk, then take off in a brisk walk to my left, even though I have no idea where I'm headed. Not the hotel—my gut tells me until I find a safe place to store this SIM card, not to stay in one place for too long. It's harder to shoot down a moving target.

Up ahead on the corner, I spot a café, the terrace bustling enough that they won't care when I spend an hour or two at an inside table. I spot one at the back corner next to an out-let, and far enough away from the crowd for anyone to spy over my shoulder. I order a sandwich and an Orangina from the waitress and take everything out of the bag.

I'm not the most computer-proficient person on the planet, but this is not all that complicated, and Harbhajan walked me through the steps in plenty of detail. Slide the SIM card into the reader, plug the reader and the first of the thumb drives into the USB slots, open Windows Explorer and start dragging. I do this a second time, then copy the files from the SIM onto the laptop, just in case. I tuck them into a folder I name Xerox, then bury it deep in the programs folder.

Once I'm done, I stack everything back in the bag and drop the SIM card into the change section of my wallet and fish out the original, the one that came with the burner. I slide it back in, and it beeps with a flurry of incoming messages, all from Katie.

OMG first up lemme just say THANK GOD. Ever since you went silent I've been positively frantic. I must have called your phone like a trillion times, and if you ever pick up those messages I'm sorry for the things I said. I can't tell you how relieved I am to know you're okay.

I can't help but smile. Katie texts just like she talks, and I picture her standing somewhere in her scrubs, her thumbs tapping furiously on the phone.

So the guy from Scott Markets. Doug I think? As I recall he was a swipe right on Hinge. We texted a bit then both lost steam. But he's the one who said Peter's stuff was worth $$$. He told me to come see him at Scott.

And I didn't give Adam your number, at least I don't think so? It's been so long I honestly don't remember. Sorry!

Oh! Almost forgot. Emily saw you on the news and now she won't leave me alone. I haven't told her anything but you know how she is. If it were anyone else's mother I would have blocked her ages ago.

And yes to telling me what's happening there. I'm going to hold you to it. The second you land I better have you on the other end of my phone.

ps SO DAMN RELIEVED you're alive xx K

I look up, staring out the window at the people on the terrace, disappointment burning in my chest. Doug made contact with Katie, not the other way around. He's the one who planted the idea to sell her ex's stuff, not her. It was all Doug. Was it a coincidence that Adam filled in for Doug that day, or was matching with Katie some convoluted scheme to get to me? Was meeting Adam serendipity, or was it planned?

And speaking of Doug, how do we even know he's real? Anybody can pose as a fictional person on a dating app. Anybody can come up with a fake name and upload a fake picture. Doug could be *anyone*. Doug could be Adam—which would mean that our origin story, the way we met and fell in love, is a load of bunk.

I try to think what this means, if Adam searched out Katie because he knew she was my friend. What was he hoping to accomplish, and why? Did he know my connection with the Persian book? Did he think I was competition? I stare into the café, and I want to scream the questions into the half-empty room. Not that it would do me any good. The person I really want to be screaming at is Adam.

I check the clock, just past three in the afternoon, and tell myself to get moving. I'll need to hurry if I want to secure these backups before closing time.

I do a quick search on the laptop browser and write down the addresses for a FedEx store and a public locker in Saint-Germain-des-Prés, and then it occurs to me, a potential roadblock. Public lockers will likely be digital these days, a transaction you can't do with cash. I do another quick search, the nearest place to buy a prepaid Mastercard, and jot down that address, too. I pack up my things, drop a twenty on the table next to the uneaten sandwich and get moving.

I'm sweaty and humming with adrenaline by the time I emerge, empty-handed, from the City Locker in Saint Germain, and then I stop on the sidewalk. Mustafa stands across the street, leaning against the building in jeans and dark shades, chomping on a baguette. He lifts the sandwich in greeting.

"You're getting rusty at this, just so you know. I spotted you hours ago back in the 10th, and then again in the 1st as I was getting off the Métro."

I also found the tracker he sneaked on the Android, and another in the side pocket of my bag. Mustafa has been keeping tabs on me for over twenty-four hours now, which means so has Sully. After everything, knowing they're out there watching, following my movements as I trek around the city, makes me feel safer.

"Hello to you, too, *gülüm*. You're looking very pretty today." Mustafa smiles. "And you saw me only because I let you. All the other times, I was invisible."

I eye the sandwich in his hand, a dull ache pounding in my temples at the reminder I didn't touch my lunch. Or eat breakfast, unless you count the two crumbled crackers I found at the bottom of my bag, which I don't. The shorts that fit me perfectly at the start of this trip now hang from my hip bones.

"Did you at least bring me a snack?"

A girl on a scooter whizzes by, blond hair flying out the bottom of a shiny red helmet, and I wait for her to pass. "I brought you this one and then I got hungry. You've been in there a long time." He pushes off the wall and steps up to the curb. "Come with me. He is waiting."

I follow Mustafa up the one-way street, the two of us moving against traffic—not that there is much of it. Only the occasional scooter or pedestrian on their way to the patisserie up the street. But up ahead I already see it, the busier street running along the Seine. We take a right and there's the Maybach, three tons of German engineering with grilles and rims polished to a bright shine, double-parked alongside a battered van, its back doors thrown open to reveal stacks of crates overflowing with leafy greens. Just beyond, two men ogle the car from the curb.

As we approach, I unwind my bag from my shoulder and hand it to Mustafa. "Thanks for the escort."

Mustafa takes it with a grin, his black eyes flicking up and down the street. The checking is smooth, so natural that anyone not looking for it would never even notice. He whisks open the back door, positioning his body so the two men on the sidewalk can't see the man inside. A human shield and bodyguard all in one.

The second the door clicks shut, the driver slides back into traffic. I turn to Sully with a wry smile. "Running into Mustafa was a nice little surprise, which means I must be out of practice. I forgot how you make it your business to know everything."

He smiles, that same sweet smile that used to make my blood sing. "You came to me, remember? I can't help you unless we know the danger."

We, as if Sully and I are on the same team, and I probably shouldn't like the way that feels as much as I do. Being with Sully always felt like living in a bubble, one that's warm and protected and secure. One snap of his fingers and the real world and all its problems fade away. How amazing would it be to disappear into that bubble for a day or two, to tell his driver to take us to wherever Sully is staying and leave me there? I hold my breath and his gaze, and I know all I have to do is say the word. One word, and the dam inside him would break. He would reach across the seat and pull me onto his lap. He would kiss me and give me whatever I want. My skin tingles with the certainty.

"This man you married," Sully says, breaking the spell. "He's made quite a few powerful enemies."

"No offense, Sully, but this isn't exactly news. You don't get almost blown up and go into hiding if there isn't someone powerful after you, someone who wants you dead. But who? Why? *That's* what I need to know."

He lifts his hands, spreads them in the air. "Strangely enough, no one is taking credit. But the chatter I'm hearing is that he's become a risk. The French police officer you spoke to is not the only one chasing him. That British man you met, Alexander Finneas Pearson, he works for MI6."

I nod, not all that surprised. "Makes sense. Finn knew about my criminal file, and he said to tell Adam to call him, that he could help. And moving stolen artifacts across international borders will get plenty of foreign intelligence involved, including the MI6."

I think of the SIM card, sitting in a locker in Saint-Germain-des-Prés, and the lieutenant colonel's words pound through my head on repeat, that the illegal artifacts trade is a billion-dollar business. The third-largest international criminal activity after drugs and weapons. How many of the contacts would be willing to kill Adam purely out of risk of exposure? Dozens, probably. The MI6 was closing in, and Adam was keeping score.

"Yes, but if the authorities were indeed circling him, that would be a business killer. These clients of his, many are also clients of mine. If they hear even a vague rumor the police are watching, they will scatter."

That's because criminals are allergic to the police.

But Sully also hides and launders money for plenty of perfectly legitimate clients—at least they look that way on the surface. People with respectable jobs, who come from respectable families with recognizable names. Musicians and A-list actors, corporate CEOs and politicians. Not just the top 1 percent, but the top 1 percent that run the world. They see Sully's services as a way of preserving their wealth, not a borderline illegal method of avoiding creditors and taxing authorities.

Like Margot Fazzari, for example.

"What about Margot? Did you dig into her?"

He nods in that guarded way he does, a gesture that's not quite a yes. "Apparently, Adam had something that belonged to her, something very valuable. He was supposed to deliver it to her on Capri, but he didn't show."

"An artifact?"

"Multiple items, it sounded like, including a golden ring. Margot is not your husband's biggest fan."

Golden ring. Two words that shoot a hot warning up my spine. "If it's a ring shaped like a belt buckle, I had that ring, Sully. I wore it for days before giving it to a woman, a friend of Adam's. She was supposed to bring it back to the owner in England, but she was killed before she could leave Paris."

"The Dutch art detective."

"You know her?"

"Only by reputation. She was well-connected and very, very smart. Her death has everyone talking. Specifically, why she and Adam were working together to return a ring that he'd already sold to Margot."

So Adam screwed over Margot. Took her money and didn't deliver the ring.

I shake my head because even then. "Would Margot really kill for an eighty-thousand-euro ring?"

"With people like Margot, it's not about the money. What does she need with money? She has more than she could ever spend. But for Margot that would be a great betrayal. She wouldn't like getting fooled."

Still. Would Margot really risk everything—her freedom, her reputation, her business and wealth—for a tarnished band of gold? I can't make it make sense in my head. Not for a stupid ring.

But.

The SIM card holds Adam's meticulous record of every one of their transactions. Pictures, prices, bank information, the works. If Margot found out he'd kept notes of her crimes, if she knew the MI6 and French police had him in their sights and he was carrying around evidence that could take her down, too… Now, *that* would be worthy of murder.

"I can see your mind turning, Stella. Does this have something to do with where you've been all afternoon? You've had a very busy day."

There's no use denying it, not to this man. Sully knows me too well, and he knows I've found something I can use as insurance to keep myself alive. Not only that, but because he's been tracking me, he knows where I've stashed them.

I smile. "Always be prepared. You taught me that."

Sully purses his lips, his gaze heavy on mine.

"Yes, but Margot is a Fazzari. She is… How does your government say? Too big to fail. Margot will take whatever steps necessary to protect her dynasty. She has her own version of Mustafa, and he is ruthless."

"Let me guess. A Moroccan man they call Aljazaar."

Because now I'm remembering something else Kat told me that day in the museum. She said that Aljazaar works for Adam's client, a woman. And yes, okay, so there were hundreds of women in the contacts on the SIM card. There's no reason to automatically assume this particular client is Margot.

Except for her yacht in the bay of Capri.

Except for her apartment here in Paris.

Except for all the ways this mystery keeps pointing back to her.

It's all been leading to Margot. I can feel it.

Sully confirms it with a nod. "You would be wise to stay away from that man, Stella. He is very dangerous."

"And I'm stubborn."

"Some might call it reckless."

"Maybe. But I can't let this go. Not until I see Adam. Not until he looks in my eyes and tells me the truth."

The driver pulls to a smooth stop, and I look out the side window. We are back on the tiny one-way street in Saint Germain where Mustafa had found me. I spot him a little farther up, leaning against a parking pole.

I turn back to Sully, who reaches across the console for my hand. His skin is warm, soft.

"Stella, *aşkım*." His use of our old endearment—*aşkım, my love*. "Please be careful. Do it for me. You do not want to back Margot into a corner."

"I'm not planning to back her into a corner." I lean over and give Sully a lingering kiss, a thank-you and a goodbye wrapped in one, then pop open the door. "I'm planning to give her what she wants."

The Maybach pulls away from the curb, and I slide the burner from the bag Mustafa just handed back to me. Margot's cell goes straight to voicemail, just like I knew it would. Women like Margot do not answer unknown numbers, ever, for any reason. I wait through a generic recording in Italian, followed by a beep.

"Hi, Margot. It's Stella Knox. I have something that belongs to you."

Two seconds later a text hits my phone.

Tonight, 9 pm. 1 Rue des Saints-Pères. Try not to get arrested this time.

THIRTY-TWO

There's nothing special about the door for 1 Rue des Saints-Pères except for its size, a giant slab of wood covered in glossy black paint tucked behind a brass-and-iron gate. I step back, searching the facade for a bell, when I hear a buzz, followed by a sharp click of a lock disengaging. The gate slides open, disappearing into the French stucco wall.

My gaze lifts, searching the corners of the vestibule, and there it is, of course—the subtle blinking light of a camera. I'm being watched.

"Step inside the vestibule, please." The voice is low and male, bleating from a speaker next to the bell. The accent is not French. Not Italian, either.

The gate is all the way in the wall now, opening up a space of about five feet before a pair of arched oak doors. I step into it, and the gate glides back out of the wall, clicking closed behind me. Trapping me here—an extra layer of security and a stark reminder that no one gets in or out of this place without express permission.

Once the gate is back in place, there's a second or two of dead air before the locks in front of me start disengaging—multiple locks, a good half dozen of them, one by one. Slowly.

Finally, the heavy door swings open to reveal a man. I take in his wavy hair and piercing eyes, his fashionable clothes and the Rolex strapped to his wrist, and my mouth goes dry. I try to breathe, but I can't because look. Look what I missed.

Lucas smiles and gives me a little bow. *"Bonsoir, Stella. Tu es en retard."*

Good evening, Stella. You are late.

By a full seventeen minutes, and every single one of them was on purpose. It's a trick Sully taught me, one that establishes dominance. Never let the opposition think they have the upper hand.

But still. I didn't notice what was right in front of me. That French of his is perfect. Too perfect.

I wet my lips with my tongue, somehow finding my voice. "You're not American, are you?"

He shakes his head, though he doesn't look the least bit sorry about it. *"Non.* I am not."

"You're not French, either." It's more a statement than a question, because France is not the only country in the world where people speak French. He raises a brow, and I can't believe I missed it before now, the wickedness simmering just under the surface. "You're Aljazaar."

He smiles, a hardening of his lips into a thin, tight line.

"Is your name really Lucas?"

"Lucas Matéo Fournier, at your service." He doesn't bother trying to sound American this time, just lets his accent fly. "Now please. Don't make me wait any longer."

I step inside, thinking it all makes sense now. Why this man pretended to work at the embassy, why he fed me all that nonsense about strange American expat cravings. He smelled my fear and desperation and said everything I needed to hear: that he was on my side, that his job was to be my advocate— and I swallowed it, no questions asked. He manipulated me, the fucker, and I readily believed him.

It's also why he gave me Adam's phone, because Lucas didn't think Adam died in that bombing, either. He knew if Adam would reach out to anyone, it would have been me. I wonder if Lucas was there the day of the bombing, watching Adam and Kat race out the square, or saw me when I chucked the phone in the Seine. I wonder if it was even really Adam's phone Lucas gave me.

He motions for me to follow him into a bright foyer, a generous space with high ceilings and checkerboard tiles and an elaborate staircase with a simple red runner. Pretty, but not particularly impressive, and without one stitch of furniture. No rugs or decor or so much as an Ikea print on the walls. Just a big, blank space to serve as a checkpoint on the way to upstairs.

I unwind my bag from my shoulders and hold the strap in a fist, raising both arms to my sides. "I'm not armed. Not wearing a wire, either."

He takes the bag from my fingers and drops it on the bottom step. "Still. I'm sure you'll understand if I check."

I stand as still as I can while Lucas feels up every inch of my body, and this isn't some standard pat-down, nothing like Mustafa's or the hurried check you get at the airport. This is him running fingers up and down my limbs, pressing into my armpits and my crotch behind the seams of my jeans, getting entirely too familiar with the skin underneath my bra and the edges of my panties, probing every fold and every crease, dipping into collars and hems and waistbands. His jacket falls open as he works, giving me a clear view of the gun on his hip—a move I'm certain is on purpose. I stand perfectly still and remind myself to breathe while he searches every inch of my body, because I have zero doubt that he'd use it.

On me.

On Adam.

Yet another reminder of why I'm here, because of my husband. Because this man with his hands all over my body wants to hurt him in service of the woman waiting somewhere up-stairs. If Adam were here right now, nothing I could say or do would matter. He'd tell me that to keep him safe—to stay safe myself—I should be anywhere but here.

Sully's voice runs through my head. *Margot will take what-ever steps necessary to protect her dynasty.*

But Adam and Margot and Lucas don't know that side of me. They don't know that when I'm backed into a corner, I can be ruthless, too.

I look at Aljazaar, this stranger who injected himself into my orbit. All those things he told me that day on the bridge, gazing out at the Notre Dame in the distance. About the lieu-tenant colonel, all those questions he asked me about Adam. *Did you know of your husband's illegal activities? Were you will-fully involved in any of them?* All that time he was feeling me out, seeing how much I knew, planting little seeds that would hopefully lead me—and him—to Adam.

Lucas straightens, swiping my bag from the step. He punches the button for an elevator at the back of the room, and the doors ding open.

"Let's go. Margot is waiting."

The elevator doors whir open, and this is more like it. This is what I was expecting for a house of this size and stature. Walls paneled in silk and hung with ancient tapestries. Rich mahogany bookshelves stuffed with art and gold-leafed books. Elaborate statues arranged among Greco-Roman sculptures plopped on marble pedestals. Paintings from Old Masters hung four and five rows high next to mosaics and religious icons in tempera and gold. A riot of history's greatest gems and master-pieces, a priceless museum all for one woman. Opulence à la Margot Fazzari.

She stands atop an antique Persian rug in the center of the room and spreads her arms wide, smiling big and open like we're old friends—which I suppose in some sick way, we could be.

"Stella, *amore mia*. Finally, we meet in person."

Even here, in the privacy of her own home at well past nine at night, Margot is painfully put-together. Body-hugging dress a dark forest green over five-inch red-soled heels. Shoulder-length hair shiny and smooth, as fragrant as if she just stepped out of a salon. Smoky eyes and glossy lips and flawless, dewy skin. Margot Fazzari may be forty-six, but she doesn't look a day over thirty.

She nods to Lucas, still standing in the open elevator, and he hits the button. The doors slide closed, leaving the two of us—just me and Margot—up here all alone.

I stand here, dirty sneakers sunk in Margot's priceless carpet, and let her give me three air-kisses.

"What tricks you must have, to capture all these men's hearts. First Sully, now Adam. Tell me, what is it about you that makes them find you so captivating? Are you sure you're not European?" She laughs, the sound high and merry. "Champagne?"

She turns away before I can answer, stepping to a built-in bar along the far wall. On the other side of the windows, the Seine sparkles in the moonlight, while just beyond, the iconic facade of the Louvre is lit up from below.

"You have a lovely home. It suits you."

Technically, I've only seen two rooms of it, but by now I get the setup. A cross between a palace and a museum, the well-guarded top floors of an eighteenth-century building that runs the length of an entire Parisian block.

She plucks a bottle of Cristal from a silver ice bucket, then fills two cut-crystal flutes. "Thank you, darling. Your husband helped me decorate."

I nod because I'd already noticed some of his pieces. A bronze statue of a Bacchus, a potbellied boy with one chubby arm held high in the air, which is an exact match to the one on our living room shelf at home. Ditto with the framed Chagall print hanging on the wall, the marble bust on the coffee table next to a carved wooden box. Fakes, Adam assured me—excellent ones I asked Katie to remove from our house just in case. What he didn't tell me was that he'd stashed the real ones here.

She swipes two flutes from the bar and whirls around in a cloud of perfume. "Let's toast to old friends. Because we are that, aren't we, Stella? Friends."

Margot and I are not friends. We have almost nothing in common, no connected social circles or similar upbringings for us to talk about. The only reason our paths ever crossed is because of Sully and now Adam.

I give her a close-lipped smile. "Are we, though? Because I feel like friends wouldn't try to kill another friend's husband."

She hands me a glass, the crystal so heavy it's practically lead. "You say that like your husband was innocent, dear. Now come. Let's make a toast, to us."

She holds her own glass high, and that's when I see it—the flash of gold that catches the light. It's on her pointer finger, a band in the shape of a belt buckle, and I don't have to wrench it off her hand to know what the inscription says.

Gift of love, to one who wishes love, but in Greek.

I tap my glass against hers, then bury my nose in a sip, golden bubbles with just the right amount of tartness. I need a moment to regroup, to give myself a pep talk, to tell myself that coming here wasn't a mistake. That while Margot might think I've walked into a trap, I am the one holding the literal key. That I won't become a sacrifice like Kat.

"Let's stop playing around, shall we?" Margot says. "You said you had something that belongs to me. What is it?"

"Every single transaction ever made between you and Adam. Pictures, prices, banking information. The list is very long and detailed. Adam stored it on a SIM card."

Despite herself, she looks almost impressed. "A SIM card,

how clever. Small. Easy to conceal. A million of them out in the world, and no one thinks of them as anything other than a tiny little plastic thing you shove into a phone. Very resourceful of him to think of it."

"The most resourceful part is where he hid it. I've been carrying it around for weeks now." I step to the window and press my face to the glass, looking down on the busy street. "When I decided to come here, it was to trade the SIM card for Adam's freedom. For you to leave him alone. But now that I'm here, now that I've seen this place and you, I've changed my mind." I whirl around, my gaze finding hers. "I want the ring, too."

She holds her hand up to the light, admiring the golden band. "Now, why would I give you this ring? I paid your husband handsomely for it, and then he tried to deceive me, the bastard. Though he deceived you, too, didn't he? As the French would say, *on est dans le même bain*. You and I are in the same bath."

Margot may be Italian, but her French is just as effortless, and I don't miss the way she leans on the words, the way her lips curl down with a sneer. She wants to wound me with them, but I don't give her the pleasure.

"It's boat. In English we're in the same boat." I lift an unaffected shoulder. "And without the ring, I'm not handing over the SIM."

I'm taking a chance to argue this point, because I already know that Margot did it on purpose—positioned her hand just so the gold would glint in the light, made it impossible for me to *not* notice the ring. She wanted me to not just see it, but also grasp the implications of the ring being on her finger. That band is both a prize and a threat. Margot murdered Kat for that ring. Why wouldn't she murder me for the SIM?

She leans forward, her friendly smile gone. "You're just as stubborn as Kat was, do you know that? Even at the end, she was such a righteous bitch. Do you know what she called me? The Veruca Salt of plundered artifacts."

I can't help myself—I laugh. Veruca, the spoiled little girl from *Charlie and the Chocolate Factory*. An overindulged heiress who wanted things for the simple sake of owning them. Kat was right. The comparison is perfect.

Margot points at me with a manicured finger. "Careful. Kat laughed, too, and you see what happened to her. Did you know she and Adam were working together?"

"I know she was an art detective. That she chased down stolen artifacts and returned them to their rightful owners. She was supposed to take the ring back to the Oscar Wilde Society at Oxford University."

"Not just the ring. Other pieces, too. An Avar treasure, a fifth-century Greek bust, a Byzantine mosaic of an adolescent Jesus Christ. They were fakes, just like all the others." She tilts her head, studies my expression. "Oh, you did not know? Your husband sells forgeries, dear. Excellent ones, but forgeries nonetheless. He has made a lot of money this way, but this is not a good way to do business. This is a good way to get yourself killed."

Forgeries. The word is like the click of a teakettle, spreading heat through my veins. All these treasures Adam is selling, they're forgeries?

I think about all the lists and pictures he stored on the SIM card, the statues and the masks and the icons decorated with ancient pigments and gold leafing, all those exorbitant prices. Is that what Adam's been doing in his workshop all day every day, constructing replicas good enough to fool collectors like Margot? Is his staff in on it?

"What about Kat? Did she know?" From everything I've read about her, she's one of the good guys. A hero in the art world, not a forger.

Margot's lips purse in a pretty sneer. "Kat was his partner.

She helped him come up with the scheme. I would have never known if not for Antoine. Do you know Antoine, dear? He has a lovely shop in the 18th."

I nod. "Yes, I know Antoine."

"Anyway, Antoine is the one who alerted me to their scheme. Apparently, he and Adam had a huge row about the ring. Adam offered to split the profit, but Antoine was a better man. He took the ring and was going to return it to me, the rightful owner. I'd already paid your husband handsomely for that ring. That makes it mine."

"No. That makes you complicit in their crimes."

"Look around you, *amore*. Do you think these artifacts come with origin paperwork? Do you think vendors like your husband have licenses to sell these things to me? Or to anyone, for that matter. If I didn't own these antiquities, they would have been burned, or destroyed, or hacked into a million pieces in their countries of origin. I am the reason these antiquities still exist, because I have the money and the means to bring them here. To cherish them and keep them safe. Every piece in this apartment is one I saved from the rubbish heap of history. One day the world will thank me."

"Except they won't, because you're holding these pieces hostage, locking them away for only you to see and enjoy. People can't go to visit them in a museum. Artists and historians can't study them. None of these things belong to you. They belong to their own culture."

Margot rolls her eyes. "Oh, please. Stop pretending to be so noble. As I recall, you are part of this world, too."

"Was. I *was* part of this world, but only once, and it was a stupid, stupid mistake. Twenty-six nights in a French prison helped me see the error of my ways."

"Yes, and from what I understand, you were much more trustworthy than your Dutch friend. Luckier, too."

I don't know how to respond to that. I don't know how to

respond to any of this, because this is how Margot sees herself, as a hero. As a protector of the world's historical beauty. I'm trustworthy because I took the hit without dragging Sully's or her name into it. I didn't try to pass off fakes as genuine artifacts like Adam and Kat. They are the guilty ones in this scenario. Not Margot.

Behind me, the elevator dings.

Margot's gaze doesn't stray from mine. "In a weird way, I suppose it makes sense. That you and Adam would have found each other, I mean. Does he know about your history?"

A week ago, I would have said no. Hell, just yesterday I would have said no. But now, after my text conversation earlier today with Katie, I'm guessing the answer is yes, though I still don't entirely understand why Adam sought me out. I shrug. "I don't know. We haven't discussed it."

Margot's brows twitch upward, the Botox version of feigned surprise. "No?"

"No."

She smiles, and her gaze flits away from mine, focusing on something just beyond my head. "Let's ask him, then, shall we?"

Something about the way she says it, with satisfaction and an almost giddy glee, catches my next words in my throat. I whirl around, and my fingers lose their grip on the glass. The flute slides from my fingers and hits the carpet with a dull *thwunk*, splattering icy champagne on my legs, but I barely feel any of it because there he is.

There's Adam.

THIRTY-THREE

ADAM

Msida, Malta
Sixteen days earlier

> *The secret to life is to enjoy the pleasure of being terribly,*
> *terribly deceived.*
>
> —*Oscar Wilde*

Stella stops in the middle of the two-lane street. "Where the hell are we?"

In a somewhat questionable neighborhood of Msida, a tiny fishing village on the northeast coast of Malta—though Stella already knows this. We've just come from exploring Lookout Point with its ancient Manoel Fort in neighboring Valetta, until Stella announced she was hot and hungry, not a good combination on the best of days. It doesn't help that she only got a few hours of sleep last night, thanks to a hotel air conditioner that makes an ungodly noise to produce barely tepid air. All day today, she's been grumpy as hell, and I hate to tell her, but it's adorable.

I show her the GPS map on my phone, the little blue dot that indicates we're exactly where we're supposed to be. "We're not lost, if that's what you're thinking."

She takes in the empty storefronts that line the road, the dingy apartments and long stretches of unmarked buildings. "Really? Because I don't see this Nono place anywhere."

"It's Noni." A four-star restaurant, chosen not because Yelp assures me it serves the best octopus Bolognese in town, but because of its location, right next to a plain brown door with a man waiting for me behind it, holding an envelope containing two shiny new passports. One for me, one for Stella.

I check my phone, then point farther up the street. "Noni is just up ahead."

Stella does an about-face, turning back from where we came. A dusty road lined with even dustier parked cars. "That can't be right. Check the map."

"I just checked the map. I've been checking the map all this time. Seven minutes. Less than a kilometer. We're on the right track." I point to my phone as if to prove it.

"Then let's choose another lunch spot. Or better yet, let's go back to the one we saw in the harbor. That one looked good."

"The harbor is a mile back. Noni is only a few more blocks."

I bite back the rest of what I want to say—that she's being unreasonable, that I'm hot and hungry, too, that this is our last day in Malta, and I'm not leaving this island without those passports. Just because I haven't seen the *Aphrodite IV* lurking in the harbor doesn't mean Aljazaar isn't here on this island, watching. Waiting to strike. Wherever he is, he's like a time bomb, ticking down in my ear. New names. New identities. Those passports are my insurance policy, a plan B for when— not *if*, but *when*—things go sideways.

I step closer, hook an arm around Stella's neck. "Babe, please. Let's keep walking for just a few more minutes, okay? I promise you, we're close."

She crosses her arms, huffs a sigh. "You always do this, you know."

Her cheeks are shiny and flushed an unnatural color, two hot-pink circles as bright as her shirt, rumpled and damp from the heat. She looks miserable but beautiful, her hair in tight red ringlets around her face.

"Do what?"

"Make me think I'm the unreasonable one when look around, Adam. This is *not* a nice neighborhood."

Stella is right about that. But what she doesn't know is that I was here not all that long ago, in the week before she arrived, and so I know that only a block from here, the landscape changes. This dusty road gives way to a pedestrian street, vibrant and spinning. Music. Bars. Shops and cafés packed with people spilling out onto the sidewalk. And Noni sparkling in the hot afternoon sun, next to that plain brown door.

She juts out a lip. "Adam, please. All I want is a mountain of pasta and a glass of bubbly water with more than two ice cubes. Is that too much to ask?"

"I'll buy you every ice cube in the freezer when we get there. I promise." I smile, nudging her along. "Now come on. It's only a little farther."

She caves with another sigh and lets me lead her down the empty block, which is already starting to improve. Up ahead, a flash of purple flowers tumbles from a stone planter, and just beyond, a pair of pedestrians linger on the corner. She trudges ahead in silence, veering to the sidewalk to catch a little shade.

I click off the screen, slide the cell phone into my pocket. "A little fun fact about Malta," I say, only partly to take her mind off the heat. "They're one of the few countries that sells passports."

Stella nods, wiping her brow. "They call it a golden passport, and it costs a fortune. Malta is part of the EU, which means their passport is like a winning lottery ticket."

Free to travel in the European Union without visas or passport checks at the border. Free to live and work in any of the twenty-seven EU countries. Free to travel visa-free to countries all over the world, even for dual citizens of countries like Russia and China and the Middle East, which are not always welcomed. For people like them, for people like me, these perks are well worth the hefty price tag.

"One-point-three million a pop," I say, grinning like I'm kidding, "though we'll need to act quick. I think I read somewhere that the EU is trying to put an end to the program."

Stella snorts. "Yeah, because it's a magnet for money launderers and criminals."

She's not wrong about that, either. Even though Malta claims to vet all the applicants. Even though they impose a "strict" residency requirement of a year, plus a minimum amount of capital applicants must invest in the country via government bonds and housing to prove they're building a life here.

But every rule comes with a loophole or two, and money launderers and criminals spend plenty of dough to find them. I should know. It's how I skirted the rules myself, by throwing money at the problem until *poof*—it went away. Like magic.

"Still, you have to admit, Malta doesn't suck. A tiny island in the middle of the Mediterranean filled with palaces and prehistoric temples, World War II shelters and war rooms. If I had 1.3 million to spare, I'd pay it to live here. Wouldn't you?"

At the corner she stops, eyeing me from the sidewalk. "Live here. With all the money launderers and criminals?" She can't tell if I'm serious or not.

"Why not? We could buy a charming farmhouse overlooking the sea. I'll restore it and fill it with art and antiques. I'll panel the walls and put in a claw-foot tub big enough for two, in front of a bay window with the prettiest view. And on weekends I'll bring you here and stuff your belly with pasta. I hear the Maltese chefs make a mean octopus Bolognese."

I take her by the shoulders and turn her ninety degrees, and there it is—the pedestrian street with, at the far end, Noni. A dozen or so tables topped with white linen and crystal, shaded under a striped awning.

She turns back, tapping a finger against her chin, pretending to think. Humoring me. "The beaches here aren't bad, I suppose, but what about me? How would I while away my days while you putter around the house?"

"By filling the house with babies. I was thinking at least five. Maybe six."

Her face brightens, her brows inching up her forehead. "Seriously? Babies, do you really mean that?"

Up to now, Stella and I have only spoken about babies as a vague possibility in a very distant future. Stella thinks my hesitation is because of Babs, because I was there when the doctors told Julia what she was in for and it scared the living daylights out of me, and I've always let her believe it. I let Stella think that I couldn't bear to relive that moment because it was easier than explaining the real reason.

"There's nothing I'd love more than making a whole bunch of babies with you." And maybe it's wishful thinking, but I *do* mean it. For an instant, just for a split second, I let myself go there. I imagine a whole squadron of kids, little redheaded boys and girls who look just like Stella, before I pull myself back. The passports. Margot and Aljazaar. First things first.

"I can't make all those babies by myself, you know. You're going to be a very busy man."

I grin. "I think I'm up for the job."

"Okay, fine. I'm in." She nods, wiping her face with the hem of her shirt, revealing a slice of her flat stomach. "But can we please make all these babies in Paris? Or maybe in a pretty stone house in the South of France? Malta is just *so fucking hot*."

I laugh and wind my fingers through hers, and I tell myself I still have time to fix this. That once we get to Paris, I can find a way to placate Margot and her Moroccan lapdog, and we won't need those passports waiting for us behind the wooden door. That we can board that homeward plane, fall back into our old life with Stella none the wiser.

So maybe I don't tell her the whole truth—not yet, but soon—but I do tell her the truest thing I know.

"I don't care where on this planet I end up, as long as it's with you."

THIRTY-FOUR

STELLA

Paris

Adam stands at the edge of the room, wearing clothes I've never seen before. Faded jeans and a gray shirt over plain white sneakers, almost as white as his face. The jeans hang low on his hips and his cheeks are sunken, his bones prominent like he dropped ten pounds in a week, which it's quite possible he has. His jawline is scruffy like he needs a shave.

My body wants to run to him, but my feet stay planted on the carpet. "What are you doing here?"

Of all the millions of questions beating through my head, that one seemed the most pressing. It's been six days since he disappeared down that alleyway for his sunglasses, six days filled with grief and terror and a constant struggle to make sense of all these new parts of him. Is he here to apologize? To retrieve the SIM and whatever other clues I haven't found yet? Is this the last time I'll see him?

He steps into the room, then stops at the carpet. "Lucas called me from your phone. He told me you were here." His gaze flicks to Margot, and I hear the words he didn't say: *Lucas told me you were in danger. That's why I'm here.*

I glance at Lucas, still standing in the hallway by the lift, and *dammit*. Why did I not anticipate he'd set up a trap? Lucas would know how to get past the lock screen on the Android. He would know who's hiding behind the name John Doe. I think about my text string with Adam on Signal, the one with Katie on the burner, and I try to recall if there's anything in there he can use against me, because for sure Lucas has read those, too. I don't *think* so, but I can't be sure.

"I broke the heart."

Adam nods. "Where?"

"Not here."

"And the white card?"

"Same place."

Margot and Lucas listen intently, and though they may not fully understand the meaning behind our words, Adam and I do. He knows I found the SIM card. He knows I know what's on it and have stashed it somewhere safe along with the white card. He knows that's why I'm here, to trade it for our lives.

"I'll give you everything," Adam says, turning to Margot. "The evidence, your money, every cent of it back with interest. Just let Stella go. She's innocent. She has nothing to do with this."

Margot scoffs at the word *money*, just like Sully predicted. Margot owns jets and mega yachts. She owns houses all over the world, coveted real estate in the most expensive cities, ones she's filled with priceless artifacts. However much money Adam tricked her out of with those forgeries, a few hundred or a few million, it's a drop in Margot's diamond-encrusted bucket. *Selling fakes is not a good way to do business. It's a good way to get yourself killed.* There's no amount of money that will result in us walking out of this place alive.

But that SIM might. I'm counting on it.

My gaze flits to Lucas, and the gun he's still wearing strapped to his hip. One swipe of his arm and it'll be pointed at me and

Adam. I keep him in my sights, directing my next words to Margot. "I've already said I'll give you the SIM."

"No, you said you'd trade it for the ring, which isn't the same thing at all." She reaches for the bottle of champagne and refills her glass. "I want both, and I'm sorry to say that ever since your husband arrived, your negotiating powers have diminished substantially. Tell me, dear. How many copies of the SIM card did you make? How many did you hide all around Paris?"

Two, including the laptop. Not that I'm planning to tell Margot that. And not everything is hidden in a locker in Saint-Germain-des-Prés. One is tucked in a FedEx envelope, headed for Katie back in Atlanta. She doesn't know to expect it—I didn't send her a warning text because I'm not *that* stupid—but the note I taped to the backup drive says if the box has arrived before my call letting her know I'm safe, she's to get in her car and drive it straight to CNN. I know Katie, and I know she'll do it, no questions asked.

"The SIM is in a City Locker in Saint-Germain-des-Prés." I chose the neighborhood on purpose, a good twenty minutes from here through a city center jammed with evening traffic. "I'll give you the number and the combination, but it closes at ten. Lucas, what time does that fancy watch on your arm say it is? You'll have to hurry."

Lucas doesn't answer. Doesn't check the time, either. He doesn't move at all except for his eyes. His gaze shifts to Margot, awaiting orders.

She waves a hand through the air, gold bracelets chinking. "Oh, please. You think Lucas is worried about a little thing like a locked door?" She takes a sip of her champagne, looking down the glass at Adam. "And by the way, dear, your wife is far from innocent. But I suspect you knew that already."

It's the subject Margot and I were discussing before Adam walked in, whether he knew how closely our businesses were aligned. He doesn't answer, but a shock wave ripples across his features, a tiny earthquake before he washes it away. But I still see it, the answer in how he looks at me, the way he licks his lips. His face says everything.

"*You* ordered me to find the lost Diwan of Hafez," he says, turning to Margot. "You told me to stop at nothing to get it for you, so when an American flight attendant was arrested for smuggling it over the French border, of course I followed that lead. I needed to know where she got it."

I shake my head, his words echoing around me like the blood in my ears. From the start Adam knew I was holding back, keeping this whopper of a lie by omission, and he pursued me anyway. I think about the way he looked at me that day at Scott Markets, like he knew me already. His eyes scanning my face as though it were familiar, his slow grin when I told him my name. The way he pursued me, gliding quickly and seamlessly into my life, dropping to his knees four months to the day after we met. As if this had been his plan all along. As if *I* had been his plan.

"Did it make it any easier for you?" I say, blinking away tears. "To lie, I mean. Did my lies make it easier for you to justify yours?"

"*No.* No, it made it more difficult, a *lot* more. I never meant to fall for you. I thought you were my competition. And what was I supposed to say when you walked into that booth, that seeing you changed everything? I didn't give a damn about the Pooh book. From the second our eyes met, it was only you. Every single thing I've done since that day, every choice I've made, has been for you."

"What are you talking about? What choices? To lie to me for all this time about what you do and how much money you make?" At this point, I don't even care that Margot and Lucas are listening in. "I know about the trust, Adam. Julia told me."

"Then you also know my answer——Babs. I started down

this road because of her. Because my sister was drowning in medical bills and her idiot husband had his head in the sand. Babs deserves better than merely surviving. She deserves all the best doctors and therapists, the best care and alternative treatments her shitty insurance refuses to pay, a future after her parents are dead and gone. It was a business born out of necessity. I don't make all this money for me. I make it for her."

"Maybe that was true when you first began, but now? Now you make enough for a hundred kids like Babs."

"True, but I can't just stop. These clients of mine…" His gaze shifts to the side, just for a second, but it's long enough. I know he'd say more if not for Margot. "I'd love to be able to extricate myself, believe me."

"What about Architectural Antiques? You could have paid Babs's bills with your legitimate business."

"Are you kidding me? All it takes is one builder to go belly-up before they can pay my bill, or a shipment to arrive covered in mold and I can't make payroll. And in the meantime, what happens to Babs? What happens to my stall of employees, people I love like family? I can't let them down, either."

I stay quiet, because I don't know how to argue with that. People do a lot of things for money. Good and bad and everything in between. And didn't I do the same with Sully? Choosing to give my time and my heart to him, agreeing to do all those "little favors." I justified it by my feelings for him, with the way I longed for him to need me as much as I needed him. My love for him was real—I know that. Except for the cash his lawyer gave me, I made it a point not to take a penny, but all those trips, all those private plane rides and penthouse hotel rooms, all the jewelry and gifts… Isn't it the same thing? When it comes to money, I'm certainly not one to judge.

"So all that talk of preserving history…"

"Is true. That feeling I get from restoring a pair of iron shutters, or removing twelve coats of paint on an ancient staircase to discover the most perfect oak beams." He pauses, gives me a soft smile. "There's only one thing I love more."

Before I can stop it, I feel myself smiling back. I don't mean to, but it's instinct. After everything, Adam still has that effect on me.

Still, though.

"All these illegal artifacts, how can you sell them when you know where they come from? Ripped from history so that people like Margot can hang them on a wall. How do you do it?"

"People like Margot," she says, setting her glass on the bar with a hard smack. "What's that supposed to mean, my dear?"

Adam ignores her, his gaze locked on me. "I think people can change. Don't you? But only the people who really *want* to, who regret their past choices and are committed to making better ones moving forward. I'd like to believe they can change themselves and their whole entire circumstances."

I blink in surprise, because they're *my* words. I said them to Adam after our lunch in Luxembourg, while finishing our bottle of champagne. I was grumpy about my mom hitting me up yet again for rent money, and Adam wanted to know why. "Maybe this time is different," he said at the time. "I believe people can change. Don't you?" My answer was referring just as much to Emily as to myself.

And now here's Adam, adopting the answer as his. Asking me to believe that he's changed.

"Yes. I think people can change." I hesitate, pivot so I'm facing him dead-on. He's still staring at me, his expression so pained it hurts to see. "I'm just not sure you're one of them."

He swallows. Nods. "You should know I'm not proud of what I've done. I'm not trying to justify it, or say that I didn't have a choice, because you always have a choice. But from day one, I had a rule. I would only ever sell to collectors who I was certain would respect these pieces and their history. Who would protect them as well as—better, even, than—any museum."

Behind me there's a loud crashing, and I whirl around to find Margot, her elbow resting on a marble pillar—an empty one. The priceless Ming vase it once displayed lies in shards on the ground.

She looks at me and smiles. "Oops."

"It's a forgery," Adam says, more to me than to her. "Not real."

Margot pushes off the pillar, stepping over the pile of porcelain on the ground. "Oh, it's not? What about the Israeli death mask that dates back to 1200 BC? Is that one fake, too?"

She marches to a far wall and snatches it from a hook, a flat oval sphere with two round holes for eyes, a tiny nose and a full row of teeth. She hurls it in Adam's direction, but it doesn't quite get there. It hits the floor and shatters into a million pieces.

"That's enough," Adam says, but Margot is just getting started.

She whips a bowl off a side table and pitches it like a Frisbee. Adam steps aside and it hits the wall and explodes. Next is a Roman fresco she wrenches from a hook behind the couch. It goes sailing over the bar, scattering a line of liquor bottles like bowling pins. They smash into the mirror with an unholy racket.

Her next words are just as loud. "*Pezzo di merda!* I paid you a lot of money for those things."

"I'll pay you back, I swear. Every cent, with interest. I'll double what you paid."

"Look around you, Adam. This isn't about the money. Why on earth do I want your money? What I want is for you to pay for the betrayal."

"I'll get you the real items, then. The vase and mask and mosaic and everything else. You have my word."

That seems to give her pause. She tilts her head and studies him, a greedy gleam in her eyes before it disappears into a shake of her head. "I'm sorry to say it, Adam, but your word no longer means anything to me. I no longer trust you, and once trust is gone…" She doesn't finish, other than to give another shake of her head. "It's why I couldn't wait for you to bring me the ring."

His gaze dips to her forefinger, and for the first time tonight, Adam shows real anger. "I told you I needed more time. You didn't have to kill Kat for it."

"Kat's death is on *you*." She stabs her finger, gold flashing, at Adam's face. "She knew too much. You should have kept her out of it."

"She came to me, not the other way around. She'd been tracking the Saint Mark mosaic—did you know that?"

Margot can't help herself. She turns to me with a bright smile. "The Saint Mark mosaic is a very special piece, and not only because it's more than 1,600 years old. It's my favorite piece in my Saint Moritz home, one of the last and most beautiful examples of art from the early Byzantine era, salvaged from the Kanakaria church in Cyprus."

Adam corrects her. "Not salvaged. Raided by the Turks in the 1970s. Most of the churches were destroyed during the Turkish occupation, but some of the icons and mosaics survived to be sold on the black market."

"Like the Saint Mark mosaic," I offer.

He nods. "The point is, Kat knew that I'd sold it to Margot. She had been tracking our transactions for a while, and she had enough evidence to report us both to the authorities. She was going to take us both down."

"Well, we couldn't very well let her do that, could we, Lucas?"

My gaze flits to Lucas, who's moved from his spot by the elevator to take up position by the couch. It's a strategic spot, halfway between Margot and Adam, though Adam would be crazy to try anything. Lucas has removed the gun from his holster and is holding it now, trained on Adam's chest.

Adam holds up both hands, swallowing hard. "Margot, listen. I have a lot of money, millions and millions of euros, sitting in three numbered accounts in Luxembourg. I'll give it all to you, but only if you let Stella go."

Luxembourg, where sometime during our two and a half days there, in a café or at the hotel or while we explored the tunnels under Bock Cliff, someone slipped him a white card with three rows of numbers written in blue pen. I was right—those numbers open three bank accounts stuffed with illegal money.

Yet here we are, talking about money again. Promising it to a woman who already told him she doesn't need a penny of it. Adam is trying to buy time.

I watch his gaze flit around the room, and I know he's looking for possible weapons, or maybe exits. His eyes settle on an elaborate brass sword fastened to the wall above the couch. Big bulbous handle inlaid with stones, engraved and sharpened double-edged blade. It looks like something Mulan would have used, and heavy enough to slice a man in two. There's no way in hell I can lift it.

Margot turns to the leaded windows overlooking the Seine. The glass is smooth and black with night, a mirror reflecting the rage that twists her features. "And the SIM?"

"I'll get that to you, too."

"What about the copies? And think twice before you lie to me again. Because your precious Stella is smart."

Adam doesn't deny it, and neither do I. Margot Fazzari is a lot of things, but she's not a fool.

"Do you know what else I think?" She turns away from the window, aiming her scowl first at Adam, then me. A warm hand wraps around my own. Adam, squeezing my fingers, urging me to stay strong. "I don't need the SIM or the copies. Not if the two of you are dead."

She gestures for Lucas. His expression goes stony just like the rest of him—muscles tensing, fingers curling into his palm.

"Wait, wait," Adam says, but he doesn't look at me. His gaze is trained squarely on the revolver in Lucas's right hand. "I'll give you everything, and then you can kill me. Stella is innocent. She has nothing to do with this."

Margot shakes her head. "As one of my favorite French authors, Anaïs Nin, once said, *'Nous ne voyons pas les choses comme elles sont, nous les voyons comme nous sommes.'*" I look to Adam for help, but there's no need, because Margot translates, "'We don't see things as they are, we see them as *we* are.'"

I frown. "What's that supposed to mean?"

"It means you're screwed."

Lucas stabs the air with his gun, thrusting the barrel in our direction. "Let's go."

"Go where?" Adam says, not moving, but I already know the answer: anywhere but here. Because cleaning blood from the trunk of a car or off some remote Parisian sidewalk is easier than sopping it up from a priceless Persian. Heaven forbid our deaths ruin one of Margot's precious antiques.

I look at her, this entitled princess hoarding the world's money and its treasures, and I feel it then, the anger and rage surging in my chest. My fingernails dig into my palms hard enough to draw blood, and I can't help myself. I can't resist one last parting shot.

"Surely you don't think I came here without insurance." Margot's gaze swings my way. I look her dead in the eye. "Because you should know I'm smarter than that."

"What are you talking about? What insurance?"

My insurance, a thumb drive tucked in a box in a FedEx cargo jet, zooming across the ocean to Katie. As Zoé would say, *collatérale*. Margot doesn't know what it is, but she can see from my face that I'm not lying.

"It's too late. By the time you wake up tomorrow morning, the whole world will know what you've done. To Kat, to us."

"What insurance?"

"And even better, they'll know what you have here in your house, on your yacht, hanging on your walls in Saint Moritz. Kat was right. You are the Veruca Salt of plundered artifacts."

Her expression hollows out, satisfaction draining away like the yolk from a cracked shell. Her cheeks flood with blood, and her mouth twists into something tight and dark.

"*Tuez-les,*" she says to Lucas in French. "*Maintenant.*"

Kill them. Now.

Before he can make a move, Adam lunges—not for Lucas, but for the hand holding the gun. Adam might be big, but Lucas is faster, and he's a trained fighter. He holds Adam off with an arm, but Adam does manage to get in a punch or two. He bats the arm holding the gun away, right as Lucas squeezes the trigger. The shot is deafening, as is the crystal decanter behind the bar when it explodes.

Margot hustles backward, moving well out of the way, and so do I. I step to the wall and rip a sword off the hook—not the one Adam spotted but a smaller one, the size of my fore-arm. Much more manageable and it looks just as sharp. It's an act of adrenaline, of desperation, and to do what? Scare Lucas? Stab him?

"Be very careful with that," Margot says, her expression panicked as I lift it over my head. She holds up both hands in a calming gesture. "That's Napoleon's sword from the Battle of Marengo. It's irreplaceable."

I don't give the first shit about the sword. I'm fueled solely by panic now. Lucas has Adam pinned against the bar, both of them grappling for the gun, and Lucas's expression says he's winning.

With a roar, I launch myself in their direction, and either the noise or the motion distracts Lucas just long enough for Adam to pull back a fist. He smashes Lucas in the throat, sending him sprawling into a table. Sending everything on it, gold-dipped objects of glass and porcelain and plaster, sailing over the smooth surface and crashing to the ground.

"The Incan headdress!" Margot cries, shoving both hands into her hair. "You idiots! You broke the Incan headdress."

Lucas falls on top of it with a sharp crack—at least, that's what I think it is, the sound of the plaster snapping in two underneath Lucas's big frame, until I see Adam. Until I see how he staggers backward, his expression of surprise when he glances down at a spot in the center of his shirt, where red blooms like a rose on his chest.

"Adam!" I scream.

He goes down hard to his knees.

Lucas swings the gun at me, dragging himself up the table with his other arm, but I've already dropped the sword, let it fall point-first in the Persian carpet by my feet. Margot goes for it and I go for Adam, falling to the floor, reaching for his hand. The rose is growing ugly and big, soaking the front of his shirt. I press the heel of a hand to it to stem the bleeding and, as gently as I can, help him to the ground.

"I thought I could figure this all out," he says, intertwining his fingers with mine. "I thought I could find a way to come back to you."

"It's okay. You're here now, and you're going to be fine." My voice is all over the place because clearly he's *not* fine. His eyes are wide, a vein pulses erratically in his neck, and suddenly nothing else matters. The lies, the blood antiquities, not even Lucas's gun aimed at his head—I don't care about any of it. Nothing matters now but this moment with Adam. This singular slice of time, just me and him, alone in a room full of people. Me saying the only thing there is left to say: "I love you. I'll never stop."

Two black sneakers step up on either side of his head—Lucas, moving into close range, positioning his body above Adam's for the kill shot. I squeeze my eyes shut and wait for it, which means I don't actually see what happens next. I only hear the stampede of boots clomping up the stairs, the shouting in urgent French. Margot's gasp. The dull thud of metal skidding across the floor.

My eyes open, and it takes a few seconds before my brain registers what I'm seeing. Big men in uniforms, carrying big guns. The lieutenant colonel standing in shock at the doorway, his eyes as wide as those kids at the Galerie d'Anatomie Comparée as he takes in Margot's treasures. Margot's look of horror when she realizes he's come for them.

Adam's lips, wet and red, as he tries to speak. Nothing comes out, not even the softest sound, and yet I hear his words clear as day: *I'm so sorry.*

THIRTY-FIVE

The Pitié Salpêtrière is like every other hospital waiting room on the planet. Floors of tired gray linoleum. Unnaturally bright thanks to the cheap bulbs overhead, casting the room in a sickly green glow. The air is laced with the scent of latex and sanitizer and fear, wafting off my fellow emergency room comrades. They're slumped on chairs or milling around like schools of fish, their faces long with strain. Their loved ones are lying behind those double swinging doors, too, their bodies hooked up to monitors and machines that pump blood, fill lungs, keep them alive, but for how long?

I shiver, not from the air-conditioning but from terror. From the bullet lodged dangerously close to Adam's heart. That's what one of his surgeons told me in excellent English, that he's lying in an operating room somewhere with his chest spread open with a giant metal claw so the doctors have room to work.

The image of Adam, ghostly pale, leaking blood onto Margot's Persian rug, flits across my mind like a film on repeat. Of the paramedics shoving me out of the way so they could strap an oxygen mask on Adam and send a bag of fluids rushing into his veins. I didn't catch half of what they said as they worked, but I understood the urgency in their voices, the gravity dragging down their expressions.

Just like his surgeon's face when I asked if he'd be okay. Nobody dares to answer that question. I pick at a speck of his blood on my jeans and try not to scream.

A big body sinks onto the stool next to me, passing me a steaming Styrofoam cup. "Here. Brought you a cuppa."

I look over to find a scruffy Finn, his hair mussed like he just rolled out of bed. He looks like me, like he hasn't slept in days, and I'm only a little bit surprised to see him here, though I don't have the energy to muster up much of a response. I blink at the liquid in the cup, beige water with a milky film on top. "A cuppa what?"

"Earl Grey, supposedly. The milk is a bit gone off, but at least it masks the grocer bag."

"I have no idea what any of that means." I take a sip and wince. "This is awful."

Finn slumps farther into his seat. "I know. That's why I only brought one."

I set the cup on the tiny table beside me. "Was it you? Who called the police, I mean."

For hours now, the scene has been flashing across my brain like a horror movie interrupted halfway through. What if the police had stormed the place five seconds later? What if they'd come five seconds earlier? All the what-ifs, all the alternative endings are making me crazy. I know I need to stop overthinking, but I don't know how.

"Not me. An anonymous call from an untraceable number. A burner, most likely. Whoever it was spoke perfect French."

Eleven million people living in and around Paris, sixty-eight million in France. It could have been any of them. Call it a hunch, but I don't think it was one of them.

"Why didn't you just tell me you were with MI6?"

"Would you have confided in me?"

I shrug. "Probably not right away, no. But I might have come around."

"There are some very smart people back in London who think otherwise."

"The same people who told you I was here, I'm guessing."

"You guess right." He wriggles in his chair, crosses and uncrosses his legs. "Jesus, these chairs are shite. Any news?"

I sigh, my gaze wandering to the big double doors that lead deeper into the hospital. I will Adam's surgeon to appear in the twin windows, but there's nothing behind them but a plain white wall.

"Every thirty minutes or so, one of the surgeons comes out to scare the living crap out of me, but the only thing they tell me is that he's still in surgery."

"Well, if it helps any, this is the best place for him to be. Jacques Chirac, Ronaldo, Prince Rainier of Monaco, Gérard Depardieu, Princess Diana. They brought her here after the car— Shit. Forget I mentioned that one, eh?" Finn looks over with an apologetic wince. "The point I'm trying to make is, these docs are world-class."

A finger of fear shimmies down my spine. My eyes sting from exhaustion, from the harsh lights overhead, from terror. Everything.

Finn blows out a sigh, letting his gaze run over the faces in the room. "Look, I don't know how much you know, so I'm going to tell you what I can and leave you to fill in the blanks yourself. Does that sound okay?"

I nod, grateful. There's still so much I don't know. Still so much I don't understand. "Yes."

"This business your husband is in, it's supremely complicated, and not just in terms of the finances. It's the structure, the way the antiquities trade has this baked-in moral ambiguity. Every country has their own rules, and not every country is serious about enforcing them. There's a lot of gray area when it comes to things like origin paperwork or vendors operating without official licenses. But these relics Adam is selling, make no mistake—they don't call them 'blood antiquities' for nothing. By trading them, Adam is financing terrorism."

Finn's words thrum, hot and angry, like a heartbeat under my breastbone. He said the relics *Adam* is selling. He said *Adam* is financing terrorism. Even now, after everything, I have an inexplicable urge to defend him. "That seems like an awful lot to put on one man's shoulders."

"Not just him. Adam is one little cog in an enormously intricate machine that, on the surface, often looks legit. An antique dealer burying an Egyptian mosaic in a container filled with tiles carrying the proper paperwork, sneaking it past customs agents who are too overworked or undereducated to know the difference. World-famous museums purchasing these artifacts without bothering with due diligence so later, when we confiscate them, they can say 'oops, sorry, we didn't know.' But did they really not know, or did they simply turn a blind eye?"

"By your tone, I'm guessing the latter."

"The point I'm trying to make is, the art world has no morals. Absolutely zero. From the gallery owners and auction houses and museums, and this has been the case all throughout history, starting with the British. All this history, all this beauty, but in the hands of cold-blooded killers, the same people trading drugs and weapons and humans. Some seriously dodgy assholes."

"*Le marché noir.*"

Finn nods. "Them, plus every other criminal organization you can think of. And the kind of money people pay players like Adam only ups the ante. Higher prices drive higher demand drive more looting in conflict areas. It's a vicious cycle."

"It wasn't a criminal organization who tossed Kat out of that window, though. Margot copped to killing her. She was wearing the Oscar Wilde ring that Kat was trying to return."

Finn looks away, but he doesn't look surprised. "What happened to Kat was a goddamn shame. She was a hero, like your husband was trying to be."

"That's not what Margot said. Margot said Kat and Adam were working together. Apparently, they were selling forgeries."

I picture her face when she elbowed the vase from the stand, the fury as she hurled that mask at Adam, her almost gleeful expression when it hit the floor and shattered into a million pieces.

And then I think of something else.

"Hang on. Adam said Kat was going to report him and Margot to the authorities. That Kat had evidence, that she was going to take both of them down."

"Kat did, or she tried. She bypassed the Dutch police and went straight to Interpol. They offered her protection, but Kat didn't want it. She said it would interfere with her work."

"Is that why you came after Adam, then? Because Kat reported him?"

"No, I'd been chasing Adam for much longer than that. Your husband is good. I've been watching him for years now."

"But why Adam? You just said he is one of a hundred. Why wouldn't you go after the terrorists, the looters, the guys running le marché noir? Seems like there are so many bigger fish."

Finn looks at me then, and he stays silent. He holds my gaze, his eyebrows raised, and for so long that I fidget in my chair. He's giving me space, waiting for me to figure out for myself why Adam.

Because Adam is a big fish?

No, that can't be right. Finn just called Adam a little cog. He talked about all those seriously dodgy assholes.

And then Finn's other words come back to me, the ones he said to me on the bridge. He said Adam was not the bad guy here. He said he was on Adam's side.

Understanding hits me in a flash of heat. Finn *is* going after them. That's why he's here, talking to me now, waiting for the surgeon to give us news. Finn is worried about Adam. He's worried about the fate of his witness.

"Adam turned himself in, didn't he?"

Finn gives me the tiniest ghost of a smile. "About four years ago. He called me up out of the blue and gave me an address for a bar on the east side of London. He told me to leave the handcuffs at home. We drank beer and shot the shit for a while, and then he told me he'd met a girl. He said she was a game changer. The kind of person that comes along once in a lifetime."

Tears flood my eyes because four years ago… Finn is talking about me. I'm the game changer. The reason Adam wanted to make a change, not just for himself but his whole entire circumstances—because of me. He flipped because of me. It's too much. I pinch the bridge of my nose with two fingers and let the tears fall.

"He offered me a deal that day. He said he'd start compiling evidence, irrefutable proof that would take down everyone, from the big names running the show at the top of the pyramid all the way down. You might not understand what a carrot that is for someone like me, but I'm here to tell you it's like winning the jackpot. Criminals don't do things by the books. They don't write receipts or keep ledgers for people like me to follow their tracks."

But Adam did. He kept receipts and saved them onto a SIM card like a ledger. One giant register of names, amounts, transactions. That score Adam was keeping was for Finn.

"Did he give you the proof you were looking for?"

"He gave me a steady stream, mostly suppliers and customs officials, occasionally a fellow dealer. I kept pressing him for the big players, but he said he needed more time. He promised me it would be worth the wait. But that deal we made all those years ago, he did have one stipulation, though."

"Which was?"

"You. You were off-limits. I wasn't to approach you, at all, ever. He said you didn't know anything about what he was doing, that you were innocent. He wanted your record wiped clean."

I look away so Finn can't see my surprise. All this time, I thought it was Sully who did that, wiped my record clean, though it makes more sense that it was Finn. How else would he know to bring it up that day on the bridge? Because he was the one who buried it.

"And Kat knew what he was doing?"

Finn shakes his head. "Like I said, Kat worked alone, but she was one of the good guys. That's all she's ever been, which in the beginning put her and Adam on opposite teams. She didn't know he was working with me, and she almost blew his cover. But by then he'd come up with a way to salvage some of the artifacts, and he needed her help. He started making forgeries, really good ones, to sell to his clients, and giving Kat the real pieces to return to their rightful owners. For the record, I advised him against it. For the most part, these relics are one of a kind, and people in the industry like to talk. It was only a matter of time before one of his clients figured it out."

"Like Margot did with the ring."

"Exactly. It was reckless, but I don't have to tell you Adam is a stubborn bastard."

"She tried to kill him for it."

"And what do you think the rest of his buyers will do if they find out Adam is alive? What do you think they'll do to *you*?"

"Me? I had nothing to do with any of this. Until a literal bomb ripped my life apart, I had no idea Adam didn't make his money selling reclaimed floor tiles."

"Come on, Stella. Do you think any of that will matter? Adam kept receipts. He was working with me to take down all the most powerful fuckers. He had proof that would put them away for a really long time. Unfortunately for you, as his wife, that makes you fair game."

Again, not surprised, because what was it Zoé said? That my connection to Adam puts me in danger. Finn is only confirming it. No matter what happens behind those big double doors, there's no going back. No long airplane ride back to Atlanta, to my job and my house and my old life. Even if Adam doesn't survive the bullet in his chest, I'll still be a target.

"I tried to warn you, so you know. I said you were digging your own grave."

So Finn was the source of that mysterious text way back at the beginning of all this, the "friend" reaching out from an unknown number. "You probably don't have many friends, do you, because that's not how it works. A real friend would have been supportive instead of threatening, and he would have given me concrete advice, not vague messages. So...what now? I live the rest of my life looking over my shoulder, running from danger?"

I think of Sully in his bulletproof Maybach, the way he surrounds himself with men like Mustafa to make him feel safer, and in some weird way, I suppose it does. Because that's the thing about danger—it heightens your sense of being alive. Makes you intensely aware of your heartbeat, your lungs filling with air, the touch of another person's skin. Because how can you feel anything but alive when you're being chased by people who want you dead? But the feeling is only temporary. Sooner or later, these people will penetrate your defenses. It's only a matter of time until one of them succeeds.

The thought is like a heavy, heavy weight, pushing down on my shoulders. I've lived like that, once, and it didn't take me long to realize it was unsustainable. I might as well save everyone the trouble and give myself up now. It'll be faster and less stressful that way.

"I'm not like you, Finn," I say. "I'm not physically or mentally prepared to live on the run, and I certainly don't have the means to pay for protection. What do I do now?"

"I wish I could help you, Stella. I really do. But I'd never get protection past the higher-ups. Not unless you have something to trade."

I can sense Finn watching the side of my face, his steady gaze waiting, hoping. Adam said he was compiling proof. Stockpiling *collatérale*—not to protect his own hide, but to save mine. Finn thinks I might have some.

I think of Adam's words when he gave me the heart in Venice. How he leaned in, his gaze intent despite all the people and noise in the *piazzetta*. *If anything ever happens to me, just remember you always have my heart.* A message and a gift, all in one.

I stare at the double doors, willing Adam's surgeon to appear in the glass. Is he alive? Is he dead? There is no sense of time inside a hospital waiting room—nothing to indicate how long I've been sitting here, waiting to hear my husband's fate. The windows stay empty and still.

"What if I do?" I say, turning away from the doors, looking at Finn. "Have something to trade, I mean."

THIRTY-SIX

Paris
Three months later

A chilly breeze whips up from the Seine, sending white-blond curls dancing across my cheek, tangling in my earrings. The terrace is sheltered behind a glass windscreen, but the morning sun is milky at best, and dark clouds gather in the distance. September in Paris is a fickle bitch, but I won't be here long. I chose this spot, a busy terrace on a busy square, on purpose.

The waitress catches my eye, and I order a café au lait, even though caffeine is the last thing I need. I'm jittery enough, my foot already bouncing with nerves. I shift on my chair, crossing and uncrossing my legs and scanning the people passing by on the street. No one followed me here, at least I'm certain of that.

"*Quel terrible gâchis,*" an elderly woman two chairs down says, *what a terrible mess.* She bats a spotted hand at this morning's newspaper, spread out on the table before me.

I look down, pretending to study the article, even though I've already read it twice since purchasing it from the newsstand on the corner. Another one of Finn's successful stings, this time across the German border, three enormous reliefs and six bronze statues that once belonged to Josef Mengele, recovered from an underground bunker in Bad Dürkheim. Pieces that were lost for decades, vanished into the hands of Soviet troops until early last year, when Kat and Adam met a German businessman looking to sell some Nazi memorabilia.

But here in France, the war is still so fresh, the memories of the bombings and Vel' d'Hiv' roundups still so horrific. Finn was right; those reliefs and statues are blood antiquities, and no amount of money will ever wash them clean. For this woman, for people like her in Europe, profiting from Nazi anything is an unforgivable offense.

I match her expression, pursed lips coupled with a slow head shake. *"Je n'en reviens pas."*

A colloquial expression of shock, literally, *I'm not coming back from it.*

My French is excellent these days, thanks to a month locked away with some extremely fussy nuns in Normandy. My pronunciation, too, so honed by the sisters that I sound just like one of them—a Parisian. It comes in awful handy when trying to fade into the background.

And the expression is an apt one—I'm *not* coming back, not to Paris or to the States. Not to my house, not to my friends or my old job. I am Estelle Tremblay now, citizen of France via Malta. I got the golden passport, though this one didn't cost me anywhere near 1.3 million. It cost me my old life, though, which in the end wasn't all that much of a sacrifice, since it would mean living always in fear and without Adam.

"Bonjour, aşkım," Sully says, sinking onto the chair next to me. He's in faded jeans and a puffy coat, a black baseball hat pulled low over his eyes. Still, I'm surprised to see him outside the protection of his Maybach, despite his scruffy disguise. I was expecting Mustafa.

I look around for him, but wherever he is, he's well hidden. "Why are you here?"

"To see you, of course." He reaches out, tugs one of my curls. "The blond is starting to grow on me, I think."

I laugh. "Speak for yourself. I still do a double take every time I pass a mirror."

And it's not just the hair. It's also the colored contacts and the way the combination makes my skin even paler while magnifying my freckles, a constellation of dark dots scattered across my cheeks and nose like one of those filters on TikTok. At first I tried straightening my curls, but there's no controlling this hair, and Finn says brunette is too close to my natural red, so who am I to argue? It's not like I have much experience in the witness protection department.

I lean closer to Sully, lowering my voice so only he can hear. "Any developments I need to know about?"

Sully sits back in his chair, his gaze sweeping the street—both at the reminder of danger and by force of lifelong habit. Because all those people who wanted Adam dead, Sully knows them, too. He keeps his ear to the ground, listening for chatter of any leads on a redheaded American widow, but so far, nothing.

It's helped that I've moved around a lot. The nuns, a safe house on the outskirts of Munich, an ordinary row house in a suburb of Utrecht. While Finn worked his way through the names on Adam's SIM card—a literal Who's Who of corrupt sheikhs and third-world politicians, mob bosses and terrorists, gallery owners with questionable morals, greedy collectors like Margot with too much money to burn—I bounced from place to place, never sitting still for long. Until he'd rounded up the worst of the bunch—as Finn called them, the dodgiest of the seriously dodgy assholes—staying in one spot was too dangerous.

"Everything is fine," Sully says, settling back in his chair as the waitress delivers the café au lait. She asks if he wants anything, but he declines with a shake of his head. As soon as she's gone, he adds, "You worry too much."

It's true, I *do* worry, and I meant what I said that day to Finn. That I wasn't like him, that I wasn't physically or mentally prepared to live on the run, and it's something I'm working on. Finn's guidance has helped, and so did the training from MI6 and Mustafa. Between all of them, they've taught me how to lie low, how to trust my instincts and listen to my gut, how to never get comfortable enough to drop my guard. How to spot whoever might be following me, how to play with them like a cat with a mouse, leading them around in dizzying circles before shaking them off. Mustafa and MI6 are the best in the business, and now I am, too.

It also helps that I never told Finn about the white card.

Those three accounts were one of the few truths I held back in the weeks after that awful night at Margot's. I didn't know how much money Adam had stashed away in Luxembourg, but I suspected it was plenty, and I knew I would need it. For Julia and Babs, for me. Starting over is expensive, staying hidden even more so. There's more in those three accounts than I will ever need.

Sully reaches over, helps himself to my coffee.

"Order your own. Want me to call the waitress back over here?"

"You don't need it, not where you're going. There's your ride." He tips his head to the car rolling to a stop at the curb. Not the Maybach but an ordinary SUV, generic and black with dark tinted windows. So dark I can't see who's inside.

I lean over and press a kiss to Sully's cheek. "Thank you. For everything."

My words are a little vague, but Sully knows what he's done for me, and there's no need to summarize them for him now. That he flew all the way to Atlanta to deliver a message to

Katie that I'm safe, that she now holds the keys to an offshore account, an Emily Emergency Fund Katie is to dole out as she sees fit. He told her that I love her, but that I can't come back.

But mostly, I'm thankful that he made that 1-1-2 call. This was back before my training, and Mustafa wasn't kidding when he said he could make himself invisible. I didn't spot his big body lurking in the shadows of the Rue des Saints-Pères when I stepped up to Margot's gate, but I'm thankful he was there. And Sully's French is excellent, too. Smooth and without an accent. He was the anonymous caller. The reason I'm still alive.

"You are welcome, *aşkım*. Now go. Be safe."

With a grin, I grab my things and wind my way through the tables and toward the sidewalk, and Mustafa would be proud at the way my gaze sweeps as if by instinct over the traffic, the people loitering at the corner, the faces in the crowd as they pass by on the street. Just like he taught me, just like I've watched him do a thousand times.

At the SUV, I turn back for one last wave, but Sully is already gone.

I tug on the handle, right as another gust of wind whips up the leaves in the treetops, shooting down a fat raindrop that smacks me on the shoulder. Looks like I'm getting out of here just in time.

I slide onto the back seat next to the man I haven't seen in months, other than on a tiny iPhone screen. Thick beard. Face a warm bronze from an Alpine summer. Wisps of gray at his temples where before there was only dark hair. Adam looks completely different, and yet I would know him anywhere.

I launch myself into his arms, laughing with joy, with excitement.

"It's really you." I pull back, still smiling, taking him in. I trace a fingertip down the center of his chest, the scar where the surgeons split him open rough and lumpy under his shirt. "You're really here."

"I really am. Though I go by Noah these days." The name on one of the passports he picked up that scorching day in Malta, after we'd filled our bellies with pasta. Noah and Estelle.

"I don't care what you're called, as long as you're breathing."

And for a while there, it was touch and go. Six days in the ICU, an infection that spiked a 104 fever and multiple blood clots, followed by six grueling weeks of rehab in a remote, private clinic in Switzerland, paid for with the money from the white card. Doctors say it will take him a full year to get back to where he was before the shooting, but we can't wait that long. We need to disappear now, while Finn's roll-up of the blood antiquities trade is still the biggest story on the news. Before anyone other than Finn and Sully learns that Adam Knox didn't die on an operating table in Pitié Salpêtrière.

"Are you sure about this? You don't have to go with me, you know. You can still say no."

"And do what? Go back to asking people if they prefer chicken or pasta?" I shake my head. "No way, mister. You're not getting rid of me that easily."

He smiles. "Good, because the plane is waiting." The private jet at Le Bourget that will whisk us away to an undisclosed location. Not even I know where that is just yet.

"Where are we going? Please don't say Malta."

The truth is, I don't care where we go. Malta, South America, the Antarctic. It's all good to me. Nearly losing the man you love—not just once, but twice—will do that to a girl, make her forget about the difficulties that came before, erase all that hurt and anger. Everybody makes mistakes. Everybody does things they later regret. I am guilty of it, too.

It's what a person does afterward that matters to me more. How they commit to doing better, to *being* a better person. It's why I walked away from a man who will never change, and why I'm staying with the one who did. Who made a choice the moment we met, who loved me so much he asked Finn to meet him at a bar and started to put things right. He did that for me. I don't think he's been lying to me all this time. I think he's been trying very hard *not* to. I refuse to lose him a third time.

"Not Malta," he says. "Remember that pretty stone house we talked about in the South of France? I found us one, at the end of a long driveway, on the edge of a blink-and-you-miss-it town. How does that sound?"

How does it sound?

I turn to the window, soaking in what I can of the buildings whizzing by on the other side, committing the views to memory, making them solid enough to last a lifetime. Beautiful Paris, where I put my tears on display for a reporter who made me the face of the Paris bombing, the tragic American widow whose husband was blown to bits. The city where my heart broke before it was healed. This is the last time I will see it.

I hope this Adam of yours is worth it. It's what Sully said to me that day in the car. I wasn't so sure of my answer then, but I am now.

A new life, a fresh start together.

I turn back to Adam with a smile. *"Ça sonne parfait."*

That sounds perfect.

★ ★ ★ ★ ★

AUTHOR'S NOTE

Like every story, much of *The Paris Widow* is rooted in truth.

A simple Google search will land you on more than you ever wanted to know about the illicit trade of blood antiquities, millions and millions of hits about archaeological artifacts ripped from virtually every country on the planet. From temples in India and churches in Colombia and tombs in Egypt and across Asia, these thieves are strip-mining our past, selling the world's treasures for big bucks on a black market that has a lot of gray area. Too many people pretending to be legit brokers for anonymous donors, too many precious antiquities sneaked over international borders only to land in respected galleries and museums. Like most illegal activities, the looting is hard to quantify, but some experts say the blood antiquities trade is booming to the tune of around eight billion dollars per year.

Arthur Brand is one of these people, a real-life Dutch art detective in the fight to recover the world's treasures and the basis for my character Kat. Dubbed the Indiana Jones of the illegal art trade, Arthur risks his life to go undercover and reclaim centuries-old treasures, unmask forgeries, solve museum thefts and trace stolen art to world-famous museums around the globe. Kat's career—her dogged determination to protect the world's cultural property, the risks she takes to return these treasures to their rightful owners—is a direct result of Arthur's bravery. The Oscar Wilde ring, the lost Diwan of Hafez, the Bacchus statue and the pair of bronze horses that once belonged to Hitler... These are just a few of his many real finds that found their way into my fictional reality.

In case this isn't already clear, any mistakes in this story are mine alone.

I am also grateful to:

John Jordan, for sharing his beloved Dennis and so many bottles of rosé while so thoroughly but gently correcting my very basic French, and to Erhan Cot for fixing what Google couldn't quite translate to perfect Turkish. Rebecca Messina, *grazie mille*.

Everyone at Park Row Books for inviting me into your home: my editor Laura Brown for your thoughtful suggestions and creative vision, Erika Imranyi for believing in my work, Emer Flounders and Sophie James for your publicity genius, copy editor extraordinaire Nancy Fischer and all the other tireless folks working in marketing and sales and editorial behind the scenes. You are the reason this story became a book.

Nikki Terpilowski at Holloway Lit for working so tirelessly on my behalf and offering sharp-eyed thoughts on early drafts. Thanks for always being in my corner.

On the author side: fellow Killers Heather Gudenkauf and Kaira Rouda; our Killer Author Club evenings are my favorite of the week. Jean Kwok for talking through my plot and listing off all the reasons my art detective should be female; Kat is for you, Jean. My Young Rich Widows crew, Vanessa Lillie, Cate Holahan and Layne Fargo; you ladies dazzle me every day with your brilliance. And to all those other author friends who are happy to lend an ear or talk me off a ledge—and you know who you are—thank you for making this solitary business a whole lot less lonely.

All the generous Bookstagrammers, BookTokkers, bloggers and reviewers who shine a bright light on my books, the booksellers and librarians who get my books into readers' hands, the readers who dive into my fictional worlds. It's because of all of you that I keep writing.

My dad, for all the bedtime stories, and my mom, for... well, everything else.

My favorite real-life Dutchman, Ewoud, and our kids, Evan and Isabella. You three are hands down my most precious treasures.